the
Lost Village

DANIELA SACERDOTI

the Lost Village

bookouture

Published by Bookouture in 2020

An imprint of Storyfire Ltd.
Carmelite House
50 Victoria Embankment
London EC4Y 0DZ

www.bookouture.com

ISBN: 978-1-83888-012-5
eBook ISBN: 978-1-83888-011-8

PROLOGUE

Many times she'd been told not to wander the woods during hunting season, from September to the end of October. Sure, the hunters knew what they were doing – they were careful – but her parents always said mistakes could be made, and it was better not to risk it.

She was a girl with a good head on her shoulders. She wasn't careless. And yet, the temptation was too much: if she cut through the woods, she'd be at her boyfriend's house in half an hour, which meant they'd have double the time to spend together. Moreover, if she cycled on the road, she would inevitably be seen by someone, and it would be reported back to Mamma. That was how village life worked. She was supposed to be home, studying for exams, and Mamma would be furious if she knew she'd gone out. But if she was careful, she could be in and out of the house without anyone noticing – unless, by tremendous ill luck, Mamma went upstairs to check on her. But it was just after lunch, and Mamma always let her study in peace in the afternoon. She decided to chance it. Her desire to see her boyfriend was too strong for her to be circumspect. She threw caution to the wind, and escaped through the window, jumping from the balcony onto the soft grass below.

The hunters would know she wasn't a boar, or a pheasant, or a hare! Her mamma was being overprotective as usual. Also, her own father and brother were out hunting that afternoon, and she trusted them.

And so, all things considered, the girl convinced herself she was safe, and decided to let her bike fly free down the slope, which was covered in leaves of every shade, from yellow to red. She met the uneven undergrowth, and bump and after bump, she rode on, following the tree-lined dirt path. She congratulated herself for wearing a jumper over her skirt, as the October air was now chilly enough to do so, even in the warm heart of Italy.

Her thoughts went to the boy she was going to meet; he didn't know she was coming – it would be a surprise. They were both meant to be studying for their exams, and then, diplomas under their belts, they'd be free to begin their lives, at last. They could get jobs and be together properly, like adults, not like teenagers, having to ask their parents' permission. The girl knew he loved her, for real; and he'd promised his feelings would never change. She believed him with all her heart and soul. Young she might be, but she knew the two of them were forever…

The fallen leaves were slippery under the wheels, and the scent of wet earth filled the air. Suddenly, the distant noise of a gunshot made the girl jump. She frowned, but she'd known it was likely to happen, that she'd hear shooting at some point. Maybe it was her own father's hunting party. She cycled on, faster. Soon she'd be through, and she could dismount, lifting her bike and herself over a low wall and onto the road. Ten minutes longer, no more.

There was another shot, this time closer, and voices came to her, carried by the autumn wind. The hunters really were terribly close. Blood rushed to her head, and she could feel her heart beating hard in her ears. Should she pause and try to find out where the shots came from? Or should she ride on as fast as she could, out of the tree canopy and into the open?

The girl was about to stop the bike and call out, to make her presence known, when voices followed the shot, coming from the thickets on her right-hand side – distraught, terror-stricken, and, finally, the voices turned into screams. Fear made her stop too fast, and she fell in the dirt, the wheels of her upturned bike still spinning.

While she lay with her cheek on the wet leaves, too stunned to get up, she saw a figure staggering onto the path, hunched. She recognised the brown checked shirt at once, she recognised his face, that face she knew like the back of her hand, even now that blood was pouring all over his eyes. He was faltering, falling, his arms forward – could she see her? Did he recognise her? The girl didn't know. She crawled to him, her body trembling, and kneeled beside him. This was a nightmare – it couldn't be happening. She felt as if she were watching herself from above, as if the shock had jolted her soul out and sent it wandering. Her father whispered three words, in a ragged, rasping voice, three words that were to change her life forever. And then he went limp, staring at the sky with unseeing eyes.

CHAPTER ONE

LaGuardia Airport, 2006

You did it, Mom!

My son's words appeared on my phone.

I told you I would! I typed and smiled to myself, glancing out of the wide windows to the rows of waiting planes. My decision to fly to Italy had come as a surprise to pretty much everyone who knew me. Deciding to buy a one-way ticket to the other side of the world, I'd surprised myself too.

> *I didn't believe you! I told Dad. I hope that's okay. Just so*
> *he knows I'm going to stay with him when I come home.*
> *And yes, I'm good x*

I bristled. Eli had done the right thing in telling his father about my trip, but even after three years apart, communications between Ethan and me were still fraught, and I wanted his involvement in my life to be Eli-related only. My resentment towards the man I now saw as my ex-husband – even if we hadn't finalised a divorce yet – had no place in my conversations with our son. Eli worshipped his dad, but Ethan and I had drifted away from each other in silence over the years and there was no coming back.

I was trying to word a diplomatic reply, when another message popped up:

It's awesome you're doing this. For yourself and for Nonna.
I'm proud of you.

Well, that brought tears to my eyes. My Eli, who'd gone from being a baby in my arms to a college student in the space of a heartbeat. The little boy I'd cherished, who'd heard those words from me so often – I'm proud of you – was now grown up and telling me the same. No matter the grief and strife between his father and me, we'd made an amazing human being, together.

Do you know how long will you be away for?

Guilt grabbed at me again, as it had throughout my preparations for this transatlantic trip. For the first time in our lives, Eli and I would be so far away from each other. And yet, he'd been the catalyst in the process that had led me here, on my way to unravel the secrets of my family's past.

Eli had left home a few months earlier, to study photography and filmmaking at New York University – his dream come true. His choice of studies was no surprise: I was a wedding and portrait photographer, and ever since he was little Eli had come to the studio or on location with me, playing with toy cameras and then being given his own. But while my work was run-of-the-mill, Eli's was extraordinary, and I nurtured it every step of the way. I had been overjoyed when he'd decided to go study in New York, but I hadn't realised how deeply his departure was going to affect me.

At the ripe old age of forty-three I was living on my own, and I'd left romantic relationships behind, despite my girlfriends' best efforts. I had a full life, with a job I adored and a good circle of friends, and I thought I'd be all right. But, as is often the case in life, things hadn't unfolded as I'd expected. To my surprise, empty nest syndrome hit me hard. Now that Eli was gone, the house was empty not only of him, but of the buzz of all his projects and activities, of his friends coming and going, of music playing and photographs strewn all over the living room floor.

Ethan was out of my life, Eli was in New York. And me?

I was adrift.

One night, I dreamt I was walking down a narrow street and stopped in front of an old house, its door framed by trailing white roses. The dream was so vivid it felt real, and in the morning, I couldn't shake it away. It kept playing on my mind.

The night after, the dream came back – and then again, and again, never changing. I walked down the same alley towards the same house, and stopped in front of the door, contemplating the ripe flowers that hung pure and white, like an impossible summer snowfall. I began to look forward to the dream, every night as I closed my eyes. Small details became clearer – the scene was drenched in light, sunshine all around, and there was a low buzz of bees in the air. Although I never saw my feet, I knew I was barefoot, because I felt hot stones under my soles. Each night the image grew clearer and clearer, although the scene remained unchanged – the place felt familiar, but I didn't know why.

And then I remembered: I could count on one hand the times that Mamma, my Italian mother, had spoken about her past to me, in all the years of my life; and one of those rare times, she'd mentioned how there were trailing white roses wrapped around the entrance of her childhood home, and how they filled the air with their sweet scent. Was it my imagination, or when I was little had she told me that on moonlit nights she used to step out on her bedroom's balcony, and breathe in the magical fragrance?

Sometimes during those long, lonely nights in my now-empty house – a house too big for me alone – I imagined the same: that I was standing barefoot on a balcony on a balmy Italian night, breathing in the scent of roses, watching the white moon high in the sky. The desire to find out where I came from, to discover why Mamma had cut herself – and me – off from her Italian family and locked the story away, overcame me.

And so, here I was, on a plane to Italy, a few thousand miles over the ocean. How long was I going to be away? I had no idea. Not yet.

As long as it takes… I typed, and it was time to board. Now, there was no turning back.

*

The blanket of clouds just below the airplane wing was an expanse of white and orange, sun rays piercing it and creating prisms of light – it was beautiful, and daunting in its vastness. It was a perfect shot, and my thoughts went to my camera, safely tucked in my suitcase. The phone would have to do. I took a few pictures to send to Eli once we'd landed – and then the plane began to jump a little. There was crackling over the speaker, then the captain's voice filled the air – we were to fasten our seatbelts and switch off all electronics.

I followed the instructions, covered myself with my jacket to stay warm and leaned back. I fell asleep, a jet-lagged, confused slumber that might have been an afternoon nap or a whole night's sleep, because only seconds seemed to have passed when the pilot's voice awoke me. It was finally time to prepare for landing, he said, and butterflies filled my stomach as I saw snow-capped mountains below us. The Alps! Soon we'd make our way south and fly over the centre of Italy, ready to touch down in Fiumicino, not far from the ancient city of Rome.

The pilot informed us that it was warm and sunny in Italy, that we'd need to have our sunglasses and sun cream handy because down below it was a scorching summer day.

Oh my God. I was really here. In Europe. In Italy. Away from everything I knew.

On my own.

Was I excited or terrified? A little bit of both, I thought as I watched the ground coming closer, the mountains giving way to patterned fields and cities.

I took a breath – cold, stale plane air – and held onto both armrests, waiting to land and finally, finally, set foot on my mother's homeland.

*

Stuck in between fellow passengers and bags, I waited impatiently for my turn to step off the plane; my heart was beating fast, my cheeks were flushed with excitement, and every minute spent on the plane was a minute too long. Time to retrieve my case, to navigate customs and then, with a rush of warm air, the automatic doors opened to a whole new world.

I scoured the people waiting beyond the barriers, some with handwritten signs, and glanced beyond them, towards the crowds of people coming and going, or waiting in queues. A bedlam of noise and colours and foreign voices. For a moment, anxiety held me tight as I thought maybe nobody would be there for me… and then, there she was! Matilde, my cousin! I recognised her straight away from the pictures on her Facebook page. A smile bloomed from the depths of me; oh, how I'd waited for this moment, to meet someone of my blood at last, other than my mom. She stood on her tiptoes, her chin raised, wavy raven hair to her shoulders and sunglasses pushed back on her head.

'Matilde!' I called and waved, hoping my voice would be heard above the din, and made my way beyond the barriers, rolling my case behind me. Her face lit up when she saw me; she ran to me and hugged me like she'd known me forever. She was even prettier than in her photographs; and there was definitely a familiar air in her build, in her colouring. She had a striking resemblance to Mamma and me, all three of us small, dark, unmistakably Mediterranean.

'Luce!' Matilde pronounced my name like Mamma did – Lu-chay – and my heart somersaulted. Nobody, apart from my mom, ever used the right pronunciation. I was always Lucy. We hugged tight and, at that moment, I felt the deep, heart-warming conviction that I'd made the right decision.

'It's so good to finally meet you!' I said, and silently thanked Mamma for always speaking to me in Italian. However, everyone seemed to speak so fast here; I hoped that the Italian my mom had taught me would stand the test of real-life conversations.

'And you! Are you moving over here?' She laughed, taking in my enormous suitcase.

'I like being prepared for all eventualities!' Truth was, I was so anxious to be travelling so far, and on my own, that I'd packed half the house.

'I can see that. Oh, I just can't believe you're here! My American cousin,' she said, taking my arm. 'Like in a film!' She had a light, contagious laughter. Matilde's cheerfulness shone around her like a warm aura, and I basked in it.

We stepped outside in the blinding sunshine – I couldn't believe I was actually in Rome – not exactly in the city itself, but almost!

'I'll just go pay for the parking, then we'll be off. Two minutes,' Matilde said, so fast that I had to concentrate to understand what she said – hopefully I would get used to the accent quickly – and left me and my huge suitcase alone on the edge of the pavement. With my heart in my throat, I watched Matilde cross the road, dodging cars in a way you'd never see in America. I'd read that people in Rome drove like madmen; it seemed I was getting a taste of it already, and we hadn't even left the airport. Instinctively, I took a step back from the edge of the pavement, in case someone drove over my toes. I fished my sunglasses out of the crossbody I carried, and took off the light cardigan I'd worn on the plane, letting the Italian sunshine kiss my skin.

The sky was the purest blue, and a hot breeze played in my hair – it was the kind of dry wind that would never blow back home in Seattle. Everything looked and felt so exotic, more like a holiday far away than a homecoming. For a moment, the noises and colours of this unknown place overwhelmed me. The smell of hot asphalt and car exhaust, Italian voices, loud and expressive, the chaos of klaxons… And everywhere, pervading everything, the light of the sun, a different hue from what I was used to – almost like the Seattle sun was silver, and this was gold.

I took out my phone and captured a shot of that moment; I wanted to compose a story in pictures to show Eli. And then I bent over the screen to write him a message, and let him know I'd landed safely. I was struggling to see the screen because of the glare and the sunglasses, when something startled me – '*Ciao, bella!*' a voice said. I jerked my head up from the phone. A man with tight jeans and sunglasses had just stepped past me, and he was still turning around to catch a glimpse of me.

Seriously? Seriously?

Had I just been catcalled? My jaw dropped open. Was I about to find out that all Italian stereotypes were true? I didn't know whether to be outraged or secretly pleased. A little bit of both, maybe. I looked down, embarrassed, and when I looked up again, Matilde was beside me.

'Ignore that. I apologise on behalf of Italian males, they're not all so… forward. To be fair, you're beautiful. Expect some attention,' she said, mischievously. She knew about my marital situation – I hoped with all my heart she wouldn't attempt some matchmaking, like my married girlfriends did every once in a while.

And anyway, me? Beautiful?

No, I wasn't. Nondescript, more like. Small, dark-haired and brown-eyed; average, really. I had made an effort to prepare for this trip. Even if it had all been so quick, between deciding to go and actually getting a taxi to the airport, I'd managed to squeeze in a visit to a fancy Seattle boutique and treated myself to a few linen dresses, high-heeled sandals and new sunglasses. I'd visited the hairdresser's too, trimming my long dark hair in a shoulder-length bob to freshen it up, and working in some mahogany lowlights. Still, no amount of grooming could make me beautiful, I didn't think.

We crammed ourselves and all my luggage into Matilde's Fiat 500, and the next hour was spent trying to untangle ourselves from Roman traffic.

'I hope I'm not being offensive here, but you guys drive like maniacs,' I said, grabbing the little handle over my right shoulder – it didn't seem much to hold onto, as Matilde launched herself into what seemed like a Paris–Dakar type of race.

'We do, don't we?' Matilde replied cheerily, overtaking a couple of cars in a way I was sure was illegal. It had to be. A bald man in a tiny car with a rosary hanging from his front mirror made a gesture that meant pretty much the same in all cultures. I held onto my seat, hoping I would make it out of there alive.

'I'm a conscientious driver, don't worry,' Matilde said. 'I've only been stopped a few times and almost always convinced the *carabinieri* – you know, our police – to let me go.'

That wasn't very reassuring. 'All good, then,' I said feebly, leaning back.

'You okay? You're not really scared, are you?' Her eyes were huge. 'You need some fresh air,' she said and let the window down. Hot air from inside the car blew out, hot air from outside the car blew in. No freshness anywhere.

'No, of course not.' *Yes, I am terrified!* 'Just…'

'Sorry?' she yelled over the noise of the wind.

'Just a bit…' I yelled back, and words failed me.

'A bit overwhelmed?'

I nodded. It was true.

'I can imagine,' Matilde said, and swerved in between two trucks to get onto the motorway. I held on with both hands. Good Lord, who gave this girl a driving licence? 'It is overwhelming – the whole situation, I mean.'

'It is, yes… be careful!'

'Why, what's wrong?' she said, overtaking a truck and driving so close to it I saw the little chips in its paint job. The name of the truck company flew in front of my eyes, letter by letter, in slow motion, an inch from my face.

'Watch out!'

'Relax, Luce. It's all good.' She laughed. 'I promise I'll get you to Bosconero in one piece.'

I dried beads of sweat off my forehead and decided I could not formulate another sentence in a foreign language until we came off the motorway.

A few minutes later, to my relief, we left the truck-infested motorway and drove onto an open road, covered with a blue sky so bright not even my sunglasses could dim it. Matilde closed the windows as we relied on AC, and quiet and coolness permeated the car. In the distance, on my right, I could see the Rome skyline passing by, with its domes and tall buildings, and on the horizon, the ground rising into tree-covered hills. Even further away, the blue, dim profile of a mountain range – the Apennines, I guessed.

I took a breath and relaxed slightly, leaning my head back. I began to consider the possibility of actually making it to Bosconero in one piece, just like my cousin had promised.

Jet lag and the last dregs of adrenaline ebbing away made everything seem like a daydream. Was I really here, on the other side of the Atlantic? Was that really the Rome skyline, the same Rome I'd read about in history books? Was I really sitting beside my own flesh and blood, after years of knowing nothing about my origins?

'It's so weird we had no idea of each other's existence,' I said in the silence of the car.

'Yes. All I knew was that I had an aunt named Angelina – your mamma. It barely registered with me when I was little. Like she was this mythical creature who lived far away. I don't think it felt real until you got in touch with me. Nonna Clelia mentioned her so rarely, and every time it was like this dark secret that couldn't be said aloud…'

'Nonna's name is Clelia, then?' I asked, and realised how little Matilde and I had spoken online before I'd made my way to Italy. There was so much to say and so much to find out.

'Yes. Nonna Clelia. And my papà's name is Carlo. Your zio Carlo.'

Clelia and Carlo. My grandmother and my uncle…

'They mention my mom sometimes, then?'

'Only Nonna. She mentions Angelina once in a while, like it's a secret. And my papà… he doesn't want Angelina discussed. He forbids Nonna to even mention her, which is why she always looks guilty, every time she does.'

'He forbids it? Does she not have a mind of her own?'

'You have to meet my papà. He's quite… imposing.'

'Oh.'

'You didn't know about me either. Your mamma… my aunt Angelina… she never told you about us?'

'Very little. I knew she'd left her mother and brother behind, somewhere in Italy. I didn't know where exactly, though. All I had to go with was our family name, really. I had to do some detective work behind Mamma's back.'

I explained to Matilde how I'd found out about Bosconero, and about her – though I wasn't exactly proud of my methods.

After all my attempts to speak to Mamma about our past had ended in her changing the subject and telling me about her peonies, or some old acquaintance who'd turned up at the bakery where she worked, or some recipe she'd found and was dying to try, I'd realised I would never get anywhere. So, I'd bought Mamma a voucher to attend a one-day cake decoration course; even with the low moods she was struggling with, I knew she wouldn't miss the chance. While she was away, I used the spare keys to her house. There, on the top shelf of her mirrored bedroom wardrobe, she kept some boxes – the kind that everyone has, with documents and memories and pictures. I opened them one by one and went through the contents. Mamma's cat, Priscilla, glared at me from her perch on the armchair in the corner. I knew I was being underhand, but I knew deep down that her silence on the matter of our family was eating away at her too. Something told me that her silence, her estrangement, hadn't been her choice. She was being forced to stay away, and I wanted to know why. As her daughter, it was my duty to go on this journey of discovery for her. And for myself too.

Still, I felt terribly guilty while I thumbed Mamma's documents and rummaged through her photographs, old cards and memories. Photographs of me as a baby, of her smiling with the owners of the bakery, a lock of my baby hair in an envelope, and cards I'd made for her, full of glitter and stickers. And then her copy of my wedding album, photos of Eli as a baby, as a little boy, as a teenager. Letters from a lady who used to work with her and had moved to Michigan. Old cookery magazines. Random files. Nothing that could help me find a clue.

No pictures of her family back home, no letters, no documents. No photographs of her as a child, or a young girl.

It was as if she had a phantom past, gone forever, no traces left. What could have made my mom want to scrub her history clean so thoroughly – or who could have done that to her? I was so frustrated I could have screamed. An impossible riddle, with no clues.

I started again, examining every document, every postcard, every brochure, every magazine. I was thumbing through seventies' cookery magazines full of aspics and pineapple-and-cheese sticks when –finally, finally – a black and white photograph fell out from between the pages.

A dark-haired girl in a summer dress, barefoot, standing on a doorstep and surrounded by roses. My heart began to beat harder – the trailing roses from my dream, the one Mamma had mentioned! I turned the picture around. On the back, there was an inscription: *Bosconero, Summer 1959.*

Something had survived the purge.

'Bosconero…' I said aloud, and tasted the word on my lips.

The sound of my voice in the empty house almost made me jump. I began gathering the papers and putting them back in the plastic boxes Mamma used to store them, trying to make them look undisturbed. Priscilla glared on.

'Give me a break, cat.'

I packed everything away again, except the photograph, which I tucked into my purse. Surely Mamma wouldn't notice it was missing, but on the drive to collect her in Seattle to take her home,

I wondered if the guilt was written all over my face. Probably. My mother's radar certainly told her that something was afoot, because after the initial smiles and account of her day, she began stealing glances of me as we drove.

'Luce?'

'Yes?'

'I know there are things playing on your mind. And I'm sorry I can't answer your questions.'

I wasn't sure how to reply. The fact that I'd just been rummaging through her stuff weighed on me. 'I know you're sorry, Mamma. And I'm sorry too, that you feel you can't speak about your past.'

'Don't feel sorry about me. We must forget all about this.' She lifted a slender, olive-skinned hand over her shoulder, as if she were throwing everything behind her. 'Let's just all live our lives. Don't you think that's the best way? The only way?' She'd been looking out of the window, but now she turned to watch me, to study my face.

I couldn't keep my real feelings bottled up. I couldn't keep acting behind her back. And so, my reply was truthful.

'Actually, no... oh, Mamma, I don't want to upset you, it's the last thing I want! You always protected me, you took care of me so well... I want to protect you and take care of you now. But... This is eating you inside. I can see it, I can feel it. And you feel it too, don't you?'

'I'm fine!'

'No, you're not, Mamma! And I'm tired of seeing you like this. So... sad.'

'We all have our burdens to bear. I'll bear mine.'

'Stop playing the martyr!' I snapped and berated myself for it. She didn't deserve that. How could I have spoken to her so harshly? I was afraid of looking at her. But when I did, catching a glimpse of her quickly before I laid my eyes on the road again, she wasn't crying – she was composed, her mouth set in a hard line, in a way I'd seldom seen throughout the years. Her inner steeliness had come out. This was the face she wore when she needed all her strength to get through something – and there had been plenty of moments like that, having brought up a daughter all alone, without the support of a family.

'I want what's best for you, Luce. I always did. And that is why I kept you away from all that. To protect you.'

'This is not protecting me. This is burying your head in the sand. Instead of a family history, we have a black hole.'

That was too much for her. She shut herself in silence and stayed there for the rest of the drive back to her house. The tension between us made the air thick with unanswered questions. I parked in her driveway, unable to take it any more. 'Tell me more. Or give me your blessing to search for myself. Please. It's not just your past. It's my past too.'

'If you keep searching, you'll only bring trouble to our door,' she said, and although her voice was sweet as always, I could feel her resolve.

'So be it,' I insisted. 'It's better than standing on a big, gaping hole.'

She seemed to try to find another way to convince me. '*Amore mio*, please listen. There are reasons why I just don't want to go there. You need to trust me that these reasons are legitimate.'

'Can I not decide for myself?'

'I don't want to talk about it, I don't even want to remember.'

'But you do remember. You just don't talk about it.'

Mamma had always put me before herself, so I tried to play that card: my own desire to know where I came from. And it wasn't just a strategy – it was true. 'What about me?' I said softly. 'I don't know anything about our family back home. I don't even know who my father is…'

Mamma brought a hand to her forehead. 'You don't understand.'

'What, Mamma? What do I not understand? Please tell me.'

'What you don't understand is that I'm not just doing this for me, but for you.'

'But how can it be good for me? Not to know what my roots are, where they are. And how can it be good for you, to have left all you loved behind…'

'*Amore mio*, listen—'

No. I couldn't listen any more. 'I don't know who my father is! I don't know who my grandparents are! I'm forty-three, all alone again and I know nothing!' I couldn't restrain my frustration any longer. There was a moment of silence as we sat in the car, my heart pounding and my chest rising and falling heavily. 'I'm sorry, Mamma, you did so much for me, but—' I began.

'Maybe you're right,' she interrupted me.

'Really?'

'Maybe it's not the best for either of us.' She looked up at me, and there they were, those dark, fiery eyes that she seldom showed.

'No, I don't think it is,' I said, tentatively.

'But I have no choice. Not knowing… is better than the alternative.' She squeezed my hand and stepped out of the car, opening and closing the door behind her without a backward glance.

Later that evening I sat on my bed with my laptop, and Mamma's picture in my hands. She was smiling, posed to step out, as if the photograph had caught her in motion. Even if the image was in black and white, I could guess the vibrant colours of her surroundings, and the beauty of the roses that crowned her; and from her summer dress, her bare shoulders and feet, I knew that the sun was shining on her… just like in my dream. It was as if the recurring dream had been a soul-calling, a way to express a need so deep, so repressed, that it had no other chance to come to the surface.

I dived into every type of social media I knew of, and swam among dozens of Nardinis for the hundredth time. But now I knew where to look – Bosconero – and this made the search so much easier. Yes, there were a few Bosconeros in Italy, but only one where someone with the surname Nardini lived.

That was how I found Matilde.

There, a tiny little root… A tiny piece of my history. It took all my courage, but I wrote to her.

Hello. You probably have no idea who I am…

'And here I am. Look,' I said now, taking out the photograph from my purse. Matilde glimpsed it quickly, then returned her eyes to the road.

She nodded, her profile in shade. 'The family home is still there,' she said. 'And so is the rose bush. We call the house Rosa Bianca, because of its trailing roses.' Rosa Bianca: white rose…

My heart did a somersault of longing. 'Rosa Bianca… I can't wait to see it!'

'And I can't wait to show you, Luce!' Matilde said. 'I grew up in that house, pretty much. Papà and I lived down in Bastia, a bigger village at the foot of the hill, I'll take you there… but he worked a lot and I was always up at Rosa Bianca with Nonna Clelia. In fact, Nonna said to me once that my room used to be your mamma's.'

I couldn't believe I was about to see with my own eyes the place Mamma had seldom mentioned, but always with such emotion – like a lost promised land.

'I can't quite wrap my head around this!' Matilde turned towards me for a moment and then brought her eyes back onto the road. 'I thought I was alone. I mean, I'm an only child, I have no cousins on either side... At least I thought I didn't!'

'Same here. It's all been so quick. We've only known about each other's existence for... what is it, a week? It's a weird feeling...'

'You can say that again. But weird in a good way. Like I said, Papà is not... well, he's not an easy person to deal with. I feel bad about saying this, because I know he loves me so much. He and Nonna brought me up. Nonna is so gentle, but Papà can be a bit... suffocating. To find you...' She gave me a broad smile. 'Is like this incredible gift from life.'

'Thank you. I feel the same, Matilde.'

I wondered why there was no mention of her mom, but I didn't ask. If she wanted to tell me about that part of her life, she would do so in her own time. I thought that her choice of words and her demeanour whenever she mentioned her papà was a bit off. It was like she had a lot more to say than she was allowed to. She chose her words carefully, like she was bound by loyalty.

We left Rome behind and made our way onto smaller roads, towards the hills in the distance. On both sides there was gentle countryside, now, open fields dotted with maritime pines and cypresses, Roman ruins and ancient churches – I had to remind myself that they were real, and not a film set. The landscape was so beautiful and serene; it seemed to me that everything was full of promise, of possibilities, of discovery. Matilde lowered a window and let the breeze inside. Gone were the smells of asphalt and car exhausts; the warm, perfumed breeze now carried a scent of greenery baking in the sun, of fennel and laurel, and – it seemed to me – of the distant sea.

We drove in silence for a while, as I soaked in the beauty all around us. The landscape was changing again now, the gentle fields turning into something wilder and more primitive as we made our way up into hills covered in dark woods, with grey stone mountains on the horizon. Valleys covered in almost-black trees loomed at both sides of us. We were in the Apennines, the mountainous backbone of Italy, beautiful and wild. From the busy roads around the airport, to the sun-baked, serene countryside – and then, into this ancient forested place, with villages perched on top of steep hills. The name of our village – Bosconero, Black Wood – was beginning to make sense.

I felt like I was moving away from the modern world, into a timeless place – it was all was so different from my suburban home in Seattle and everything I was used to. Ethan was the traveller in the family – I'd never looked beyond our yearly holiday in Colorado. Europe had always felt like a different planet. I kept looking from left to right, not wanting to miss anything. How much I wished that Eli could see all this! It was a photographer's paradise. I took some pictures on the phone, my faithful camera still packed away, but just a few – I wanted to see everything with my own eyes, and not through a lens. Not yet, anyway.

'We left the region of Lazio now, and we are in Umbria,' Matilde said. She pronounced it Oombria, making it sound a little ominous. 'I think it's the most beautiful place on earth, but then I'm biased!'

'It's breathtaking. No wonder Mamma is homesick,' I said, almost to myself.

There was silence between us then, and a strange anxiety began to take hold of me. Why was I so apprehensive? Surely Matilde's warm, cheerful welcome was a good start?

'Do they know I'm here?' I asked, trying, and failing, to keep the apprehension out of my voice. 'Nonna, Zio Carlo?'

'Kind of… kind of no,' Matilde replied, and I could feel her anxiety now.

'Oh.' I'd suspected as much, but hearing right out that I was here without their knowledge, and therefore a surprise meeting with them awaited me, was scary to say the least.

Would they blank me, refuse to see me? Be angry, furious? Would they reveal something, anything that would make me regret I'd even come? Then I would know why Mamma had wanted to keep all these secrets…

'Luce? Don't worry. We'll make it work,' Matilde reassured me.

'I hope so. Do they know I got in touch with you at all? That we've been talking online?'

Matilde shook her head.

'They don't know of my existence at all, do they?' I asked, and seeing Matilde's face I knew the answer at once. 'They don't know Angelina has a daughter.'

'I'm sorry. It's all been so quick. I needed some time to figure out how to break it to Nonna, and Papà, and then… and then you said you were coming over here…'

'Well. It'll be quite the surprise for them.'

'You can say that again,' she replied, and something in her voice made my anxiety go up a notch.

I didn't hold anything against Matilde. I understood why she'd kept quiet about me – I could see where she was coming from. I hadn't told Mamma I was coming to Italy either, and although I believed in my decision, and in my right to make it, I wasn't looking forward to telling her where I was. Yes, this was the best way: Matilde and I reaching out to each other and dragging the family back together, before they knew what was happening.

The Fiat 500 began to climb up a steep hill. 'I'll go slow so you can see the landscape,' she said, and I thanked my lucky stars that she would not zoom up those bends the way she'd zoomed out of the airport. The road was so narrow that I wondered what would happen if a car came the other way. She must have read my mind because she said, 'It's tricky when it rains a lot, or when it snows. They have to close the road so the snowplough can go up, turn and come down again.' It was difficult to think of winter and snow when everything was shining so brightly and the sky was the purest blue – how wild and isolated it must be when the cold season came. We drove along a valley with scattered sheep on the slopes and, beyond it, a small, dark hill crested with stone buildings.

'We're nearly there. Are you ready?' Matilde said.

'I don't know... am I ready? I have butterflies!' I held my breath.

Bosconero seemed to appear as if by magic, perched on the hill like a crested crown, shining under the sun among the dark woods all around.

CHAPTER TWO

Bosconero looked like a small citadel, its red-roofed houses protected by a cluster of high walls. Both houses and walls had been built from the same stone, a light brown colour that shone in the sun with pink undertones. The stone walls towered above us, enveloping the village and almost covering it from view, except for the top of what looked like a medieval tower on one side and a church belfry on the other. The vague scraps of memories Mamma had reluctantly painted for me were now gaining substance, taking shape in front of my eyes. Somewhere up there, waiting for me, was the house with trailing white roses over its door...

'Is this how you imagined it?' Matilde asked.

'I'm not sure... this is beyond my imagination. Like a film, a travel ad and a history book all mixed together!'

'I know what you mean. I'm used to all this, but if I look at the village like I'm seeing it for the first time it takes my breath away too.'

Matilde's little car climbed the last few miles up the steep road, as the sunshine turned dappled, straining to filter through the woods on both sides. We passed the high stone walls and drove into a cobbled square, enclosed by the biscuit-coloured buildings I'd seen from a distance. The light of the sun, already blinding, was reflected on the stones and turned the square into a nest of heat and radiance.

My sandalled feet touched the cobblestones, and I pushed my sunglasses up on my head, squinting in the orange-yellow-golden light. I looked up into the blue, the top of the tower in my line of vision, bright against the cloudless sky; and then I gazed all around me, spinning to take in the buildings that framed the square, their stone façades all the same hue of sandy-brown with brightly coloured painted walls and windows. The air smelled of sunshine, heated stones and pine trees combined with coffee and the aroma of flowers, wafting from the boxes in the windows; that must have been the smell of home, for my mother.

Mamma, sono qui. *I'm here.*

I'm standing where you must have walked as a child...

And somewhere not far from here are your mother and your brother.

'You okay?' Matilde laid a hand on my arm. I almost jumped, so immersed in my imaginary conversation with Mamma.

'Yes. Jet-lagged, I suppose!' It was impossible to try and put into words the tangle of my thoughts. 'I'm badly in need of a coffee,' I said, trying to defuse the emotion of the moment. 'But first, if it's not too much bother...'

'Nothing is too much bother for my American cousin!'

'Well, I'd like to see Rosa Bianca.'

Since Matilde hadn't told Zio Carlo and Nonna Clelia of my arrival – or my existence – I wanted to take my time, but it was hard to pace myself, now that I was there. My grandmother was a couple of hundred yards away from me – how could I wait any longer?

'Oh... Nonna is there. So that would mean you meeting her right away... Are you ready for that?'

'Yes. Yes, I am.'

A determined look came over her all of a sudden. 'You have all the right in the world to see our family home. Papà won't be there anyway, and Nonna... I'm sure she'll welcome you.'

But she didn't sound sure.

Well. Whatever was ahead of me, I would face it.

'Will you get into trouble with your papà? Just tell him it was all my doing,' I said, considering the absurdity of it. Two grown women, tiptoeing around like naughty little girls. But I had to be mindful of Matilde – I couldn't just walk in and topple her family dynamic overnight.

'Probably. But it makes no sense. She's your nonna as well as mine. You should be able to see her when you want. None of this makes sense,' she said.

'Well, it's not your fault, and it's not my fault either. Whatever this falling-out is about, it came from our parents.'

'True. And we'll sort it!' Matilde took my arm and began to lead me across the square.

'That's my girl!' I said. I pushed my sunglasses back down – even if I'd wanted to see everything without a filter, in its real, vibrant colours, the light was blazing and almost blinding me, in contrast with the inscrutable dark woods all around the village. Stretching my legs and feeling air and sunshine on my skin was bliss after all those hours being cooped up on a plane and frightened for my life in the car.

We made our way into the heart of the village. The houses were so pretty, with their stonework, brightly painted wooden doors and balconies with wrought-iron fences. Faded frescoes of saints or of the Holy Family, some of them enshrined behind a glass case with a small bouquet and a candle, were dotted everywhere.

'It's almost deserted now, because it's the hottest part of the day. Everyone is inside having their after-lunch rest.'

'A siesta! That sounds good. We should have that in America too!'

'It's good for hot climates. Everything shuts until four in the afternoon, but they're open late in the evening, in the freshest hours of the day. Anyway, this place will be filled to the brim later on. See?' She pointed up. Only then did I notice lines of red and white bunting hanging from balconies and street lamps, across the small street, as well as ribbons of fairy lights. 'It's our Summer Festival. There will be dancing, and food and live music…we'll have a great time!'

'A welcome party for me!' I joked.

As I walked on, I brushed my fingers along a warm stone wall. Everything seemed so ancient. Hundreds of years of churches, castles and homes built one on top of the other, in layers. I could breathe history all around me.

My ancestors had lived in these homes; some of my family still did. Down the generations, our blood was mixed with these stones. The story of my family was one of the thousands that weaved the bigger tapestry. To cut my mother and me off from all this was simply impossible – this landscape, this place, was ingrained into me, it made me who I was, even if I was born thousands of miles away, even if there was so much I didn't know.

We came to the end of the road and Matilde led me down a narrow alley, barely wide enough for two people. An immaculate white cat looked up at us, unfazed. I briefly glanced at it as I walked on, and when I looked forward again, there it was – Rosa Bianca.

This was it, this was the place Mamma had burnt in her memory, and that she had painted in words, even if only in broken sentences here and there. Snippets of a life she'd tried to forget, but couldn't.

I was in a foreign place – and yet, it was so familiar. The trailing roses still bloomed under the summer sun, garlanded around a door painted sky-blue. The house was a two-storey, cream-coloured building with balconies running the full length, decorated with red and pink geraniums in terracotta vases. I could picture the few memories that Mamma had shared with me. So it was here – in the kitchen I could half see, half guess through the window at the left of the door – that she'd made fresh pasta with Nonna Clelia, to be had on feast days. And the balcony upstairs, with its ornate banister – it was from there, on summer nights, that she'd looked at the moon making its progress across the sky, over the hills. And these under my feet, these were the stones she'd walked on barefoot, when she'd played with the children in the neighbourhood…

'Nonna! *Sono io!*' Matilde called, and then again. But there was no reply – only silence.

We waited for a few minutes, but nothing stirred; and then, I thought I saw a little movement, a slight twitch of fabric at the upstairs window, a face peeping from the white linen curtain. I froze. Perhaps I was imagining it. Maybe I was tired and jet-lagged and overwhelmed by it all…

'That's strange – she's usually always home at this time of day…' Matilde said.

'Never mind. I'll meet her soon, I'm sure,' I said. If my eyes hadn't deceived me, if really that had been Nonna Clelia at the window, she didn't want to open the door. My heart sank. There was no point in telling Matilde what I'd seen.

Had it all been for nothing? Maybe I'd come all this way, and I wasn't going to meet any more of my family anyway. The idea was too dismaying for words.

We stepped away, my sandalled feet clicking on the stone.

CHAPTER THREE

Matilde was saying something, but there was a low buzz in my ears, and I was too choked to speak. I walked on, trying to swallow back embarrassing tears. And then – 'Angelina!' a voice said from behind me.

I stopped in my tracks.

'Angelina! Angelina! It's you.'

I turned around, shaking all over, and saw an elderly lady, as small as a bird, on the doorstep of Rosa Bianca. She stood there, eyes wide, wearing a flowery cotton dress and an apron, her hair tied back in a grey-white bun.

She was my mother's twin, and looking at her was like looking into a magical mirror that showed myself at ninety years old – the same huge brown eyes and high cheekbones, the same hairline, high on her forehead and with a tiny dip in the middle…

Yes, she looked like Mamma.

She looked like *me*.

Everything seemed to retreat further and further in the distance, as my surroundings melted away and noises were muffled. This beautiful old lady was all I could focus on. There was nothing I could do but stand and stare, fighting the inner battle between wanting to run to her, and fearing the consequences.

'It's you!' she repeated. 'Angelina!' Her arms stretched out to embrace me.

'Nonna, I'm Luce. Angelina's daughter,' I managed. 'Your granddaughter.'

'Luce…' my grandmother whispered. 'Am I dreaming?'

She might have been confused, due to her age, or the shock; there, on her doorstep, stood her long-lost granddaughter, who'd materialised in front of her from America…

'It's not a dream, Nonna! I'm here!' I said, reaching out to her, and she threw her arms around me, holding me close. She was so small and frail. Now I couldn't hold back my tears any more. It felt like hugging Mamma – familiar scent, familiar body shape. This was the woman who'd given birth to my mother…

We had to wrench apart from each other and, when we did, we were both crying – instantly letting go of so much sorrow, so many years of separation.

Matilde was now crying too. 'Matilde! Thank you, *tesoro mio*!' Nonna said. 'You brought me back my granddaughter!'

She led me inside – the scent of roses pervaded the house as well. For a moment we just stood there, unable to speak; then Nonna broke the spell.

'Come, come. Let's sit in the garden and talk.' She led me to her kitchen, which was immaculately tidy, and then through the back door, into her small garden. On the cupboard to the left of the door, I noticed a little tray with a few pill bottles and boxes, and a square box with an arm cuff attached – I realised it was a blood pressure measuring device. She was an old lady, so it was to be expected that her health would need attention, but I resolved to ask Matilde about the medicines I'd seen, and enquire if Nonna was in good health.

I followed Nonna and Matilde outside, and I was embraced by soft shade, perfumed air and cricket song. We stood under a pergola covered with more trailing roses, angels' bells, hibiscus and passiflora, while from all around us came the scent of lavender, basil, thyme... It was enchanting.

'Your flowers are incredible, Nonna!' Matilde said. 'Still in bloom even in this heat!'

'They've been here forever. They're old and sturdy. Like me!' She laughed. She spoke Italian with exactly the same accent as Mamma, and words from the local dialect peppered her speech. I was once again thankful to Mamma for having spoken Italian to me, and for teaching me many local words – even if I couldn't tell the difference. The way Mamma spoke was my only experience of Italian – I wouldn't have recognised dialects from other regions. In the US, there are different accents and local expressions, but the words Nonna came up with seemed to come from a whole different language. I wondered if someone from the far north of Italy would have been able to understand someone from the deep south, had they both spoken their native dialect... There was so much I didn't know about my own culture.

Nonna sat on a wrought-iron bench covered by a flowery pillow, and patted the place beside her. I sat, and she took my hand in hers.

'Will I make coffee?' Matilde said.

'Thank you, dear, and there's cake in the tin. I made it this morning.'

Matilde disappeared inside, and I was left alone with Clelia. 'Oh, Nonna! I'm so happy to meet you at last!'

'It's a blessing from God,' Nonna said. 'A true blessing that you're here. Tell me, Luce, do I have any other grandchildren?'

'No, there's only me. You have a great-grandson. His name is Eli. He's nineteen and he's... just wonderful. I was married, but not any more.'

'El-i,' she pronounced carefully, with a smile. 'I would love to meet him!'

'I hope it will happen soon, Nonna!'

'And… Luce… how is my daughter? How is Angelina?' she asked, her voice suddenly trembling. All her features were tense, expectant, like everything depended on the answer to that question.

'She's good, Nonna. She worked in a bakery all these years, she never married. She brought me up alone. She misses her home, she misses you… She doesn't talk about it, but I can tell. Especially recently.' I bit my lip, holding back the impulse to blurt out all my questions at once.

'I miss her too, Luce. Did she explain to you what happened all those years ago? Why she left?'

I shook my head. 'Nothing. I'm here to see you and Carlo… and to find out the truth. It's a thorn in Mamma's side… and I don't want to live with a blank page for a past,' I said – my voice was trembling too, but determined. Now that I was here, nothing would stop me until I discovered why my mother left and why I'd grown up without a family. The questions pervaded the air, the space between us. The moment was still, and there was perfect silence for a moment, except for the cricket song, and the bees buzzing all around us.

'There has been so much silence! So much silence. Between Angelina and me, between Carlo and me too. We haven't spoken about what happened. We pretended it never happened.'

It?

What was it that blew the family apart?

'It's time that you know, *tesoro mio*,' she said, and my heart gave a jump as she used the term of endearment Mamma had always used for me – *tesoro mio*, my treasure. 'I'm going to tell you everything, Luce.'

Matilde came back with a tray of coffee and slices of cake. I took the hot cup from her with shaking hands; I was now desperate for sugar, and my head was spinning. The first sip was a lifesaver – the caffeine began coursing through my veins, and I was ready to listen.

'My two granddaughters, together,' Nonna said, looking from a beaming Matilde to me, and back. She closed her eyes for a moment, and she seemed to draw strength to start her story.

When she began to speak, her voice was soft but clear, and it had an almost hypnotic quality. I listened and lost myself in the images she conjured, as everything she said came to life before my eyes.

CHAPTER FOUR

You know, my memory is so bad now, I can't remember things that happened last month, last year. But those days, when I was a child – and later, when the war came... I remember almost every little thing that happened then. Maybe it's because all these years, I wasn't allowed to talk about it. All this time, Luce, I kept my secrets buried deep inside. So I went over the memories by myself again and again: when I sat at the window in winter, and on the doorstep in summer, when I listened to the radio and when I went to church to pray, when I cooked Sunday lunch for the family and when I knitted Matilde's baby clothes. When I went into Angelina's room to dust and sit on her bed and touch her things and cry.

Every time I saw my daughter's chair empty. All those times, I remembered.

That way, recalling things I was supposed to hide so deep that they would seem forgotten, I called to me all the people I'd lost because of our foolishness, and felt them close again.

It was only yesterday, Luce. Only yesterday...

I sat under the shade of a beech tree, at the edge of the dark woods. My head was bent over a book – a precious, rare thing that I treasured – and my sister, Nora, sat beside me on the grass, playing with a daisy chain I'd made for her. She was only three years younger than me but, being the second, she was considered the baby of the family; I was the big one who took care of her, though I wasn't even seven years old. The bright summer day was coming to an end, and soon it would be time to gather the sheep and go home, where more chores waited for me.

I looked up to the sky and then at the small herd of sheep I minded – oh, how I wished to be in school right now, like other children from Bosconero! The ABC book I'd borrowed from the local teacher was so very hard to decipher, though I tried and tried. Going to school was my dream, but my father was away in America, and it was left to my mother and me to support our family. Nora was the apple of everybody's eye – we were inseparable, mostly because Mamma worked so hard that she didn't have time or energy for her. Mamma spent her days at the *lavatoio*, the washhouse, doing laundry day in and day out, and with the little money she earned, she tried to keep the family afloat.

My papà had gone looking for a better life for us; he was tired of scraping a living in those mountains, with the sheep and the back-breaking work on the land they stole from the woods. He'd heard of people finding fortune overseas, a few from Bosconero as well. Mamma didn't want him to go – she was afraid he would not come back – but she relented. What else could she do?

I closed my book and stood, ready to gather the sheep for the night. Bianco, our shepherd dog, stood to attention beside me. Nora, even if she was only little, knew to stay put while I did what I had to do – Bosconero children grew fast, and she was no exception.

But then I heard Mamma calling me – 'Clelia! Clelia! A letter from Papà!'

My heart jumped in my throat. We gathered the sheep as quickly as we could inside the stone shed – there was no way that they could be left outside at night, not on those mountains, where wolves roamed. Mamma scooped up Nora and, with the precious letter in her apron pocket, we rushed to the village. None of us could read; we needed Nin to read it for us. Nin's full name was Caterina, but everyone seemed to have forgotten it, including maybe herself. People brought her papers to read, they asked her to write letters for them, and she could make *medicine as well. She knew things nobody knew, she saw things nobody saw, living at the edge of the woods like she did. The local priest didn't like her: he never really said she was a witch, but we all knew it was what he thought. One day, though, he became very sick himself, and in spite of his protests his housekeeper called Nin for help. Nin gave him medicine, and he lived. He didn't change his opinion of her – he still thought she was a witch – but now, he reluctantly greeted her every time he saw her, instead of turning his head away. Nin smiled and returned his greeting: she wasn't one for holding a grudge. And maybe, who knew, she was a witch indeed. I wasn't afraid of her, though. No woman in the village was afraid of Nin.*

Mamma, with Nora in her arms, and I made our way along through the village's high stone walls, and stepped on the cobblestones, barefooted as we always were. We wore shoes only on a Sunday, to Mass. We walked across the village through narrow, winding alleys, until we reached the end of Bosconero – there, outside the walls and at the edge of the woods, was Nin's house.

We spotted her from a distance, working, as always, around her beehives. When she saw us, she straightened and waited; she didn't wear any protection from the bees she kept, but she was never stung.

Nin always seemed to float in between youth and old age; when you saw her from afar, her face was smooth, and her white hair seemed blonde. But when you came close, you'd see her face was wrinkled and her hands wizened.

'Nin, he wrote!' Mamma said, giving Nora to me and fishing the precious letter out of her apron. You know, my mamma's clothes were old and mended a thousand times over, but she was always clean and tidy. That was your great-grandmother, Luce, she was full of dignity and pride, even living in poverty like we did.

When Mamma showed her the letter, Nin simply nodded and raised her arm to let us in. Once inside, she held Mamma's hands in hers, and the letter between them.

'It's good news,' she said in a soft voice. Because she always knew, when she touched the letters, whether it was good or bad news. I saw Mamma melt in a smile, and I smiled too, sensing the change in atmosphere, the easing of anxiety.

'Thank you, Santa Maria!' Mamma exclaimed.

We sat by the fire on low wooden stools; Nin opened the letter, carefully, and began to read it aloud.

My dear Venturina, Clelia and *piccola* Nora,

I am able to send you this letter because a fellow Italian here agreed to write it for me. I only stepped off the boat a few hours ago, but I could not wait to write to my girls. This city is very big and full of people, I have never seen the likes. There are many of us here, all looking for work. But there is work aplenty and nobody starves. Everyone has a chance. Venturina, *amore mio*, it was the right decision for me to come here! As soon as I can, I will send you the boat fare. I pray for the day we will be together again. Life in America will be good for us, you'll see. Clelia, be a good girl and look after Mamma as you always do. I miss you and you will have grown so much when I see you next. I am so proud of my little Clelia. Please give a kiss to Nora from her loving papà. I will ask my friend to write another letter as soon as we find work.

Your loving husband and father,
Giovanni Nardini

*

Mamma dried happy tears. 'Grazie, Nin, grazie! I'm sorry we have nothing to give you today,' she said. 'But I will pick some good herbs from the fields and bring them to you.'

'That would be lovely,' Nin said, and turned towards me. 'I would like for you to come and see me, Clelia, herbs or not. In the meanwhile, take this,' she said, and picked a jar of liquid gold from a shelf over the fire. Her precious honey. I took it gratefully and held it against my chest, with both hands.

'She's a clever girl,' Nin said. 'I can see it in her eyes.'

On our way home, I could hardly contain my happiness and excitement! Seeing my mamma so animated after having been burdened for so long, almost listless, made me want to skip and jump everywhere I went. I tended to the sheep, looked after my little sister and did all my chores with a spring in my step – I knew it wouldn't be long until we went to America and were reunited with Papà. There, I would be able to go to school and learn to read and write, like Nin.

Every day I sat with the sheep, working on my little ABC book, looking after Nora and waiting for the letter that said we could pack our bags and buy the tickets for the transatlantic voyage.

A few weeks later, the second letter came, at last. We went to Nin full of joy – we knew the boat fare was in that envelope, we knew Papà had written to us to go reach him.

But when Nin touched it, her face told us all there was to know. Mamma turned white.

Nin gave it back to Mamma to open, but Mamma put her hands up. She couldn't bring herself to do it.

Carefully, Nin ripped the envelope open. Inside, there was no boat fare, but a bundle of the letters we'd sent Papà, tied together with a piece of string, and a handkerchief that Mamma had embroidered with Papà's initials. Nin gave Mamma the handkerchief, and Mamma sat with it folded against her heart, while Nin read the letter.

Dear Nardini family,

I write this in sorrow and I am sorry if my writing is so bad but I didn't go to school for long so I hope you understand. I am from Bastia, I knew Giovanni Nardini...

Mamma burst into tears. Not 'know', but 'knew'. I followed suit, my little sobs echoing my mother's.

...We worked together here in... Nuiork...

Nin struggled to read the word.

...Giovanni fell from a scaffolding only a few days after we found this job, he talked about you all the time. I found your address among his things, I cannot send you the rest of the things because I work day wages and they are just enough to eat so I don't have enough money to send a parcel but all there is left here is his clothes and a rosary. I am sending you the letter and a handkerchief that was there, it was all so fast, and he fell from high up so he didn't know he didn't suffer. I hope this is a consolation for you all I am so sorry and I pray every day for his soul and for you...

Nin handed the letters to Mamma; she took them and slipped them in her apron pocket, and there they stayed, together with the one letter

Papà had sent us, for the rest of her life. She wore her apron every day, except to Mass, and every day she carried those letters. Whenever she had a moment's rest, and it was a rare thing, she sat with the letters and looked at them, even if she couldn't read the words.

I never saw her crying again.

The next day I was sitting under the beech tree, Nora beside me and the sheep grazing as they always did. The light had gone from my life. Everything was the same, except everything had changed. My hopes were shattered forever. I grieved for our papà, I grieved for the life I could have had.

I didn't have my ABC with me any more. What was the point? I could never learn on my own anyway, and that road was shut forever.

And then, a young blonde woman appeared out of the woods, and made her way towards me. I peered in the distance to see who it was, and realised that it wasn't a young woman at all – she was old, with white hair and a weathered face. It was Nin. She carried a bundle of books with her. I stood, surprised.

'Hello, clever girl. Sit back down. We have work to do.'

She opened the book and, just like that, like it was nothing, she began to read aloud to me, spelling every letter. She was teaching me how to read.

'Come on, clever Clelia. What are you staring at me for? Look at the page, not at me. I brought you bread and honey as well. Feed the mind and the body. Let's get to work.'

I recovered myself and concentrated on the page, but grateful tears fell on my cheeks and I kept drying them with the back of my hand. Nin didn't seem to notice and, if she did, she didn't comment.

How had Nin known that I had wanted this so desperately? Maybe Mamma had told her. It didn't matter anyway. All that mattered was that I had hope again. To see those little black signs on the page unravel and finally begin to make sense was like a miracle to me, and hope bloomed in my heart again.

*

Years went by. With Mamma taking in washing and me minding the sheep, Nora could go to school, while I never could. But I'd learned to read and write now, and every day I brought a book to the pasture that I could read while the sheep grazed, and my dogs kept guard. Between the schoolteacher, the priest and Nin, I'd put together a small library. I couldn't get enough!

But then Mamma began having pain in her bones, her joints becoming twisted and painful, because of all the time she'd spent with her hands in cold water. She couldn't take washing in any more, Nora was in school, and I had to work for two.

Nora grew to be beautiful. She curled her hair every day, she didn't go barefoot like us but she wore shoes, and although she owned only two dresses she always looked like a city girl. Unlike me, tanned with the hours spent under the sun and my hair straight and unfashionable, in a bun on top of my head, like Mamma. I felt frumpy but I just didn't think this could ever change.

'I'm going to be a teacher, just you wait and see,' She told us.

But when she finished school, having stayed on for middle school – a rare thing at the time, when most children left after two, three years of elementary school – she announced she wanted to get married instead. With her looks and her confidence, she could take her pick; but I was outraged.

'I can't believe you're throwing away the chance of a proper education! You could have a real job! Be respected, looked up to! You would learn so much… If you marry, you'll end up like our mamma. Working until you break your back the way she did, and have nothing to show for it.'

'No, I won't. I'll marry a rich man. Not just a boy from this village. And you'll marry too, and we'll both be happy!'

I rolled my eyes. I was already a spinster by the standards of the time. And I wanted to keep it that way – getting married was the last thing I aimed for. I bit my tongue. I had a sea of tears inside me, and I was afraid that if I started crying, I would never stop; if I got angry, I didn't know what I could do. Sometimes I felt such rage inside, it burnt me.

As always when I was upset, I went to the woods with Grigio, my favourite shepherd dog – Bianco had died years before – and walked and walked until I managed to swallow my anger back. I wondered if all this rage I had to swallow and keep inside me would end up poisoning me slowly.

No, I wasn't keen on men. The ones I knew were loud and drank too much. The man who was supposed to take care of us had gone away and left us forever, even if it hadn't been his fault. I didn't want to be abandoned that way ever again, I didn't want to rely on a man for my survival. I wanted to stand on my own two feet and look after Mamma and myself. Nora could look after herself. She was the smartest and strongest of the three of us, I was sure.

And then, my outlook on life and my plans for the future changed completely when, one night in the woods, I met your grandfather.

*

Nonna fell silent; her gaze had been unfocused and gazing at somewhere far away while she was talking, as if she could see the scenes and the people she was conjuring to life; but now, her eyes were closed. For a moment, the song of the crickets was all I could hear.

'Nonna, stai bene? Are you okay?' Matilde asked, leaning towards her and stroking her back gently.

'Of course, I'm fine! Just, some things aren't easy to bring back to mind.' She smiled. 'I'd better rest a little, now,' she said, and laid a hand on my cheek. Her fingers were cool, and rough, like someone who'd worked with her hands all her life.

'Oh, Nonna, I tired you out! I'm sorry. I hope this wasn't too much of a shock, me turning up this way…'

'It was a shock, but a good one,' she said. 'I wish you could stay here, at Rosa Bianca, but my son… your zio Carlo…' She caught Matilde's eye, and that anxious look that came over my cousin whenever her father was mentioned, was suddenly back.

'I know. I know, you don't need to explain. Don't worry, Nonna, it's all good. We'll sort it out.'

'Massimo and I will be staying with his dad in Bastia, and Luce can have my little attic all to herself.'

'That's good, *tesoro*. I'll see you tomorrow, then? Will you come back? And I'll continue my story…'

'Of course. For sure,' I said, and Nonna and I hugged under the pergola, for a long time – she carried a scent of pansies and baking. When she pulled away, there were tears on both our faces: but they were tears of joy.

CHAPTER FIVE

Matilde slipped my arm under hers and led me down the alley, back to where the sentry cat was sitting, with its emerald eyes and bright white coat. We'd left behind the crickets' song and the perfumed air, and we were back into reality. Nonna's story had been so vivid that I expected to see Nin turn up at any moment, with her honey and her uncanny gift; and Nora, pretty in her city girl's dress and shoes. Poor, poor Giovanni Nardini – my great-grandfather! To die like that, so far from home… And how brave Nonna had been to keep the family going, when she was so little.

'Are you happy, Luce?' Matilde asked.

'Yes. I am,' I said, and my own reply surprised me.

'It went great! I'm so relieved. Nonna was delighted to meet you. And I can't wait to hear more of our family history… it's always been a secret for me too.'

'Relieved doesn't quite describe it, for me. I can't wait to tell Mamma… and Eli, too… at the age of nineteen, he gets to discover a family he knows nothing about.'

I sighed, having unburdened myself of such a heavy load. I could still feel Nonna's arms around me, and her faint scent of violets and baking. I truly had come home, I thought, with a sense of joy and contentment that had escaped me for so long.

'And I can't wait to tell Papà,' Matilde continued. 'Hopefully that part of our family reunion will be as successful…'

'I hope so too,' I said, but both Matilde's and Nonna's apprehension when she'd mentioned Carlo didn't bode well. No – I didn't want to think about that now, when I was still so joyful after being welcomed by Nonna, and the sunshine uplifted me even more. One step at a time was the way to go. However, there was something I needed to know.

'Matilde, I saw lots of medicine bottles on the counter in the kitchen. Is Nonna well?'

'She has some heart trouble, but nothing alarming… they keep it under control with meds. Papà and I take her to the hospital in Bastia regularly to be checked out. In fact, I think Papà is taking her down to Bastia tomorrow. Don't worry, she's good. She's strong. I'm glad to say we have very strong genes, Luce!'

I'd noticed that with Mamma, for sure. 'Thank goodness,' I replied, relieved, and went straight from a word to a yawn.

'Oh, you must be exhausted!' Matilde said, pulling me closer. 'What next? More coffee, sleep, or both?'

'Both! Sleep first, more coffee later!' I said.

The meeting with Nonna had been so poignant, so emotional that I'd forgotten all about being jet-lagged from the journey. Now that I was out in the sunshine, in the deserted, sleepy village where everyone was probably inside snoozing, it all came tumbling on my shoulders.

The air was so warm that it relaxed every muscle in my body, still sore from the flight and from nerves. A sweet scent of grass baking in the sun wafted from the hills all around us and overlapped with the scent of coffee that seemed to be ever present. I raised my eyes to the azure sky and breathed in, enchanted…

We were almost in the square when an electronic tune came from Matilde's bag. After looking at her phone, her eyes clouded up a little.

'Papà just messaged me,' she said, and once again, I sensed her disquiet. Why was everyone so on edge where Carlo was concerned? Why was he given the power to upset everyone? The idea that my uncle was a bully was making room in my mind, but I didn't want to be too prejudiced about him. I had to give him a chance and form my own opinion. 'Is he coming to Bosconero?'

'He's coming back tomorrow. Nonna has an appointment at the hospital, like I told you, so you can meet him before or after… I suppose we need to do it the right way, you know. Try and not ruffle any feathers. He's very protective of her…'

'He doesn't need to defend her from me,' I said, a touch annoyed. Not with Matilde, but with the idea of this stranger – who happened to be my uncle – not trusting me near my own grandmother.

'Oh, I know, I know… It's just that…' She was anxious again, and I hated to see her like that. Maybe my words had been too harsh – I had to remember I could not fall on them all of a sudden and upset delicate dynamics.

'Don't worry. We'll make it work. I'll just turn up and speak to him there and then. This way, he can't find an excuse not to meet me. I'll reassure him about my intentions, and… Oh, sorry…'

It was my phone ringing, now. I saw the number flashing on the screen, and I smiled to myself: Mamma. Of course, it was almost obvious that she should call me just at this moment. It was as if my thoughts had reached her, somehow.

'It's Angelina,' I told Matilde before pressing the phone to my ear. I braced myself and turned away from Matilde a little; my eyes met the cat's as I answered. He had followed us down the alley, apparently. 'Mamma?'

'*Tesoro mio*. Where are you?' she said softly.

'Oh, Mamma, I'm here, in Bosconero,' I whispered; I had to remind myself that here people actually spoke Italian and could understand what Mamma and I were saying.

Silence. Two elderly ladies who'd skipped their siesta went by, walking slowly beside the cat. He stayed put, didn't move an inch, forcing the women to walk around him, like he owned the place.

'I've just been to Rosa Bianca,' I tried to fill the silence. My heart was in my throat.

'You are in Bosconero?'

'*Sì*, Mamma.' There was another moment of silence – then a sigh so sorrowful it broke my heart. 'I met Nonna. Your mother,' I insisted, trying to be cheerful, in spite of Mamma's consternation. 'She was lovely to me, she was so happy to meet me…'

'Oh, Luce. *No…*'

I knew she'd been against the idea of me travelling here, I knew she wanted the past to stay buried, I knew all that – but for some reason, that 'No' still hit me hard. Doubt creeped in my thoughts, dispersing my previous happiness, and I almost shivered in spite of the sun and heat. Had I done the right thing? Had it all been a huge mistake?

My heart said it hadn't.

I'd finally met my grandmother. I'd gone back to where I came from. And for a woman without roots and without a father, it meant a lot. It meant everything.

'Mamma, I promise you, she was happy to see me. She thought I was you, she called me Angelina…' I said in the unnerving silence. It was like shouting down a well. There was a soft sob at the other end of the line – Mamma was crying. This alone was horrible; she hardly ever cried. 'Oh, no, don't cry! Nonna was so sweet, she asked after you! She said she wants to tell me everything that happened! Oh, Mamma, you should be here…'

For a moment I thought she'd put the phone down, but then she spoke. 'Some things should stay buried. Some things are better left alone,' she said, and although she was suffocating her tears and trying to speak evenly, her voice sounded broken. I was half heartsick for her, half exasperated.

I'd made a step forward, and I'd done it for her, too – why was she so inflexible, so uncompromising on keeping the situation as it was: twisted and unnatural? A family torn apart hurt everyone – why did we have to live that way?

'But these things you buried, the secrets, they eat you from within. You know that. It's what has been happening to you!'

'You should have let sleeping dogs lie. I left it all behind, and so should you.'

'Mamma. You know that's not true. You didn't leave it behind. It stayed with you, always. You can pretend the past never happened, but I've had enough of pretending! I…'

And then a thought hit me, and my words trailed away. If Carlo didn't know about me, did Mamma know about Matilde? I didn't think she did.

'Mamma. I'm here with your niece… Matilde,' I said tentatively.

'My niece?'

I thought there was a hint of longing in Mamma's voice, now. I pressed on.

'Yes. Carlo has a daughter.' I looked up at those words, and I saw Matilde gazing back at me from a few steps away. 'She's beautiful, Mamma, and so sweet!' I said, hoping she would offer something more than fear and disapproval. 'She'd love to meet you…'

But I was to be disappointed, because Mamma's only comment was: 'Just, Luce, please, keep safe. Promise.'

Safe.

Her choice of words took me by surprise. There was more to it than something you'd say to a daughter who'd just flown to the other side of the world, more than a conflicted family history. I could feel it.

It was a warning, and I was spooked. 'Mamma, I'm perfectly safe—' I began, but cold fingers had travelled down my spine, and I had to try hard to seem unfazed, untouched by her ominous words.

She cut me short. 'Promise.'

'Mamma—'

'Promise.'

'I promise,' I gave in. 'I'll call you…' I began, but there was silence on the other side, and I knew she was gone. I let my arm fall.

My eyes met Matilde's again. She'd moved away a few steps, but I could guess she'd heard the conversation, both my words and Mamma's – cell phones leave little room to privacy.

'*Tutto bene?*' Everything okay?

'I suppose. Yes.' I gave her a smile, but she'd heard Mamma's words, and she knew that everything was not okay. A moment of awkwardness, then we both spoke at the same time.

'Shall we go…'

'Maybe we should…'

We laughed, and the echo of Mamma's warning was dispelled for the moment. Matilde gently led me across the square and to the car, leaving the sphinx-like cat behind. 'This is the plan. I'll take you to my apartment, let you refresh and rest, and tonight we're going out. There'll be music and food stalls on the streets, you'll love it! Does it sound good?'

'It sounds wonderful,' I said heartily.

'And tomorrow, we'll sort everything with Papà. It'll all work out, you'll see,' she said, and squeezed my arm as we walked down the silent street. The whole village seemed to be sleeping now, in the blazing, scorching midday – everyone, except the two rebel ladies who were out in what had to be almost ninety degrees, and the cat who thought himself king.

The place was beautiful, and Matilde was even sweeter and kinder than I had pictured after our virtual exchanges. The family home, the pretty Rosa Bianca, seemed to have jumped out of a postcard, and Mamma's memories had finally come to life, for me. Most of all, Nonna had been happy to see me, and eager to tell me their story.

Everything looked good, for now.

And still, I was shaken. Even in the blinding sunshine, in the heat of noon and with Matilde by my side, a shiver shook me.

Keep safe. Promise.

Mamma wasn't the dramatic type, and that made her warning even more worrying.

Of course I would keep myself safe.

The question was – safe from what?

*

We retrieved my suitcase from the car – finally, I could get my hands on my camera! – and Matilde led me down an alley departing from the square, until we reached a terracotta-painted door in one of the ancient stone houses. She unlocked the door and I climbed up the steep stone steps after her, enjoying the cool and the shade.

'My palace! Welcome!' she said when we got to the top floor, unlocking another door. I followed her inside; she walked straight to the window across the room to open the shutters, and a warm light flooded the place, making the blond wood floors shine golden. I sighed in relief to have somewhere to cool down and gather my thoughts a little.

'Thank you. What a lovely place, Matilde!' I said. It was a studio attic, with a low ceiling criss-crossed by dark wooden beams. I rolled the case out of the way and went to gaze outside the window. The view was spectacular: at the end of the small lane where the house was located, I could see the square and, beyond, to the forested hills and a corner of pure blue sky. Eli would love this, I thought; he'd turn it into an incredible shot.

'It's all yours! Make yourself comfortable,' Matilde responded and patted the double bed in the centre of the room, covered with white sheets and a biscuit-coloured blanket. A pile of folded towels sat on the bed too, and a bathrobe. It all looked so fresh and inviting that I could almost already feel the cool touch of the pillowcases against my skin. I could have lain down there and then. Matilde must have noticed the longing in my eyes as I looked at the bed, because she said: 'I'll leave you to rest. Feel free to have a shower and help yourself to anything you need. Massimo and I will come and get you around six?'

'Perfect. I'm looking forward to meeting him,' I said warmly. I'd seen photographs of her fiancé on her Facebook feed: a tall, dark-haired young man with unruly curly hair and a wide smile. He was often portrayed doing some kind of outdoor activity, climbing or running or paragliding. He seemed smitten with her, and together they were the picture of happiness.

'If you have earplugs, you'd better use them. They'll start rehearsing soon,' Matilde warned me, looking out of the window and down onto the square.

'I'm sure I'll have no trouble sleeping! A whole orchestra playing on my bed would not keep me awake at this point!'

Matilde laughed. 'Enjoy your rest. See you later,' she said and kissed me lightly on the cheek.

I looked around me – what a pretty place, so cool and restful. Bliss. I was more than ready to be on my own and let all that had happened sink in.

I put my phone to charge – it was a must for keeping in touch with my family back home – washed the journey away under a warm shower, and put on a light, white nightshirt. I opened the window and closed the shutters, rendering the room almost dark, the strong white light of the sun filtering in nothing more than tiny rays on the sides. Finally, I nestled myself under the cool white sheets, and closed my eyes to the world. Not even the million questions I had could keep me awake, and I fell into a deep, exhausted sleep.

*

I woke up to the sound of music wafting from the streets below. For a moment I battled the where-am-I? feeling that arises from awakening in a strange place, and then everything came back to me. I lay still, basking in the moment. The white sunrays of the early afternoon had given way to a warmer glow, drifting through the shutters together with the music. I looked at the clock on the bedside table – almost six o'clock. Matilde and Massimo must be on their way. I went to open the shutters and looked out.

The small stage in the square was now decorated with the same white and red ribbons I'd seen stretched between the houses, and people were beginning to gather. Food and craft stalls had popped up like mushrooms in the few hours I'd been sleeping. The street party was almost ready, and the sky had turned from a light blue to the deep azure of the almost-evening.

I listened to the tunes coming up from the streets while slipping on a simple white linen dress and another pair of high-heeled sandals. (I'd brought too many pairs of shoes, probably – on the other hand, does such a thing as too many shoes actually exist?) I layered creamy green eyeshadow to highlight my brown eyes, and gathered my hair on one side with a jewelled clip, then stood beside the window while slipping my earrings in. The alley was filling up, and the square beyond it. I took a picture with my phone, wanting to send it to Eli straight away, though the lens didn't – it couldn't – fully capture the golden light and the atmosphere.

My view right now, I captioned the photo and sent it.
Oh, it was all so exciting!

Although I missed my son, and even if my mother was determined to convince me I'd just opened Pandora's box by coming here – I felt great. *A mother, ex-wife and unruly daughter, untethered*, I thought with a half-smile, looking down to the party preparing. I was looking forward to it, and unafraid of whatever was ahead of me.

Awesome. Mom, Dad didn't take it very well that you went away.

I was irked. My decisions had nothing to do with Ethan; we'd been apart three years and all we needed now was to get round to formalising our separation into a divorce. Besides, we broke up because he lived his own independent life around which I orbited, like a small, unimportant satellite. And now, he didn't take well that I'd gone away on my own? He had never cared before, so why should he now?

I took a deep breath before I typed. I was always very careful not to involve Eli in any resentment between his father and me.

I've been on holiday before. I'm fine and I'm happy. X

But this is not a holiday, it's family stuff, and he's worried about you.

He is? Did he not have a girlfriend to worry about, instead of interfering in my life? Tell him to worry about Vicky instead, I wanted to say – Vicky, his girlfriend of a year.

Despite my best efforts, I actually liked her – or didn't mind her, anyway. She was sweet and she was kind to Eli; I didn't need to know more. Yes, every time I thought of her and Ethan together I felt like throwing up, but – but choices had been made.

> *Tell him there's nothing to worry about and to give my regards to Vicky.*

Oh, God. If ever there was a passive-aggressive message, this was it. I squeezed my eyes and brought the phone up to my forehead.

> *Vicky and Dad broke up last year! Did he not say?*

They did? No, he didn't say. Because we don't talk.

'You ready?' a silvery voice called from beneath the window. Matilde came into view, so cute in an off-the-shoulder black top and jeans. A tall, dark-haired man stood beside her, looking up at me with a friendly smile; I recognised him immediately as Massimo.

'*Arrivo subito!*' I called out to them, waving.

> *I'm sorry to hear that,* I typed quickly. *Anyway, tell him I'm okay. Gotta go, street party tonight, wish you were here, tesoro mio, take care… I'll send you pics though not as beautiful as the ones you take, Mom x*

I pondered for a moment whether to take my camera, but it was heavy and fragile, so I decided to stick to my phone for the night – I didn't want to have tourist written all over me, prancing about with a big camera around my neck.

Outside, the warmth of the late afternoon enveloped me, after the cool of the stone-walled house. The sweet, romantic sound of a lone accordion filled the air now, and I could smell roasting meat and baking bread wafting from the stalls. It was a joyful sensory overload, and such a novel feeling, after the last few months of greyness inside. Life seemed in full colour all again, of a sudden.

'You look great,' Matilde said and hugged me – she was wearing a sweet, floral scent that was perfect for her.

'So do you! And you must be Massimo!' I said and offered my hand to the lanky, smiling guy beside her.

'That's me,' Massimo said with one of the open smiles I'd seen in Matilde's Facebook pictures. He took my hand and bent down all the way to my five foot two to kiss me on both cheeks, the Italian way.

'I'm so glad to meet you at last,' I said.

'And you! You speak perfect Italian, by the way. I thought I'd have to dust down my elementary-school English!'

'Oh, no, my mom always spoke Italian to me. Though maybe I'm a bit rusty, I suppose.' I shrugged.

'Doesn't sound like it. It's great to have you here.'

'Thank you,' I replied, grateful of this warm welcome. He had kind eyes, I thought.

'You must be hungry!' Matilde intervened. 'We're taking you for an aperitivo!' She wrapped an arm around my shoulder, and we walked down the alley, towards the square.

The lone accordion played on the stage in the centre, sur-rounded by other musicians and various musical equipment – there would be a proper concert later on, I thought. The square was garlanded with coffee shops and their sun-shaded outdoor areas, and people were sitting at tables outside, drinking wine and cappuccinos, and eating colourful ice creams. Matilde and Massimo found a seat right opposite the stage.

'Is this place okay? It's my favourite coffee shop. They're very generous with aperitivo snacks,' Matilde said.

That sounded good to me. 'It's lovely!' I replied, and we sat at a small, round table. I leaned back and crossed my legs, ready for some serious people-watching. Everyone seemed dressed in their best: lovely-looking, dark-haired young people in summer clothes and elderly ladies in their Sunday clothes, hair in buns like my grandmother, holding onto their handbags. I noticed that there was a huge difference between how the older generation and the young people dressed – the former a little old-fashioned, almost out of time, while the latter were right on trend. There were children everywhere, tanned and lively, running around while balancing ice creams perilously in their small hands. A little girl in a blue dress, long brown hair held back with an Alice band, twirled to show off her skirt in front of her parents.

'*Benedetta, sei proprio una principessa!*' the girl's mother said – Benedetta, you look like a princess – and the child beamed and skipped ahead.

'Can I order for you, Luce?' Matilde asked with a smile.

'Absolutely.'

She disappeared inside, and Massimo and I were left alone. 'I'm so happy to meet someone else from Matilde's family,' he said, and I guessed that I hadn't been the only one longing for blood relatives. Matilde must have confided in Massimo about our family situation – as I would have expected, as they were engaged. She'd also said that Massimo seemed to be the only person who could reach Carlo, and who he trusted.

'I'm so happy to meet someone from my family,' I replied. 'I'm now bracing myself to meet Zio Carlo.'

'Yes. That will be interesting… Don't worry,' he added, seeing my face.

'Please tell me he's all… bark and no bite?' I struggled to translate the saying in Italian. 'Am I making sense?'

'Yes. We have the same saying. Dog who barks doesn't bite.'

'And… is that the case?'

'I'd like to say that. But… well, it's not. We'll just have to make sure he doesn't bite you.'

'Oh. Well, thank you.' I refused to revert to my earlier anxiety. And after all, I could bite back. Above us, the sky was darkening more and more and preparing for dusk, that enchanted hour hanging between day and night. Once again, and not for the last time, it all seemed like a dream to me.

I changed the subject. 'You two make such a beautiful couple,' I said.

'She's the love of my life,' Massimo said simply. 'I still have to pinch myself sometimes. I can't believe she's going to marry me. Me, of all people. How lucky am I?'

'You are lucky!' I said, and I meant it.

'Who's going to marry you?' Matilde called to him playfully, returning with two plates of fragrant focaccia and different kinds of pizza cut in tiny squares. She was followed by two waiters with a bottle of red wine, glasses and a tray of yummy-looking charcuterie.

Massimo smiled and looked down – I could see he was embarrassed, to have been caught being sentimental in public. 'This girl I know…' he said, still smiling.

Matilde laid down the goodies she was carrying and gave him a kiss on the cheek. 'Well, we'll see. If you behave! I got a cappuccino for you,' she added.

'No wine for me tonight,' Massimo explained. 'I'm on call with the ambulance service.'

'Oh, are you a paramedic?' I asked.

'No, just a volunteer. I did a course over two years, but that's all. It's a service for our villages. You see, some places are so isolated, the official ambulances would take ages to get there. We also take old people to appointments, deliver prescriptions, even just check on them.'

'Sounds great,' I said. 'What a gift to the community.'

Massimo shrugged. 'We just do our bit. Now, Luce, let me tell you something about Italians, in case your mamma didn't teach you. We really enjoy feeding our guests,' he said, and gestured to the buffet Matilde and the waiter had laid in front of us.

'And ourselves too.' Matilde laughed.

'Oh, yes, it's fine by me!' I was starving, and cheerfully tried a bit of everything. The focaccia was so good, with its rosemary flavour and coarse salt, and it went down a treat with the wine Massimo had poured for me. The fancy-looking cheeses and cured meats were amazing, and helped to offset the effects of the wine from my miraculously self-filling glass.

'Is this hitting the spot?' Matilde asked.

'Mmmm. Mmmm! Yes!' I swallowed and answered. It certainly was. Italian food in Italy was not like Italian food in America. The flavours were so much stronger and nuanced. My taste buds had died and gone to heaven.

Suddenly a small crowd of young men appeared out of nowhere and surrounded Massimo. They began to greet each other in a very Italian way, all hugs and handshakes. They all leaned over to kiss Matilde twice on her cheeks.

'We're about to steal your fiancé, Matilde,' one of them said.

'Steal away! I'll be celebrating with my cousin. Guys, meet Luce, from the United States of America,' she said grandly. 'Luce, the ambulance service volunteers.'

'*Piacere!*' There was a flurry of greetings as they all leaned over to kiss me too. Oh, how I wished that Eli could have been here, I thought for the millionth time since I'd arrived. Two of these guys didn't seem that much older than him, just by a few years, while the third one was closer to my age. They introduced themselves: there was Andrea, the oldest of the three, with salt and pepper hair and smiling eyes; bearded Roberto; and Giacomo, who was uncharacteristically blond and blue-eyed. I knew that Italy was quite diverse, but most people I'd seen up till now were dark, like Mamma and myself.

'How's the baby, Giacomo?' Matilde asked.

'Look for yourself.' Giacomo took out his phone and began passing it around, to a chorus of *awwwws*. On the screen there was a little girl with straw-blonde hair, tiny in the arms of her mother. She was perfect.

'*Congratulazioni!*' I added my voice to the good wishes.

I noticed Matilde's eyes lingering on the picture for a moment, Giacomo's phone in her hand, almost unwilling to pass it on. There was a longing in her eyes – I could see it. Maybe only women who'd gone through the longing before could recognise the signs. I smiled inwardly. All that was ahead of her – there was so much promise, in her future.

'Are you getting any sleep?' Roberto, the bearded guy, asked Giacomo. 'Because when my son was born, we hardly slept for about a year…'

The new father shrugged. 'Nah, she sleeps great. She's easy.'

'She's *bellissima*,' Massimo said. 'Thankfully she takes after her mother and not after you.' There was a burst of laughter. 'We have a bit of time yet. Can I get you guys a cappuccino?'

'Why not, sure,' they agreed and pulled up some free chairs from nearby tables. Andrea, the oldest of the company, sat beside me.

'I don't speak English,' he said, with a heavy accent. '*A parte questa frase!*' Apart from this sentence. I laughed.

'It's okay, I speak Italian.'

'*Bene, bene.* So, how have you been liking Bosconero, so far?' he asked.

'I'm loving it. It's beautiful, and I'm getting such a warm welcome from my family.' My family. It felt good, to say that.

'I'm glad you love our village,' he replied. I noticed that his eyes were light brown, an unusual colour – like amber. His skin was dark from the sun, and he wore a smart short-sleeved shirt and jeans.

Maybe it was the wine, or because I was far from home and felt free, but although I never usually noticed this kind of thing, I had to admit he was attractive, in an exotic, interesting way.

'I can't wait to explore the area,' I said. 'I'm a photographer, and so is my son. I promised him to send him plenty of pictures.'

'Oh, a photographer! That's interesting. I'll show you around a bit, if you want?'

'Sure, why not?' Oh God. Had I actually blushed? I caught Matilde's mischievous look with the corner of my eye. How embarrassing.

I took a sip of wine and joined the general conversation, feeling silly. The guy was just being nice and welcoming to a foreigner; why on earth had I got that rush of blood to the head?

Ridiculous, that's what it was.

'Time to go, *ragazzi*,' Andrea said after a few minutes, pushing back his chair.

Massimo kissed Matilde and whispered: 'I'll see you later.'

With waves and a chorus of '*Ciao*'s, they walked away, leaving behind a cloud of aftershave that lingered for a moment.

'They're Massimo's best friends,' Matilde explained once they'd left. 'They all grew up together. I do a shift a week in the ambulance service too. Andrea is there all hours.'

I helped myself to another generous bit of focaccia and some hard cheese with the most incredible flavour. 'Will Massimo be away all night?'

'I think so, yes. But we'll have lunch tomorrow together, if it's okay with you?'

'I'd love that.'

'We talked while you were asleep, and we planned a meal with Papà. Just us four…'

I stopped chewing for a moment and it almost went down the wrong way. I downed the rest of my wine. 'Yes, good idea. Did you speak to Carlo as well, while I was sleeping, by any chance?'

'Not yet. But don't worry,' Matilde said, and laid a hand on mine. 'Massimo will work his magic. He's the son Papà never had.' She rolled her eyes. 'He hopes we can sort the family situation out before we…'

'Before you…?' I smiled. I could guess what she was about to say.

'Well, you know, before our wedding. We don't have a date yet, but it'll be before next winter.'

'Oh, I'm so happy for you, Matilde! This is wonderful news.'

'I know! You see, this is part of it. Meeting you, having you over. Part of why I was so delighted when you got in touch. Massimo had just proposed, and we talked, and I told him it would be like an impossible dream, getting the family together. A wonderful, impossible dream. But here we are, you and me… I know it's not the whole family, but it's a start. To have you at my wedding… and Eli… and maybe Zia Angelina…'

'I hope so too,' I said, and took in Matilde's pretty face, young and hopeful. For a moment I imagined her and Eli together, the two cousins, chatting and laughing at Matilde's wedding, weaving back together what had been torn apart. 'I can be your wedding photographer!'

'I saw your website, you're so good. It'd be amazing!'

'We'll make it happen,' I said, determined.

'Shall we go and join the party? Do you dance? Shall we dance, later on?' she said, as we stood and joined the crowd.

'I haven't danced in years!' Between her cheerfulness, the wine and the festive atmosphere, my worry about the prospective meeting with Carlo was almost easy to cast aside.

Twilight was now turning into night, and the village had come truly alive. Lines and lines of fairy lights were lit up, all at once, taking my breath away, and a dance orchestra had taken the place of the lonely accordion. A beautiful, unmistakably Italian-looking woman in a tight dress was singing, and couples of all ages were beginning to dance – elderly people, young ones, children. Matilde and I wandered around; she knew everyone, and she introduced me to so many people, friends and even distant relatives. Nonna wasn't around, she explained, because she wouldn't be up for a busy party, with her heart troubles. The photo collection on my phone was getting bigger and bigger – portraits of people, shots of the stony houses, of the church and the medieval tower, and then pictures of the food, of the hills in the distance, of the fairy lights dancing in the evening breeze. They would be the record of an enchanted time.

I knew I would treasure that moment forever, lost in music and beauty and enveloped by the warm Italian night. We danced, we strolled, we ate some more – they were roasting boar meat, hunted locally, cooked there in front of us – and I found room to try a little bit, because the aroma was irresistible.

'Are you up for walking a little?' Matilde finally said. 'I'd like to show you a beautiful place, not far from here. It's called Collina Cora.'

'In the boar-infested woods?' I laughed.

'Don't worry, they're shy creatures, I promise! The fireworks are about to start, and I'd like to take you up the hill, to see them properly.'

'Are we not up the hill already?' I was a little giddy with the wine, and my cheeks were warm.

'Another one,' she said. 'See?' She pointed at a smaller, darker hill in front of us. 'That's Collina Cora.'

'Okay. But what about the boars? Are you sure they're shy?'

'A hundred per cent sure. They're more scared of you than you are of them.'

'Seriously?' I raised my eyebrows.

'No. Come on.' She laughed and took me by the hand.

'Oh, great!' I muttered, but I was looking forward to the fireworks. Matilde bought a bottle of red wine and slipped it in her bag, and we made our way through rugged paths in the woods, our phones acting as tiny torches. The night was illuminated with the fairy lights from the festival, and even under the tree canopy we could hear the voices and music and buzz of the party.

We stepped out of the village walls, through a dark, wooded stretch; I took off my sandals, and walked barefoot. It was better than tottering on high heels in the woods. We came onto an open valley, nestled between hilly ground, and walked on the soft grass all the way up the slope, while I dangled my shoes in one hand and my phone, lighting up the way, in the other.

'Look. Roman ruins,' Matilde said, showing me some grey, crumbly walls with the aid of her phone light. Then she raised her light, and what I saw took my breath away. 'With a medieval church on top of them.'

It was a half-ruined church, with hollowed-out walls and arches, covered in moss. Matilde was perfectly blasé about it, while I was enchanted. In the US, you only see Roman ruins or medieval anything in theme parks.

'Come, sit. The fireworks will start in a moment,' she said, and pulled the cork out of the neck of the bottle. She took a sip and passed it to me. I was already tipsy, but drank some anyway, feeling wonderfully carefree. The warmth spread in my veins.

Collina Cora was in perfect darkness, while Bosconero shone on the hill across from us, the fairy lights dancing slightly in the breeze.

I sighed, a long, deep sigh straight from my soul, and relieved a tension, a sense of constraint, like a band around my heart I didn't even know had been there. I leaned back, stretched my legs out with my ankles crossed, and relished the moment. The heat of the night, the beauty of the lights down the valley, the presence of the only member of my family, other than my mother and my son, that I'd ever known; everything contributed to my sudden perfect, unbound joy.

At that moment, I realised how much my empty home had really affected me. I seemed to have grown to believe that life ahead of me stretched lacklustre and dull, but it wasn't true. There was so much to enjoy, so much to experience, in this new phase of my life.

It seemed that, by going back, I had moved forward.

Popping noises interrupted my thoughts; the fireworks had begun, showers of red, gold and blue, multicoloured stars exploding and leaving bright plumes that vanished against the starry sky. Matilde was *oohing* and *aahing* like a little girl, and when the spectacle finished she laid her head on my shoulder. I wrapped my arm around her – a wave of affection for her swept me, even if we'd just met.

'Tomorrow we have lots on,' she said. 'It'll be a great day.'

'It will be, yes,' I replied, and I believed it. When I looked into Matilde's unwritten face, so young and full of hope, it was almost obvious to believe that only good things would happen.

'I just have to pop in at work for a couple of hours, then I'll take you everywhere,' Matilde said, and I remembered that she worked in a travel agency. 'Unless, of course, Andrea takes you sightseeing…'

'Matilde! He was just being nice. Stop it!' Did I just blush again?

Matilde laughed, and I joined in – I couldn't help it. I did feel silly. In three years of separation from my husband, I'd never looked at another man twice. I'd been too scarred by the failure of my marriage, by how useless and unlovable it'd made me feel. Every time someone showed some interest in me, or tried to flirt, I froze on them; and I ducked every attempt at blind dates, or 'dates with my single friend', that my girlfriends threw at me.

But tonight: tonight I blushed, and got flustered. And, to my surprise, it felt good.

Matilde rested her cheek on her hand. 'I think he likes you.'

'He just saw me for five minutes!'

'Yeah, well, I noticed the way he was looking at you.'

'Well, he's probably the kind of guy who would flirt with anyone, I'm sure! He's handsome, and he knows it,' I said, rather judgementally.

'No, actually. Flirting is not like Andrea. His wife fell for someone else, a few years ago. It was a huge blow for him. He has a teenage daughter, and he lives for her. We know him well. He's not the type to flirt around.'

'I'm so sorry,' I said, touched. I knew what it was like to have your marriage crumble around your ears. It was something I wouldn't wish on anyone. 'But I'm not that way inclined, anyway.'

'You don't have to marry him! Yes, you're here for a reason, a crucial reason, but you're also on holiday. You should go and have some fun, don't you think?'

'Well, we'll see.' I shrugged. Time to change the subject. 'I really like Massimo. He's smitten with you, it's clear to see!'

'And I with him. Some say we're too young to marry... I'm only twenty-two and he's a year older than me, but if you know it's the right person, why wait? I've never been happier than since I met him. It hasn't been easy, growing up with my papà, but now I have Massimo... he's all I want from life. To marry him and be a wife and mother. Old-fashioned, eh? I know, it's terrible!' she said and chuckled.

'Of course not! It's what you want. And being a mother is a lot of work, but the best job ever. As for being a wife... I don't think I can give lessons on that. I failed miserably.'

'Don't say that. It does happen, people break up and it doesn't mean you failed anything! Maybe you just weren't meant for each other...'

Weren't we? Because when we'd married, I was so sure. And so was Ethan.

How can love fade away, if it's so strong to start with? Is there such thing a soul mate, a love that lasts forever?

With the way my life had gone, I was given to say no.

Ethan's love for me seemed to have faded through the years, in spite of all the promises he'd made. The irony was that it was me who'd initiated the separation. We lived separate lives; what was the point? It was a charade, one I couldn't live with any longer, one that reminded me every day of what we'd lost.

'And you're clearly a wonderful mom to Eli,' Matilde continued. 'He's lucky! You know, my mother was never around for me. I'd like my children to have a happy family. I want to be there for them.'

So Matilde's mom wasn't around? She made it sound like it had been a choice, not a tragic set of circumstances, like her mother had died young. Maybe she'd left home? Once again, I refrained from asking; I didn't want to spoil the moment, and Matilde would tell me when she was ready.

'I understand. I never knew my father either…' I said. The conversation was getting quite tragic.

'Oh, I'm sorry!'

'Yeah, don't be; it was my normal, you know. Mamma and me. It's just the way it's always been. But I do wonder…' I shrugged. 'Well, one thing at a time! I'll sort this side of the family, first!' I laughed softly. Silence followed, and I felt compelled to bring Matilde and me onto happy territory again. 'So. Did you start organising the wedding already?'

'Well, I think I'm off to a good start,' she said and began pressing buttons on her phone. I leaned closer to her, our heads together, to look at her screen.

A picture came up, shining in the dark. It was a dress, a wedding dress – white and simple and beautiful, like a Grecian goddess. The model was wearing a flowery wreath and held a wildflower bouquet, held together by simple thread.

'Oh, Matilde!' I gushed, and she smiled. The light of the smartphone in that sea of darkness was reflected on her face. 'You'll look stunning in this. It's gorgeous.'

'It took me ages to find! I went to lots of expensive shops, and everything looked so… so meringue-y. I didn't want to look like someone from a soap opera!' We laughed. 'And then I found this. Vintage, homemade and unique. This girl in a nearby village scours around for old wedding dresses and restores them. I would have loved to wear Nonna's wedding dress, by the way, but our family was so poor, she got married in her Sunday dress, the one she used for Mass, with a crocheted veil…'

'Oh…' I treasured every detail Matilde revealed about our nonna, and about the family.

'Yes. So, this was my best option!'

'It's perfect for you,' I said. The Grecian style, with a high waist and the simple drapes that fell to the model's legs, would look amazing with Matilde's dark colouring. 'Well, it's settled, then. I must be at the wedding. I will be, no matter what your papà says.'

'Thank you. It would mean the world to me. Also because my mother won't be there.'

It was the second time that she'd mentioned her mother. Maybe, I thought, she needed to talk about the matter – was she trying to tell me something? So, this time, I decided to enquire. 'I hope I'm not being intrusive, Matilde, but… what happened with her?'

'I haven't had contact with her in years. She left us. She literally disappeared. I suppose my father is not an easy man to live with… but I don't understand why she never wanted anything to do with me. Since I got engaged… you know, thinking of having children and all that… it stings even more.'

Her mother didn't want to have anything to do with Matilde? That sounded outrageous to me. Why would a mother do that to her daughter? If I thought of ever abandoning Eli… But I couldn't judge this stranger. I didn't know what could have brought her to such a terrible choice.

'I'm sorry, Matilde.'

'Me too. You know, I wonder…' she said and echoed the words – I wonder – I'd often used to talk about my father. When someone so important disappears from a child's life, or was never there, they're left with an almost unbearable barrage of questions, doubts, an endless series of why? And you never stop asking yourself why they left, if they remarried, if you have siblings, what happened next. I wasn't immune from those questions, even if Mamma parented for two and gave me all the love I could ever want or need. I waited in silence for Matilde to gather her thoughts and continue. '… I wonder why she didn't take me with her when she went. I mean, if her life with Papà was hard, did she not think it was going to be hard for me too? Maybe she didn't care. Anyway, she disappeared. Left no trace. She didn't want Papà to ever find her.'

She said that without bitterness, only sadness, and I felt so sorry for her.

'There might be things you don't know… though it's hard to understand, or accept.'

'Yeah.'

The conversation had been a rollercoaster for both of us. And it had stirred old questions in me, questions I thought I'd buried deep, or even fooled myself I'd never had. Maybe the wine had something to do with the see-sawing, intricate emotions that had come pouring out.

'And anyway, you have your whole life ahead of you, and you're getting married soon!'

'Yes. And I found you as well. Life is good,' she whispered in the dark.

My heart swelled at her words. Tiny dancing lights rose from somewhere off the grass: fireflies, shining against the black of the night, enacting some arcane Morse code with their lights off, lights on dance. We drew our breath, enchanted.

'*Lucciole!*' Matilde murmured – fireflies.

We sat among the dancing lights; *a happy present can heal old wounds – if only you let it*, I thought in silent gratitude.

CHAPTER SIX

Matilde stood on the doorstep with a metal tray – the name of the coffee shop we'd been in the night before was emblazoned on the side of the steaming cappuccino, and a plate with two fragrant croissants was waiting for me. The smell was incredible.

'Good morning!'

'Oh, wow!' I said, barefoot and still in my nightie. A breakfast like this, on my doorstep; it was something I could get used to.

'Cappuccino and croissant,' she announced, as I closed the door behind her and went to sit on the bed again. She was dressed in a smart skirt and silk top, with her hair pinned up and full make-up. She was going to work, I remembered. 'I hope you don't mind having been woken up so early.'

'With breakfast in bed, I can't complain!' I said, my voice still full of sleep, rubbing my face with my hand.

'Also, I have to relay a message. Andrea asked Massimo for your number.'

'Oh, did he now?' I took a gulp of cappuccino. I needed caffeine to process that piece of news.

'Yep. He did. Massimo said he would ask me and I would ask you.'

I laughed. 'It's all very high school... What are we, sixteen?' Mmmm, strawberry jam in the croissant...

Matilde rolled her eyes. 'Oh, come on! Can I give it to him or not?'

'I suppose,' I said as soon as I'd swallowed. 'But I want to see Nonna again... if she's around I'd rather go see her.'

'Of course, but remember I said that Papà is taking Nonna down to Bastia, to a visit at the hospital. So if you're okay with it, you can go with Andrea, and see her in the afternoon.'

'If he calls.'

'Texting him now... There. Enjoy your breakfast; I'm off to work, back at lunchtime. Papà will be there,' she said, and leaned towards me to kiss me on the cheek.

'See you later, and thank you so much!'

Matilde closed the door behind her and I rested the cup on the tray. I opened the shutters – it was another sunny day, and Bosconero was my oyster. A tiny little oyster of incredible beauty, with lots to explore and infinite possibilities for pictures and discoveries. I drank the last sip of my cappuccino, enjoying the sunrays on my face, turning the sheets and my nightie from white to gold. Then, I had a quick shower and dressed in jeans, trainers and a simple white shirt with sleeves rolled up; I donned my touristy wicker hat and sunglasses, and, with my camera around my neck, I was ready. At that point, my phone chirped.

'Hello?'

'Luce? It's Andrea,' a heavily accented voice said on the other end of the phone and to my shame – although I didn't even want to admit it to myself – I started tingling. Half of me said *silly girl!* and half of me simply gave in to the excitement, silencing the inner scolding. Maybe it was time to stop thinking a little less, and enjoy life a little more.

*

Half an hour later I was sitting in Andrea's car, the sunroof down and the wind in my hair. The whole situation was so unexpected, and looked so much like a commercial or a travel brochure, that it was almost dreamlike.

'Where are we going?'

'Surprise. It's a magical place. You'll love it. Do you trust me?'

'I trust your knowledge of the place,' I said, diplomatically. Andrea was wearing sunglasses and a polo shirt over dark jeans, his dark colouring betraying all the hours he spent under the sun. He was the kind of man you would look at twice in a crowd – though he seemed unaware of his good looks, and unassuming.

We drove up and down a few hills between Bosconero and this mysterious place he was taking me to, and sometimes the bends were so steep I was looking down a wooded chasm, my heart in my throat. Thankfully, he drove better than Matilde.

Finally, we began to climb a ridge, towards the top of what seemed more like a mountain than a hill. Andrea's car, a fancy little thing that I would have pictured in a city rather than climbing mountains, held its own admirably.

'This is breathtaking!' I said, looking down as we drove further and further up. A green ocean sprawled beneath us, and the hills were its waves. 'And a little bit terrifying!'

'Nah, I've been here a million times; she knows the way,' Andrea said, patting the dashboard. 'You see, my daughter studies archaeology in Rome, so I've explored around with her quite a bit, for her university courses. But I don't want to give too much away!'

'Archaeology? Wow. It's fascinating,' I said. 'You must be very proud.'

'I am. She's all I have,' he replied, and I knew what he meant – I shared that feeling, when it came to Eli.

It was hard to talk with the roof down, over the noise of the wind, so we were quiet for a bit, while we drove up a road lined with a canopy of trees so thick that the sun almost didn't make its way through. We stopped as the small road ended, losing itself into the dark woods.

'It's all on foot from here,' Andrea said, lifting a backpack from the back seat.

'So this is where it turns out you're a psycho killer who'll hide my body in deepest woodland, and I'll never be found?' I joked.

'You read too many thrillers. Come,' he said, and offered his hand. I took it with a familiarity that surprised me, just as it surprised me how Andrea could be flirting with me in such a light, gentle way, so that it never came across as cheap or pushy. *Gentle* was a word that described Andrea well, I thought.

I let his hand go as soon as I found my footing on the uneven ground, the camera weighing around my neck. The air was fresh out here, and heavily scented – a deep, rich fragrance of underwood. The white, naked light of Bosconero seemed a distant memory, as we stepped in shade that was almost gloom. Suddenly, I felt flat stones under my feet – I looked down to see a half-hidden, overgrown path was taking shape beneath us.

'It's like a lost city in the jungle!' I said.

'You'll see!' Andrea replied, and I could feel he was enjoying my excitement.

We followed the stone path, making our way slowly among the weeds, until the woods opened up and we were swallowed by bright light once again.

In front of us stood a hamlet of stone houses, some whole, some half-crumbled, that looked completely abandoned. On our left, the ocean of hills, broken by secluded valleys, lay silent and still.

'This is Frassino. It takes its name from the trees surrounding it. *Frassini*, as you can see.'

'I have no idea what *frassini* means,' I said, staring at the place, already planning a photographic tour for Eli.

'Wait, let me see…' Andrea rummaged in the backpack, and took out a tiny Collins dictionary. I smiled. It was such a thoughtful thing to do, to carry a dictionary for us. '*Frassino…* Ash. Ash tree.'

'I see,' I said, and walked on, too curious to wait.

'Mind your step,' Andrea warned me, and placed a light hand on my back. He led me to the first house that stood in front of us, and stepping over its threshold, mossy and worn, was like stepping back in time. There was a silence so thick inside that house that I could almost hear it.

'Look,' Andrea said, moving to stand beside a ruined wooden table. My jaw dropped open – there were still dishes on the table, covered in dust. Behind the table was a fireplace, and the framed picture of a landscape sat on it. On the left was a low cot, covered in blankets so dusty they looked grey; above the cot, hanging on the stone wall, a simple wooden cross.

'It looks untouched! When was this abandoned?' I asked. The sound of my voice was almost like a sacrilege, as if I'd been caught trespassing in somebody else's house.

'After the war. Many of the villagers died, the rest emigrated. It's not easy to live so isolated. Hikers come up here, and my daughter's department did some study on the place, for a modern archaeology course. But it's an unspoken rule – nobody touches anything. Everything is like it was left.'

'If this was in America,' I whispered – this place called for reverence – 'people would squat up here. Have parties, you know.'

'Not here. I think they tried, but the atmosphere… Well, nobody seems to come partying here, for some reason.'

'You're spooking me, now,' I said, and suddenly noticed the framed black and white photographs on the wall. Stern-looking people, the men with big moustaches, the women with veils over their heads.

I swallowed.

'Look. There's still soot above the fireplace, and here's the iron rod they hung the pot on.' Andrea showed me.

'I feel like we're trespassing,' I said, uncertain, but I still clutched the camera and took picture after picture.

'You know, these houses are for sale. Guess how much they cost?'

'Oh, they must cost a fortune!'

'One euro.'

'One... euro? Seriously?'

'Yes. There's no electricity, no water, not even a proper road. The government is trying to revive the place, entice young families. To no avail. And I think it's not just because of how cut off it is. I think it's because of the spirits that inhabit it. The ghosts...'

'Seriously?' My heart was beating like crazy, and my mouth was dry.

'No, silly! Come on, the best is still to come.' He laughed, and I did feel silly.

But somehow, as I stepped through empty home after empty home, catching glimpses of furniture, fireplaces, wood-and-straw chairs nobody had sat on for decades, the presence of ghosts didn't seem like such an impossibility. Memories were thick, the desertion of the village too sudden, almost... unfinished. As if the men and women who left had done so too fast to carry the whole of their stories with them.

'Did everyone leave at once?' I asked.

'Pretty much, but some elderly people were left behind. They refused to go. Nowadays nobody would be left to live so isolated, but back then... it was a common way of life, to live halfway up a mountain with no water or electricity, and to be cut off from everything when the snow came in winter.'

'I think I would have done the same.'

'Would you? Would you have stayed?'

'Well, I'm not saying I wouldn't have emigrated in search of a better life," I explained. "But if I'd chosen to stay behind, here in my own village, I would have refused to be taken to a retirement home or a hospital somewhere. I would have chosen to die here.'

'Yes. I see what you mean…Well, this is getting a bit morbid for a date!' Andrea laughed.

Date?

'You have to see the chapel,' he said, and took my hand again. The feeling of his fingers holding mine was strange – sweet and yet alarming.

Ethan had been my high school sweetheart, and then my husband. This was unexplored territory, as uncharted and new as these woods felt to me. I didn't take the hand away, and Andrea was still holding it when we climbed two steps and entered the tiny church.

I drew a breath that seemed to suck away all the air about me, and again I stood with my mouth open. The walls and the ceiling were covered in frescoes, their colours faded, but otherwise intact.

'Oh, my goodness,' I whispered.

'I know,' Andrea replied. 'These were made approximately seven hundred years ago, give or take.'

I took a few, slow steps, my chin up, turning round and round. 'It's incredible.'

'See here, around the walls? It shows stories from the gospel, but the protagonists are common people… My daughter explained all this to me. And this is the story of Saint Emidio… he's supposed to protect from earthquakes,' Andrea said and pointed towards the ceiling. The simplicity and austere beauty of the frescoes was extraordinary.

'It's like a seven-hundred-year-old comic strip.' I smiled. 'Isn't it?'

'Yes, it is! I never saw it that way.'

The chapel was empty, but for a few benches covered in dust, a small stone baptismal font, and a bare altar nestled in the back. I walked slowly among the benches, thinking of all the children who must have been baptised here, the weddings celebrated, the Sunday Masses attended by the people who toiled all week over this unforgiving land…

All around the alcove was a small step, and on the step lay scattered papers. I crouched and touched the dusty papers – they were tiny rectangular images of Saint Emidio, with a prayer in the back. I wanted to take a picture of them, but it was too dark, so I resolved to take one outside, and then return it to its place. Everything was untouched around here, and I didn't want to be the ignorant tourist who took something away. I tucked it in the camera bag.

'So, impressed?' Andrea said, as we stepped out into the light.

'You can say that again. What do you have in that backpack?' I asked, as we walked back to the car.

'You saw what I have in there; it's the dictionary.'

I laughed. 'It's full! It can't just have a mini dictionary in there!'

'It's a surprise.'

'Oh, okay then.' I was intrigued.

Before we made our way into the woods again, I turned around towards the lost village, and bid its homes, and its ghosts, goodbye.

*

After a brief walk through the woods, Andrea led me to a small opening, shaded by the canopy of trees. There we sat, and Andrea magicked a picnic out of his backpack. I don't know how he'd managed to fit everything in: wine, cheeses and dainty, delicate pastries that looked like individual works of art, together with a tablecloth and napkins. Like Mary Poppins' bag. I decided to take some pictures, and grabbed my camera.

'Oh, no,' I exclaimed, as I discovered the prayer card in my camera pouch.

'What's wrong?'

'I took a prayer card from the chapel, in Frassino. I wanted to take pictures of it and return it, but I forgot.'

'Don't worry. Take the photographs whenever you have time, then I'll bring it back.'

'Thank you.'

'So... Massimo told me this is the first time you have met Matilde! A transatlantic family reunion, then?'

'Exactly. And not the smoothest. You see, there has been a falling-out between my mom and the rest of the family, many years ago. I'm trying to build bridges.'

Andrea nodded. 'Families can be complicated, for sure. But they're always worth fighting for. That's what I think, anyway. Did you meet the matriarch then, the fearsome Signora Nardini?'

Fearsome? My nonna?

'I did, yes. But I haven't heard anyone referring to her as fearsome. Or a... matriarch!' I struggled with the Italian word. I'd guessed the meaning of it because it was similar to English, but never pronounced it before. 'She's such a sweet little thing...'

'Oh, yes, of course she is! I hope I didn't offend you... it's just that... well, my great-grandmother knew her. She was a friend of the family, of your great-grandmother Venturina, your great-grandfather Giovanni...' It was like a tongue twister, I thought. 'But then she refused to have anything to do with Clelia Nardini ever again. Whenever her name was mentioned – you know, it's a small village, everyone is discussed, sooner or later – she refused to join the conversation. We never knew why. She said your nonna disquieted her. She loved Nora, though – you know, Clelia's younger sister. Apparently, Nora was a sweetheart and adored Clelia.'

I was annoyed. And a little bit insulted too. Why on earth would that woman not like my sweet grandmother? 'Well, maybe your great-grandmother held a grudge, or something.'

'She wasn't the type, really. She was always helping everyone. She taught Signora Nardini how to read and write…'

She taught her how to read and write? 'What was her name?'

'Caterina. But they called her Nin.'

Nin! The wise woman, or, someone said, the witch. I remembered how she taught Nonna, and how she gave her honey that day, when the letter arrived with terrible news…

'That's weird. Nonna told me some things about her childhood, and Nin was so kind to her… It didn't sound like she disliked her at all.'

'I don't know what happened there,' Andrea said, shrugging his shoulders. 'I really do hope I haven't offended you,' he repeated.

'No, not at all,' I said. He hadn't, but Nin had! Which was irrational, of course, Nin being long dead. Add another falling-out to add to the list.

'Nonna said that Nin had a gift. That some called her a witch.'

'True. But it must go down the maternal line, because I have no gifts at all! My mamma did, and my daughter has dreams, sometimes. In fact, she's been having nightmares, recently. But anyway… Now you'll think I'm crazy.'

'Of course I don't! Don't be silly. I'm enjoying myself so much. Thank you for taking me here,' I said, from the heart.

'No, Luce… thank you. For coming out with me, today. We're total strangers, and here you are, following me through woods and fields!'

I laughed. 'Well, you're a friend of Matilde and Massimo. And they seem to think you're a good guy.'

'I'm glad they think that. Massimo is one of my best friends, though he's quite a bit younger than me. I mentored him when he started in the ambulance service. Those days… well, that's when my marriage broke down. It was tough.'

'I can imagine. I'm sorry.'

'Well, I don't want to bore you with my woes. Tell me about you.'

'You don't bore me at all. Similar situation, actually. Separated, with one teenage son. Not teenage for long, actually! He's nineteen…'

'I'm sorry about your marriage.'

'Oh, don't be. It was me who decided to break up. We just lived separate lives, you know. We got to the stage where it hardly made a difference whether we were together or not.' I smiled and shrugged, trying to seem nonchalant, but talking about my separation from Ethan was always painful. Even if it had been my choice, even if nobody else had been involved, the long, lonely years in which Ethan had drifted away from me, breaking my heart with his coldness, were like a scar. The wound was almost closed, but the mark would always be there. 'However, we moved on from each other, we survived and we're happy now. He found someone else, for a while. And I was happy for him when he did.'

I wasn't exactly telling the truth here; when Eli had told me that his dad had a girlfriend, *happy* wouldn't have been the word I'd have used to describe my state of mind.

'And you? Did you find someone else?'

'No,' I said simply, and held onto my hat as a gust of warm breeze threatened to make it fly away. 'I didn't look.'

'Me neither… until now,' Andrea replied, and I was grateful for the wide-brimmed hat that hid my face and, with it, my embarrassment.

Things were getting too deep, too fast. Another gust of wind blew, even stronger, and I affected a shiver. 'Chilly, isn't it? Maybe we should go.'

'It's always fresh up here,' he said good-naturedly, and began to gather our things. I moved onto my knees and helped put away the food and fold the tablecloth, until everything fit miraculously again in his Mary-Poppins-style backpack. Before we left, I took a final photograph with my cell phone. I was desperate for Eli to see that incredible panorama, and I would send it as soon as we had signal again.

*

'Thank you for this. I had a great time,' Andrea said, after he'd stopped the car. 'I hope…' He shrugged – was *he* blushing, now? I smiled inwardly.

'Yes?'

'Well, I don't want to steal your time while you're over here… I know you want to see your family, that you'll be busy. But I hope we can do something like this again.'

'Of course. I'd love to,' I said, and climbed out of his car – no mean feat, as it was so close to the ground. He joined me and, before I could think, analyse, even before I had time to feel embarrassed, he gave me a light peck on the lips. Thank goodness we'd stopped in the square, and not at Rosa Bianca, with Matilde, and Nonna, and maybe Carlo, to see me kissing a stranger – or, more precisely, being kissed by him.

I walked away, and when I turned around to wave at him one last time, I saw him still standing there, looking at me. I was left somewhere between startled and contented, if those two feelings can ever co-exist; a little unexpected kiss had somehow lifted me over an invisible fence, into the next stage of my life.

I hadn't been planning on finding romance, but I believed romance might had found me.

CHAPTER SEVEN

I had a spring in my step as I made my way from the square to Rosa Bianca, where Matilde was waiting for me with Nonna… and Carlo. I felt optimistic. It would go well, I was sure. Matilde was on the balcony, and she waved when she saw me; she ran downstairs to open the door.

I took off my wide-brimmed hat and sunglasses. '*Ciao!*' I said and hugged her, both of us embraced by the trailing roses – handbag, hat and glasses threatening to drop on the floor at any moment.

'Oh, we're in a good mood! It went well, then?' Matilde was still in her work gear, but she'd let her hair down again.

'It went okay. I had fun,' I replied, non-committally. 'Is Carlo here?'

'Not yet. Any moment now. Will you tell me later?' she added, in a whisper. I really did feel sixteen, now.

'There's nothing to tell! How's Nonna?'

'Nervous,' Matilde said and lowered her voice again. 'More than I thought she would be. And Massimo has been held up at work; apparently it was chock-full, today.' Massimo's official job was mountain guide and a climbing instructor – hence all the outdoorsy pictures I'd seen on their Facebook page – and summer was his busiest period, he'd explained to me, because of all the tourists.

'Oh.' I would have liked Massimo to be there, to defuse things a little… 'And Nonna is more nervous than—' I began. Right at that moment, Nonna appeared in the kitchen, framed in the back door, and I was about to go to her when a deep, male voice called from behind me and made me stop in my tracks.

'Matilde!'

I jerked my head, and saw a tall, burly man with snow-white hair standing there, staring at me. And then I turned again, towards Matilde and Nonna, and back towards the man. The three of them were frozen for a moment, all in a line from the doorstep to the kitchen back door – and I was in between them, my throat dry and my hands tingling in panic. Carlo's expression was one of surprise – and not the good kind. The surprise turned into horror. As if seeing me was the worst thing that could happen.

I never thought I would evoke horror, ever. In anyone.

'Who are you?' he asked, unnecessarily – I knew he'd recognised me. Even if he didn't know of my existence as Luce, he knew I was here on his sister's behalf. No wonder he looked like he'd seen a ghost. In those circumstances, I felt like my mother's avatar, in every way.

'Papà! Come in,' Matilde said. Her voice was trembling a little. He barged inside, almost colliding into me. 'This is Luce. She's your niece, Angelina's daughter, and—'

Carlo ignored her. '*Mamma! Mamma, stai bene?*' he called to Nonna. Are you okay?

'Of course I'm well! Oh, Carlo, my prayers have been answered. This is Angelina's daughter,' Nonna repeated. 'She's come back to us. And Angelina is well! Your sister is well, and living in America! I couldn't wait to see you, and tell you…'

Carlo stood beside Nonna, a hand on her shoulder. Beside him, Nonna looked diminutive, fragile. Vulnerable. Carlo was protective of her against me; I felt the opposite, that I should protect her from him.

'What do you want from us?' he yelled – he was red in the face, and the aggression in him made me waver. I wasn't used to confrontation; I'd never argued this way with my mother or with Ethan and Eli. This bare-faced wrath overwhelmed me for a moment, and my mind went blank.

'Papà! She just wanted to meet us! She wants us to be a family!' Matilde yelled back. I could hear my heart in my ears, and I was trembling. But Matilde was holding her own, and I had to do the same. I composed myself the best I could.

'Carlo. Like Matilde said, I just wanted to meet you all,' I said, with all the calm I could muster.

A vein on the side of his neck was throbbing, and he still looked scarlet. 'Angelina sent you?' He was throwing words at me like stones.

'No. She didn't want me to come, actually,' I replied, still calm. But after the initial shock, anger was beginning to bubble inside me too.

'But you told her you were coming here.'

'She does know now, yes,' I said. What was he getting at?

'Carlo, please. Trust me,' Nonna said, but Carlo shook his head. 'Angelina told you lies about us?'

'Mamma never said anything about you,' I said, taking a step forward. Maybe, if only I could explain, if only I could tell him…

But he took a step *back* – not in fear, but as if I were repulsive, somehow. I felt my eyes widen, and I let go of what I was carrying in my hands. Hat and glasses fell on the terracotta tiles with a whoosh and a clatter, and none of us made a move to gather them.

Disappointment was not a word strong enough to describe how I felt.

'Look, Papà. Everything is ready in the garden,' Matilde said, and took a few steps towards the kitchen; after a heartbeat, I forced myself to follow her, and Carlo stepped back once again as I came into the room, as if I were contagious. From where I stood, I could see the table under the pergola, beautifully set up and laden with food. They'd gone to such trouble. I could feel the love in the way they'd arranged everything, from the jugs full of flowers, to the napkins folded and tied with rustic string, to the immaculate, freshly ironed linen tablecloth. I was so touched. What a lovely family meal it could have been…

'Carlo,' I began, trying to keep all resentment out of my voice, trying to sound pleading, and not angry – but he cut me short.

'While this woman is here, Mother, consider me gone.'

'Papà!' Matilde hollered again. She was white in the face, but two red spots now coloured her cheeks. She, too, had gone from disappointed to furious. In the silence that fell, we could hear everyone's heavy breathing.

Nonna was quiet for a moment, and then she spoke – seraphic, poised.

'It breaks my heart, *figlio mio*, but do what you need to do. It's been years, years and years of not seeing my daughter. And I won't turn my granddaughter away.'

She's not fragile, I thought. *She's in control.*

Carlo's face fell. 'Mamma?' He wasn't yelling any more now. Had he been just a little more decent with me, I would have felt sorry for him, because he looked so thoroughly wretched.

'Carlo. I would like you to stay and speak to Luce. But if you can't find a kind word for your niece, I want you to go.'

What? No more talking – or yelling, more like – no way out, no way to sort this out? Giving up on my uncle? I couldn't. I hadn't flown all that way around the world to give up so easily, after one quick encounter.

'No, no… We can talk things through,' I almost begged, in spite of my anger. Repairing the rip in the fabric of our family was more important than pride. 'Carlo, listen, we could...' I tried to placate him. But to no avail.

Carlo stepped towards me, and he was so imposing, in spite of his age, that I had to steel myself not to take a step back. His expression had changed – from bewildered, to furious, now he had turned algid; his eyes were icy.

'You need to leave,' he said, as calm as he'd been angry a moment before.

It was right at that moment, when I saw his eyes and heard his tone of voice, that I understood Mamma's words about keeping safe.

This coldness – those almost expressionless eyes, the icy aura that emanated from him – frightened me. Without any more words, he left, leaving each of us three, the girl, the woman and the old lady, with our own shock and pain.

Now that I'd met my uncle, now that I'd gazed into his eyes and seen the darkness in them, I understood what Mamma had meant.

Now, I was afraid.

*

'*Tesoro mio*, give your uncle some time. I'll speak to him. He'll come round,' Nonna said while Matilde dried her tears. Carlo's reaction had left a bitter, bitter taste in my mouth, but I wasn't crying; I was burning inside. Now more than ever I wanted to know – why?

'I don't understand him,' Matilde kept saying. 'I just don't. I know he's difficult, I know he has a temper, but this? Why does he not come out and tell us what his problem is?'

I didn't understand it either. Mamma had left Italy when she was eighteen; what could she have done that was so terrible that her brother refused to ever speak to her, or her daughter?

Forty-three years had passed, and there was still so much rage.

'*Venite, ragazze,*' Nonna said finally – come, girls – and broke the spell. 'We won't waste this beautiful day, this beautiful table. We'll have lunch, the three of us. Won't we, Matilde?' Matilde sniffed and nodded. 'Luce?'

'Yes. Yes, of course.'

We began to eat in almost-silence, in spite of the festive table and the summer abundance all around us, with its flowers and its golden light; but then we began to talk a little, and soon the three of us were chatting away – a bit subdued, but with a sense of closeness, of alliance, like the small family we were.

As I washed the dishes, the thought in the back of my mind was: how was I going to tell Mamma that meeting Carlo had been a complete disaster?

Or maybe – most likely – she'd known this would be the outcome. It was me who had hoped against hope.

After we cleaned everything up, Nonna dried her hands on her apron. 'It's too hot to sit outside, now. Come to the living room, and I'll continue my story.'

'I'd love that, Nonna.'

'I'll make coffee,' Matilde offered, and busied herself with the *caffettiera* while Nonna led me to the living room.

It was full of antique furniture, immaculate like her kitchen and smelling, it seemed to me, of old things and memories. The shutters were closed, and I thought she always kept them that way, so that the room would stay cool. There was no other light than the sunrays seeping in, filtered by the gossamer-thin white curtains; the atmosphere was peaceful, almost like a church… which reminded me…

'Matilde, if I don't see Andrea soon, could you give this to him?' I called, and went into the hall to slip the small sacred image out of my camera bag. 'I took it from Frassino, and forgot to return it… long story. He'll know what I'm talking about.'

'Sure, I will,' she said, and rested the image carefully on a chest of drawers, leaning against a knick-knack, then she came back with the coffee tray.

'So. Where was I?' Nonna began, as Matilde poured the thick, aromatic espresso into our cups.

'When you met my grandfather…' I couldn't wait to hear more.

Nonna smiled. 'Oh, yes. That was the Summer Festival, you know. A long time ago, but it feels like yesterday…'

Her words sucked me right back into the story once again, and I listened while sipping my hot, sugared coffee, enthralled at once as if her narration had never stopped.

*

It was the Summer Festival, and everyone was out celebrating. Back then, festivals and fairs were the only chances to meet young women and men from the villages around, and many matches were made on dancing nights… Men from around here are so boorish, I thought as I stood half hidden by the sycamore trees that, long ago, lined the Bosconero square. The young and old of the village danced in the middle to the sound of an accordion and a clarinet, the old-style dance bands around here. Yes, men were brutes with no manners, who treated women like carthorses. I didn't like any of them and I had no desire to dance.

I'd gained the reputation of being picky and difficult – I scared every suitor away, to my mother's despair. She prayed to see her daughter married and happy, and to see a smile on my face, instead of the perpetual frown of worry I'd had since Papà died. Not like my sister, Nora, who smiled and danced without a care in the world and would have no trouble finding a match, both Mamma and I were sure.

'Vieni, Clelia! Vieni a ballare!' *Come dancing. Nora called me and took my hand. I shook my head and freed myself; Nora frowned, concerned for me as she often was, and her friends laughed and shrugged their shoulders. Out of the corner of my eye I spotted Felice, leaning against a tree and looking at me darkly. He was a boy who'd known me for a long time, had set his sight on me when I was still little and was, apparently, 'in love' with me – or so he said. He wanted me as a wife – unpaid labourer in his house and farm, really – and having declared his love for me to the whole village, he could not take no for an answer, or he would lose face. There was no worse fate, for a Bosconero man, than losing face. I didn't love him back, and I didn't even like him; he treated his mother and sisters with contempt, and I knew he would treat his wife the same way. He was a tall, lanky, wide-shouldered thug who lifted sheep over his shoulder like he would a cat. If I married me, I would spend my whole life being shouted at and breeding child after child.*

'Dance with me, Clelia,' he said, and he, too, took my hand – but unlike Nora, he squeezed it so hard it hurt, and would not let me go.

'Leave me alone,' I whispered – I didn't want to give more fuel to the village gossip – and finally, after one last painful squeeze, he listened, and let go of me.

I'd had enough of celebrations already. Mamma was busy chatting with her friends and Nora was dancing, so I was free to slip away quietly, through the back streets and out into the fields.

This was where I belonged, I thought then, with sadness in my heart. The woods and fields outside were where I'd spent most of my childhood, after all. I walked under the light of the moon – the further I went, the dimmer the music grew. There was a crescent moon that night, I remember – just a sliver, but very bright – and fireflies danced all around me. There are still fireflies around now, but in those days, Luce, the fields were full of them! It was like they were having another Summer Festival all for themselves. It was beautiful, and I was a little consoled.

After a while, though, I heard footsteps behind me. The night was so silent that the sound of someone following me almost echoed through the woods. Also, I was so attuned to the place that my instinct would alert me of anything out of place. I can recall to this day the dread I felt – yes, there were boars and wolves around, but boars are shy and wolves go for sheep, not humans. I knew for sure that those footsteps belonged to someone who walked on two legs, not four, and I was just as sure that whoever was following meant me harm.

I hesitated – should I go back to the village, should I keep going, should I call out? I began walking faster, and the footsteps behind me increased their pace too. I could hear myself panting – until I was tired of feeling like a sheep followed by a wolf, and turned around to face whoever was there.

'Who is it? Who goes there?' I shouted. I wasn't a frail little woman; none of us Bosconero women were, back then. We worked too hard to be weak and fragile.

But even so, I was no match for the man who came out of the trees and threw himself on me, pinning me on the ground, my back banging painfully on the undergrowth. Felice had come to take what he thought was his by right. Oh, Luce, I remember the tearing of my cotton dress, I remember the terror and how I punched him and scratched him with all my might. And then, just when I thought all was lost, it was as if an invisible force had lifted him off me. All of a sudden I was free, and I scrambled to my feet, trying to catch my breath. Felice was now on the ground, and a slight, short man who I could hardly make out in the half-light was punching him over and over again. He held him by the collar and finally, after hitting him hard, he hissed: 'If I see you near her ever again, I will kill you.'

Felice was a whole head taller than the man, and double his size, but there was something in the stranger's voice that made me believe he'd be capable of that. And willing, too.

Felice tried to scramble away – there were dark shadows on his face, and even in the feeble light of the moon I could tell it was blood and that his nose was broken. But I wasn't done with him. I jumped on him from behind and hit him in any way I could, while the man who'd saved me was calling out for me to stop. Felice turned around to push me away, as if I'd been a crazy little cat, blind with fury and terror – I scratched his hands as he put them up to defend himself, and then his cheeks.

'If you come near me again, it will be me who kills you,' I screamed. The stranger pulled me away, and I screamed again, trying to free myself – but he let me go only when Felice disappeared, running through the trees like the coward that he was.

The stranger put his hands up, just like Felice had.

'Who are you?' I asked, but I could already see dancing spots of light at the edge of my vision, and I knew they weren't fireflies.

'I don't mean you any harm…'

But I couldn't hear anything more. At that moment, I felt my knees give way, and the last thing I felt were the stranger's arms holding me up.

*

I awoke not long later, and startled – where was I? Who was that man sitting across from me? I sat up and hugged my knees; feeling my dress ripped on the side brought back the terror I'd felt when Felice attacked me. I was cold, now, and shivering.

'You're safe. You're safe,' the strange man soothed me. There was an oil lamp burning beside us, and the light allowed me to see his face – he was thin, with big, slanted eyes and a shock of dark red, curly hair. There was something about him that inspired some kind of… I wouldn't say trust as such, but I wasn't afraid of him. Even though I had no idea who he was, and even after the shock of what had just happened with Felice. 'Do you want me to take you back to the village?'

I shook my head. I wasn't ready to see anyone. But neither did I want to be alone.

'Will I light a fire for you?'

I nodded.

'Are you hurt?' he asked, as he quickly put together a little mound of sticks and rolled newspaper, and lit it with a match. Where had he found all that? And the lamp? 'You were only out of it for a few minutes, time to carry you here, and you don't have any bruises, apart from a few scratches… but I can take you home, or to the doctor?'

The second he'd opened his mouth, I was mystified. I was expecting him to speak one of the dialects from the area, or – if he came from the south and his own dialect would be too difficult to understand – that he would attempt a tentative, basic Italian. But he spoke perfect Italian, like only educated people could. He spoke like a book would, if it could talk. Or like someone on the radio.

I shook my head once again, and inched closer to the small fire, lifting my hands to the flame. The man rose and wrapped the blanket around me, barely touching my shoulders.

'Who are you? You're not from the village,' I said, my arms still around my knees.

'My name is Arturo. I'm from Milan. I'm here for the harvest.'

Seasonal workers offered extra hands with the harvest, with the vendemmia – the grape harvest – and then with the annual moving of the sheep from higher to lower ground, and back again. But only the bigger, richer farmers and shepherds could afford to pay extra labourers, so we never had many of them in Bosconero. Arturo didn't sound like a seasonal worker, though, that was for sure.

'You sleep out here?' I asked, spotting a blanket, a bundle of clothes and what seemed like a cast-iron pan sitting by the fire. That would explain why he had been roaming the woods at that time of night. I brought my hand to my forehead. Now that I was coming back to my senses, and a little calmer, I could feel a dull ache at the back of my head, and all down my spine. Felice had thrown me down to the ground, I remembered.

'Are you sure you're not hurt? Is there anything I can do? Should we go straight to the doctor's house? Is there one in Bosconero? I'll carry you to the nearest one, don't worry…'

'No, no, honestly! No need for that. I'm fine. Just a bit sore… So, do you sleep here? In the woods.'

'Yes. I work for Miriani.' I recognised the name: he was a wealthy farmer from Bastia who had land all over our hills. 'He offered me to sleep in one of the sheds with the other labourers, but I'd rather be out here. On my own.'

I understood that; I would have been the same. Had it been winter, the cold and the wolves would have made it impossible – but in summer, if you were nice and silent and didn't make a ruckus when boars were around, it was safe. And so much pleasanter than sleeping in a crowded shed.

'Thank you for getting that beast off me,' I said, and shuddered. A wave of nausea overwhelmed me. Only then did I realise how scared I'd been, how close I'd come to… I didn't want to think about that, and to this day, I still don't.

'Any time,' he said, like what he'd done was of small consequence. I composed myself, trying to hide the fact that I was trembling at the memory. I wrapped my blanket closer around me. I was sure that Mamma and Nora were worried, as it was now the middle of the night, but for some reason, I wanted to be there longer. I wanted to keep talking to this strange man.

'You're a lot smaller than him,' I said.

Arturo laughed. 'Well, thank you!'

'Sorry, but I don't know how you managed to pull him off me and down to the ground.'

Arturo shrugged. 'I'm small, but a good fighter.'

His eyes were so dark that the flames made them shine like polished stones. I'd never met anyone like him. Small and slight, and yet strong. A labourer who slept outside, and yet spoke Italian like an educated man.

'What is that?' I asked, tilting my head and pointing to something behind him – a book, sitting on top of the clothes. There were a few others underneath, I noticed.

'What?'

'The book.'

'Oh. Well, it's a history book. I'm alone out here, so I read. That's why I keep an oil lamp, see? And if I don't have oil, I read by the fire.' He turned around and stretched to pick up the book and handed it to me. Then he reached backwards again, and his hand disappeared into the bundle of clothes, resurfacing with a pair of gold-rimmed glasses. He put them on, and his face looked instantly different, somehow. Like it didn't match the shabby clothes and the calloused hands.

'So… are you reading that now?'

'I've read it a few times. I have a lot more. Heavy to carry around, but it's worth it.'

He stood and disappeared in the shadows, and then he sat back down beside me. He carried a leather bag, a fancy one, and, Luce, it was full of books! History, philosophy, literature! It was like a treasure! I swear, had he shown me a barrel of gold I wouldn't have been more excited.

The mystery of this man was now even deeper: a seasonal worker with a bag full of books that would have been probably too difficult to understand even for our schoolteacher, let alone our priest. He laid the books down on the grass, and I brushed the covers with my fingers; I didn't even dare touch them properly.

'Can you read?' he asked.

'Of course I can! I couldn't go to school, but Nin taught me to read and write. She's a woman from our village. She came every day to the fields where I watched our sheep, and taught me. I was desperate to learn. Now I can read but I don't have enough books. No money to buy them. I have read every single book in this village, *and there aren't many. Can you imagine, if I could go to the city, in a car, maybe! And go to a real bookshop? Can you imagine?'*

I stopped abruptly. It wasn't like me, to talk so much. I never usually showed my feelings, let alone told anyone about my dreams. But everything had been so strange that night, and sitting there with all those books laid out in front of me, like a banquet…

Something in his face had changed, and it wasn't just the glasses. It was like he saw me for the first time. 'Would you like to read these?'

I felt like a child being offered a parcel of sweets.

'I would… But they might be too hard for me.'

'I can help. We can read them together, and I'll explain everything you don't understand.'

'Oh, that would be so good!' I said, and I saw him smile at the light of the fire. 'Of course, I'll understand most of it. I'm sure.' I didn't want him to think I was stupid, you see.

'You will.' He knew I would have trouble with those books, but he humoured me. Luce, he was humble, and that was yet another thing I liked about him.

Maybe, who knows… it was just then that I fell for him. When he said those two words – of course – and made me feel like I was worth something more than minding sheep or a prize for the local boys who were looking for a wife. Like I had a mind of my own.

Yes. I think I fell for him then.

*

He walked me home, taking care not to be seen – in case people thought we'd been up to no good. I told Mamma and Nora that I'd ripped my dress while walking through the woods, and they believed me. I never told them what Felice had tried to do to me, but they guessed something had happened with him, because he stopped pestering me.

Every night I went to meet Arturo in the woods, in secret; Mamma and Nora were used to me wandering the woods, so they didn't ques-

tion it. I didn't keep my meetings with him a secret because we had anything to hide – we read and we talked and he taught me so many things – I hid it because it was my time, our time to be ourselves, together. Nobody was to spoil it with questions and suspicions.

All day Arturo and I worked, with the sheep and with the harvest, but at night we studied. Nobody would have believed that was all we did. I loved listening to him, and I let him talk and talk, and lose myself in his voice. But I also asked questions when something didn't make sense to me, and he explained, always patient, starting from the beginning, breaking difficult things into easy bits. The more I knew, the easier it was to understand. The more questions he answered, the more came to mind – my brain had been starved. Who knew that a little shepherd girl would find learning so easy?

Still, despite having spent so long with Arturo, in our nook in the woods by the light of the fire and oil lamp, I didn't know anything more about him than I did when we first met.

He was a mystery to me, and that was one of the things that drew me to him, together with his kindness, his humility, his passion for knowledge. He knew things not even Nora had studied in her school. Things they teach only in big cities, to rich people. I asked myself if he'd studied to become a priest, but I knew that couldn't be the reason he knew so much, because boys in seminaries learned Latin and the Bible, like our priests had, not about Russia and communism and philosophy and literature from all over the world, places I hadn't even heard of. Every time I asked him personal questions, he changed the subject, or made a joke.

And then one night, everything changed – just like summer was turning into autumn, and the first chill was in the air. I knew that moment would come when Miriani would let everyone go, and Arturo would move on. I dreaded the answer too much to ask about his plans.

He held my hand in his – I realised that aside from that first night, when he'd carried me to his tiny makeshift home under the trees, he had never touched me before. I didn't take my hand away.

'The harvest is finished, Clelia. I would like to stay. But you need to give me a reason.'

'I need to give you a reason to stay? Tell me if you'll stay, first, then we'll see,' I said, but I sounded cockier than I felt. The truth was that I didn't know how to face life without the books and our discussions and all the new things I was learning every day.

And without him.

'Oh, now you're playing games?' He smiled. 'I didn't think you knew how to.'

I grew serious. 'Arturo. What do you want me to say? I know nothing about you. Labourers are almost always local, or they come from the deep south, from places even poorer than here. Why would anyone from Milan come here to work? Especially if they know as much as you do. You could teach, you could work for a newspaper, you could have a job none of us can even dream of! It's our people who emigrate – nobody comes here, in the middle of nowhere, to live perched up on a mountain in the middle of dark woods – but you—'

'I came here to find you.'

He kissed me, and to my surprise, I didn't pull away; I gave him a reason to stay.

*

'You are engaged?' Mamma couldn't believe it. 'But you said you'd never marry!' Arturo and I were standing in our kitchen, eager to break the news, both of us unafraid.

'I knew you'd find the right person!' Nora said.

'She changed her mind, I suppose,' Arturo said mildly. 'I hope you'll bless us, signora.'

Mamma looked from me to him and back; she saw his clothes, mended many times, and his calloused hands. I knew what she was thinking: you'll have a life as hard as mine, Clelia.

I held her gaze while, for a long moment, she didn't speak.

'I do bless you,' she said finally, but I knew she wasn't happy, and I also knew she was right in worrying about the poverty I would face. But if I were with Arturo, I could overcome anything.

Now that we were free to step out together, like a couple who were about to marry, I saw how different Arturo was when we were with other people. He seemed almost another person. Quiet, almost... stolid. No trace of the scholar and dedicated reader that he was. He behaved exactly like a Bosconero man: the same mannerisms, the same wordless acerbity. He'd learned our dialect uncannily quickly, and he could almost pass for a native. That was another trait of his character – he could pretend so well.

Only when we were alone he was really himself; only in those moments, he was my own Arturo. Oh, Luce, I hope that a love such as ours has come to you already, or will come one day!

There was no reason to wait further to get married. I didn't want people to talk behind my back, let alone ruin Nora's chances of a good marriage. Mamma gave me her wedding ring to use as mine, and Nin crocheted a veil I could wear on the day, with my Sunday clothes. Nora's teacher lent me a pair of fancy shoes, black and dainty. Arturo didn't want to marry in the church, but in the Comune only; I convinced him, for Mamma's sake – and it mattered to me too because, in a village like ours, if you weren't married in the church you weren't married at all, and I didn't want people to say we lived as man and wife without having the right to.

What a wonderful day it was! I knew Mamma thought I was a fool, to marry someone who had nothing, but I didn't care. Now that Arturo was in my life, everything seemed easy – even poverty. And anyway, I was used to it.

*

But what came after wasn't easy at all.

Arturo was alone in the world, and he wanted a family of his own. I had never wanted children – until I met him. Arturo had changed everything for me.

I lost my first baby a few months later, and then another and another. I stopped minding the sheep and began to rest at home, trying to hold onto a pregnancy; Arturo replaced me. We thought that maybe this would give the child a better chance, but it didn't.

I was exhausted with trying, a thousand times more than I would have been minding the sheep. All I did was rattle around the house. With every miscarriage, another bit of life flowed out of me. Arturo grew silent, and Mamma, seeing my pain, wrung her hands. Nora worried about my health and my affliction, but I shunned her. I was ashamed. I was ashamed that my body couldn't do the very thing women are supposed to do. Was I broken?

'You would have been better off marrying another woman, one who could give you a family!' I told Arturo. I wasn't crying when I said that. I was quite calm, having cried all my tears before then.

'It's you I love. I don't want anyone else; even if it has to be just the two of us, we'll still be happy.'

I knew he meant what he said, because I could see how much he cared for me. I could read it in his eyes. But I felt guilty anyway, because I also knew how much he longed for a child.

And so did I, more and more with every little one I lost. I was the shadow of myself, wandering around, pretty much forbidden to go to the woods and fields – forbidden by my mother's suffocating concern, by my own fear.

Arturo seemed to have come back from his silence, and made peace with it all. His life seemed to have flown on, like a river around a fallen boulder. But now, when we were side by side in our bed, and he spoke to me about history and literature, like we'd always done – and he argued how things were changing in the world, and how we were on the verge of a new era – I only half listened. My mind drifted, and always went back to my empty belly and empty arms. I couldn't get past it. I never would.

*

Finally, all that dancing at the summer festivals and prancing around in her Sunday best had paid off for Nora. She was being courted by a man much older than her, from Bastia. His name was Mauro, and he was the opposite of Arturo: affluent, loud and larger than life. They decided to get married quickly, almost in haste.

Mauro's wealth meant that Mamma's long years of hardship were over, and I was grateful for that. He promised he'd build us a house, but Mamma didn't want to leave the farm where she'd lived with Papà. In the months that followed, Mauro had our home restored until it was unrecognisable, and one of the most luxurious houses in the village – by the standards of the day, of course. What was luxury back then, like having a bathroom inside, is commonplace now. Mamma planted trailing roses around our door, and we called the house Rosa Bianca.

On Nora's wedding day, I suddenly realised why the wedding had been organised so quickly. I must have been blind, but now, as we helped her try on her wedding dress, made by a seamstress in Bastia, I could see my sister's tummy straining against the silk and lace. It was an almost imperceptible difference, because she was so slender, but I saw it. Nora was pregnant already.

Mamma noticed me staring at Nora's waist, and how I'd grown rigid, as my sister stood on the white sheet we'd laid down so that the dress would remain immaculate. Mamma held my arm and stepped closer to me, but said nothing; the seamstress was there, kneeling by Nora with pins and a measuring tape wrapped around her hand.

I wanted to scream and growl and oh, I saw red.

I freed myself from Mamma's touch, and my eyes met Nora's. She smiled, innocent in her joy, and, I believe, unawares of the dagger she'd just planted in my heart.

*

Everyone guessed why my sister's tiny waist suddenly looked thicker, but nobody could doubt that Mauro had married her for love, and not obligation. He was a kind soul, and he and Arturo became firm friends, almost brothers. With Mauro, Arturo showed more of his real self, and they complemented each other – one was loud while the other was shy; one was pragmatic while the other was a dreamer. Mauro owned a house in Bastia, but Nora wanted to be with my mother and me, so they stayed at Rosa Bianca.

It was the hardest time in my life.

I had to spend my days watching Nora's belly grow and tending to her. She was the happiest I'd ever seen her. It had been so easy for her, getting pregnant – whether she'd planned it or it had been fate, I didn't know – that she forgot what I'd gone through, with all those babies lost. She was so happy she poured happiness all around, and over me; but back then, it felt like she was tormenting me. Constantly. So many years have passed, and I can still hear her words.

'It's what I was born for,' she always said, her hand caressing her belly.

What was I born for?

'Clelia! Come and feel the baby moving!' she said after the first kick, beaming. I laid a hand on her belly and bled inside, because none of my babies had even ever quickened.

'If it never happens to you, Clelia, you can still be an aunt to my babies…'

One of the three people I loved most in the world was also the one who was breaking my heart. My little sister, the infant I'd helped bring up, tormented me. I tried to smile and be happy for her, I tried to believe she meant no malice, just joy, and an innocent desire to shine after having been the little one, the second one, for so long; but it was so hard. And certainly, in spite of my smiles, everyone guessed how I felt and the bitterness growing inside me.

Finally, the baby was born. It was a long and painful labour, and I was frightened for my sister. We were afraid that she wouldn't survive. Back in the day, the poor women of Bosconero laboured like sheep, like cows, without medicine, without fuss. Not like today, with the doctors and hospitals and the medicines that take the pain away free for everyone, the rich and the poor! Back then, women looked after each other, and those who knew a little more, and had more experience – like Nin – worked as midwives.

'Oh, Clelia, I'm going to die!' Nora wailed when the pain allowed her to speak. Mamma prayed the rosary in a corner of the room, and Nin and I helped Nora; she clung to my hand so hard, and she looked so afraid, for the first time in her blissful pregnancy. Mauro was outside, pacing and drinking liquor to get him through.

I bent over my sister, trying to pass my own strength on to her, if that was possible. 'No, you're not! All this will be over and you'll be fine and you'll have a beautiful baby!' The love I always felt for her had come rushing back, and the bitterness was forgotten. I only wanted her and the baby to survive. With all my heart and soul. Oh, Luce, how I regretted the envy I'd felt for her!

'Do you promise?' I still remember how her lips were almost white, the same colour as her skin.

'I promise, Nora! I'm here. I never let you down before, I never will. Since you were a baby yourself, I always looked after you, always protected you. I won't let anything bad happen to you, Nora.'

I kept trying to catch Nin's eye, because the truth was I had no idea if they would be fine, even if I pretended to be so sure; it was the first time I'd seen a baby being born, and I didn't know if all this pain was normal – I was pretty sure, from Mamma's and Nin's *behaviour, that it wasn't. Nin kept looking away from me, which worried me even more; the serenity she'd worn on her face when it all started had been replaced by a blank mask, broken by a tense smile only when Nora looked for her eyes. I knew all was not right.*

I unknotted my fingers from Nora's, stepped outside for a moment and fell on my knees. 'Please, save my sister. Please, save the baby. Please, forgive me for the bad things I thought…' I prayed over and over. Could it be that because of my resentment, I'd jinxed them somehow?

It sounds silly now, to recount this thought I had – but at the time, it made sense.

Just then I heard Nora screaming, and then silence. I almost couldn't get up, my knees were so weak, and I was terrified to the point of nausea. But I did get up, and I walked back inside, ready for the worst.

When I crossed the threshold, the strong, clear cry of a baby welcomed me, and my sister lay pale, but smiling. They had survived. I burst into tears of joy, to the surprise of those who were used to the impassive, almost detached mask I wore.

After caressing my sister's head and stroking her hair back from her forehead, I gazed at the baby.

'A boy or a girl?' I asked.

'It's a boy,' Mauro replied, his voice quivering. He was almost as white as Nora, holding his son, a beautiful, perfect boy, pink and fat and as healthy as a little foal. He passed the baby on to me, carefully, reverently, and my heart swelled with love. I held him for a long time because Nora was too weak, after losing all that blood. I already loved him so!

When Mauro and my mother wanted to hold him, it broke my heart to give him to them. Oh, how I wished I could have kept him in my arms, forever!

Nora slept, and when she woke up she asked for her son, but her arms were too weak still. We gave her some meat broth, after her long fast, and put the baby at her breast for a little while. She slept some more, and when she awoke again we gave her bread and walnuts, which was what women ate after they'd given birth, to make them stronger. Some colour returned on her cheeks, and her lips were pink again, and not white like they'd been after many hours of pain.

My mother showed Nora how to latch the baby on, and my sister sat back on the pillows with the baby at her breast, a look on her face I'd never seen before, not even when she'd been showing off her belly to me. Perfect happiness.

And I felt like crying again, but not from joy, this time. I said something about getting some fresh air, and when I was on the doorstep, wrapping a shawl around me, I saw that Nin was looking at me. Her face bore an expression I'd never seen before – like she could see through me.

So I went out and walked, even if it was winter and a bitter wind blew from the mountains. Arturo found me, and there was no need for words when he took my hand and kept me close to him and gave me the strength to return home and smile again and love them all.

That was also the last night Nin ever spoke to me. I have no idea what I could have done to upset her, or annoy her, but from that moment onwards, every time she saw me, she turned away.

And that was when Carlo was born…

*

'Carlo?'

I'd been listening so intently, I'd lost myself in the story to the point that I jumped when Nonna mentioned my uncle's name. He wasn't my mother's brother, then, but her cousin? He wasn't my uncle? He'd been adopted by Nonna Clelia, but his real parents were Nora and Mauro!

Of course Carlo knew about his birth parents. Nonna wouldn't have told me something she'd kept from him. It would have made no sense. But the few times she'd mentioned her family, Mamma had called him brother – did she know? Did she feel it didn't matter, as Nonna had brought Carlo up like his own, or was this another of the many secrets she'd kept?

I was beginning to realise that my family's history had even more layers than I'd imagined...

And Nin... I remembered what Andrea had told me about Nin not being fond of my nonna, but he never knew why. Nonna's story had given me only one clue: that Nin had noticed Nonna's envy of her sister's fertility, and despised her for it. But this seemed heartless to me. Conflicting feelings can exist in families – we are all only human. Was that the reason Nin had stopped talking to Nonna? I couldn't know for sure...

'You're not my grandmother, then?' Matilde had spoken, breaking the sudden silence. She'd grown pale – in an instant, I realised that *she* had not known. I couldn't believe it.

'Oh, I am! Just not by blood. I'm sorry we kept this from you, *tesoro mio*. Arturo and I brought your papà up as if he'd been ours. He is ours,' Nonna said.

'Why did you not tell me? I don't understand... Why did Papà not tell me?'

The room felt chilly, the crickets' song dim in the distance, and dust danced in the sunrays coming through shutters and curtains. I felt like I was suffocating – I wanted out, into the light and air. I wanted to give Matilde a hug and make sure she was okay.

What a way to make such a revelation... in passing, as if Matilde's feelings were just collateral damage.

'We thought it just wasn't necessary... You are my granddaughter, in every way. Nothing much changes from being my grand-niece.'

They didn't think it was necessary?

Silence and secrets seemed to be endemic in this family of mine. What else was there to discover, I wondered.

'No. Nothing much changes,' Matilde said with a wan smile, and I was desperate to take her out into the light with me.

CHAPTER EIGHT

Matilde stood on her toes, and Massimo bent over to kiss her. It was so good to be out of that house full of memories, and breathe in the scent of summer. Yes, I'd come there to uncover the whole story – but I'd had enough uncovering for a day, that was sure.

'So, how was the lunch?' Massimo enquired. 'You two don't look that great… Sorry, no offence.'

Matilde and I looked at each other. 'There was no lunch,' Matilde said quietly. 'I mean, there was. Just not with my father.'

Massimo rolled his eyes. 'Don't tell me. That old cranky… mule!' I guessed he was restraining himself in front of us.

'Yes. It's what you imagine. Papà was horrible.'

'I should have been there… I'm so sorry… but work today was just crazy…'

I shook my head. 'It wouldn't have made a difference. Not even your influence would have worked, I don't think. You should have seen the way he looked at me.'

'He didn't even let her talk. And something else…'

'What else now? Your family is never boring, that's for sure.'

'Papà was adopted by Nonna. His real mother was Nonna's sister, Nora.'

'*What?*'

Matilde shrugged. Her eyes were so sad for a moment, it broke my heart. Maybe I was dredging up things that should be left alone… Maybe Mamma was right…

'And she told you today?'

'Apparently, it doesn't make much of a difference,' Matilde said, and I could detect a hint of resentment in her voice.

'Oh, Matilde! But I suppose, in love, it doesn't,' Massimo tried to soothe Matilde, but I could see he was as bewildered as she was. Nonna didn't seem to understand the weight of secrets, or the importance of blood in identity. It seemed to matter little that Matilde's father never told her he'd been adopted by his aunt.

'I know Nonna loves my papà as if he were her son... God, even just saying that feels surreal. But... Did they forget to tell me the truth, given it's not important?' Her voice had grown teary, and Massimo took her in his arms.

'You know what?' he said. 'I'll take you both out for dinner, and we'll talk things over...'

'Or maybe we'll talk about something else entirely,' Matilde proposed as we walked on, her hand in Massimo's. *That's a good idea*, I thought, while we all digested the revelations in our own time.

'Or maybe we'll talk about something else entirely,' Massimo repeated, and kissed the top of her head. 'Until my shift begins.'

'You on call tonight?' Matilde asked.

'Yep.' I realised they meant the ambulance service. I asked myself if Andrea was on call too, if I would see him again, at some point. A flashing image of sitting in the shade with him, in front of a mini banquet, the conversation flowing... Such a carefree moment, compared to the last few hours.

Yes, I did hope to see him again.

*

We were a despondent little crowd initially, the three of us, sitting in the village pizzeria on the square. After dinner, we cheered up looking at the pictures from my visit to Frassino. In showing them the one I'd sent to Eli, with the awesome vista Andrea and I had enjoyed while having our picnic, I realised that Andrea was in a corner of the shot. Eli would wonder who he was… But then, I didn't have anything to hide, did I?

'I'm sorry, girls, I have to go. Tonight will be busy, summer festivals everywhere,' Massimo said, scraping his chair back.

'Well, say hello to Andrea from Luce,' Matilde said and winked at me.

'Will do. He's a good guy. He really is.'

'Did you hear that, Luce? He's a good guy, he *really* is,' Matilde teased me. It was good to see her smile, after the tears she'd cried because of our crazy family.

'He just took me for a drive. That's all. I probably won't see him again for the rest of my stay,' I protested.

'Somehow, I doubt that!' Matilde said.

'Doubt that too!' Massimo called, walking away with one last kiss on Matilde's lips.

I managed to wrangle in and pay for dinner, in spite of my cousin's protests, and we went for a slow stroll. Every five steps, Matilde met someone she knew. The village was overflowing again, almost like the night before, with the festival.

'Bosconero is always full, in the summer,' Matilde explained. 'There was a lot of emigration in these parts, so, in the summer, people come back from the cities and from abroad as well. Shall we go to Collina Cora? What do you think? We can watch the fireflies and talk in peace.'

'It's a yes. The wine is on me,' I said, and thanked my lucky stars for such a sweet, loyal ally in my quest.

On our way there, I took out my phone for a moment, and texted Eli, just to see if he'd noticed the strange man in the photograph.

Italy, part 1. The beauty and the food! Having a great time, I hope you're well! Miss you, my boy xxxx Mom xxxx, I captioned it. It took a while to go through – the signal wasn't great out here – but finally, it was sent.

*

It was a relief, to sit on the ancient stony steps of the ruins, darkness and silence all around us, and fireflies out in droves once again. We both had a lot to digest.

'So. Secrets and lies, uh?' Matilde said.

'More than I thought. Obviously your papà knew… But I wonder if my mom does.'

'Well, I didn't. Can you imagine? If it was so unimportant, why keep it from me? I'm still reeling.'

Light – dark, light – dark, light – dark, went the fireflies around us. The night was warm and windless and even up on that hill, where a breeze blew most of the time, everything was still. It was like sitting in an aromatic, warm cup of tea. Hot, but pleasantly hot.

'Good question. Sometimes the elderly can be a bit blunt, like they don't have a filter any more. Things just flow out. I'm not saying everyone, of course. I think Nonna was…' I looked for the right word. '… misguided.'

'You can say that again. Oh, I can't be cross with her. She's old, and frail…'

'True. As for Carlo…'

'I can't wait to be alone with Papà, and see what he has to say for himself. No, actually… I *can* wait. I wonder how he'll react, when I tell him I know. About him having been adopted by Nonna, I mean. Because it wasn't just Nonna, keeping things from me! It was Papà as well. Like a… a… a conspiracy!'

'You two have to be alone and talk things through,' I said. 'Probably he just wanted to protect you.'

'Who knows.'

'Maybe you can also tease out of him why he hates me and my mamma so.'

'I doubt it. If they didn't think it was necessary to tell me that my nonna is actually not my nonna, what else are they hiding, and what chance do I have to find out?'

'You're right, actually…' I'd barely finished the sentence when my phone chirped. I almost jumped on it with a whispered sorry towards Matilde – I was sure it was Eli, so I didn't even look at the name of the sender, and read the message straight away.

Eli told me you're in Italy.

Who was this?

Ethan? I had his number memorised, in case we needed to communicate because of Eli.

'Sorry, it's my ex-husband. I just need to check that all is well with my son,' I said. I was surprised, and a little alarmed.

Is Eli okay?

Yes, of course. I just wanted to know how you were.

All good. You sure all okay?

Yes! Why so anxious?

You don't normally get in touch, Ethan.

You don't normally go to Italy. Just wanted to make sure you're good. Can I call you?

No. No, no no no. I didn't want to hear his voice. Not now. I didn't want to be taken back to the past, now that I felt I was finally moving forward.

Signal not good, I texted quickly. Not now. I wanted to look forward, not backwards.

Sorry. Well, glad to hear you're okay. Awesome picture, by the way.

Oh, he'd seen it? Eli had sent the photograph I'd taken with my cell phone to his dad?

Because in that case, Ethan had seen Andrea.

Thanks. Take care.

'Everything good?' Matilde asked.

'Yes, everything good. Just, I don't often hear from my ex-husband, so I thought maybe there was something wrong with my son,' I replied, and composed a quick message to Eli, just to be sure. That's mothers for you, I suppose.

'Was he shocked you came here? Your ex-husband, I mean… what's his name?'

'Ethan,' I told her.

'Ethan. Was he shocked?'

'Well, I don't know, to be honest. I didn't even tell him. Our son did. Oh, such a relief,' I said, as my phone chirped again – I'd just a received an *all good* from Eli. I took a deep breath. I brought Ethan's message back up on the screen.

To say it was unexpected was an understatement.

This was the man who broke my heart, I had to remind myself. He was my husband *and* the man who broke my heart – both. It was yet another case of families being complicated, and feelings becoming tangled and unclear. Because he was the love of my life for sure, but apparently, I wasn't the love of his.

Why was he contacting me now?

It wasn't about having broken up with Vicky, I knew that. Eli had told me it'd happened over a year before, for a start; and also, his indifference to me had begun long before she'd come on the scene. Our separation had not happened because of other women, but because of the indisputable fact that Ethan and I had lived separate lives under the same roof for a long time, and that I'd been lonelier with him than without him. Once Eli was a teenager, it seemed there wasn't anything else keeping us together.

Ethan was an IT specialist, but he worked as a consultant for big corporations and was away from home most of the time. He called himself a nomad. Except his son was in school and I had a job, so we couldn't be nomads with him. He was content to travel all over the world and have me to come back to.

We both lived good lives. Separately, though.

With Eli's graduation from high school looming, I'd known I had to make a change. I asked Ethan to make a choice – to stay home more, to spend more time with me, to be a couple again… or to continue the way we were, but to break up.

He was horrified: none of the two options suited him, of course. He wanted to keep living the same life and stay together.

But I couldn't.

Three years on, I couldn't say I was happier – but I certainly felt more peaceful, now that I didn't have to fight for his attention, now that I'd given up on the façade we'd portrayed of the perfect marriage. The first few months had been bleak, but after that – well, like I'd predicted, not much had changed. We were as distant as we'd been while we were together. After about a year

Ethan found Vicky, and I was convinced they were happy – but it seemed that had been an illusion too, because it hadn't worked out.

'You lost in thought?' Matilde said.

'Yeah. You see… my son sent Ethan the photograph I…'

'Oh, I see!' She'd guessed at once.

'Andrea,' we said at the same time.

Could it really be about Andrea, though? Ethan wanted to know if I was in a relationship, if I'd met someone?

'You didn't date anyone else, since you broke up?'

'Oh, no. Not at all. I'm not dating anyone *now* either, Matilde. It was just a short outing with a guy I hardly know…'

'But you like him.'

'Yes, I do. I like him. And I hope to see him again, I must admit.'

'Well, maybe Ethan knows that.'

'How would he know?'

'Because he knows you. He knows that you didn't have a date since you guys broke up, and that this da… I mean, *outing* was your first, and that you don't take this lightly.'

'I suppose. Oh, I'm so confused. I say one thing, feel another, and think something else entirely!'

My word, what a day, I said to myself as I watched the fireflies dance in the darkness. Light – dark, light – dark. Like our lives. All of a sudden, the sound of howling dogs came from all around us – I was startled, then I just ignored it. Some kind of twilight bark, I thought.

'Let's toast to our future family reunion,' I said. It really was time for a drink. I switched my phone torch on to see what I was doing. The howls continued, and I felt Matilde tense up beside me. Still thinking nothing of it, I grasped the bottle of wine with my free hand.

Suddenly there was flapping and flurrying above us, around us. I instinctively cowered a little and covered my head with my hand. Flocks of birds took flight from the trees, black silhouettes against the stars, while howls still resounded in the dark, far and near. Matilde gasped.

Strange – the bottle was quivering.

My hand was quivering.

I was tipsy, and tired, I thought, but the quivering turned into shaking, and then swaying; the bottle fell on the grass with a muffled sound, deep red liquid spilling on the ground. In the light of my phone, I saw the bottle jumping a little, as if it was alive. Matilde's fingers burrowed in my thigh. At that moment, grey shadows detached themselves from the woods and began to run in the open fields – grunting, barking, making sounds I'd never heard before. Boars – terrified, running for their lives. I didn't have time to be afraid of them, because I realised that not just my hand was shaking, but my whole body, and Matilde, and the earth beneath us, and the woods, and, it seemed, the sky. A low rumble filled my ears and I realised my teeth were chattering. The sound of screams echoed from a distance – from the village.

'*Il terremoto!*' Matilde yelled out and sprang to her feet, dragging me with her. *Terremoto?* My mind went blank. What…

Earthquake.

We clung onto each other, shaking with the ground we stood on. The lights of Bosconero disappeared right in front of us, as if they'd never been there.

CHAPTER NINE

It's hard to recount what happened in those moments. I remember that one whispered word – *terremoto* – and then watching a sea of darkness swallow Bosconero whole. After that, my memories are like pages torn off a diary.

Everything was a blur, with images and noises melting in terror: stones falling behind us, the rumble from the belly of the earth louder and louder in my ears, and the two of us throwing ourselves forward, rolling downward on the grass, down the slope. That jump forwards was what saved our lives, I realised a few moments later, when we scrambled to our feet and ran down the hill, the ground still jerking underneath us: I glanced over my shoulder, and saw that the steps where we had been sitting were now buried under fallen stones. The Roman ruins and what was left of the medieval church was now a small rocky mound.

We kept running down the slope, but a final, mighty shiver shattering the earth made us fall in the grass at the bottom of the hill. We curled up against each other, Matilde whimpering, while I was too stunned to make a sound. I was still clutching my phone, but I couldn't find the torch button.

'Massimo! Massimo!' Matilde was calling towards the darkened village. I couldn't speak. Everything was pitch black around us: no more fairy lights hanging between the houses, no more street lights on top of the hill, no lights at all, except the cold, indifferent stars high above, watching us from afar, undisturbed.

That terrible, terrible sound coming from beneath us, deep and deadly, rose once again. I could feel it in my guts, in my bones. Matilde and I clung to each other, and I tried to cover her, to shield her, as the sky was falling and the earth was rumbling...

Then everything stopped.

The earth was still and silent again, and the only noises left were the screams coming from the village, and the rising howls from all around us. It took me a while, but I managed to switch on the torch on my phone. We scrambled to our feet, leaning on each other, arms linked, and ran through the woods in the feeble light, until we stepped onto the village square.

'Massimo! Nonna! Massimo!' Matilde was calling over and over again.

We were swallowed by cries and moans and surrounded by strange shapes – mounds, where buildings used to be. My brain couldn't process what my eyes were seeing. The tiny torch could barely make out the scene, but what we saw didn't make sense.

Where had the houses gone?

Matilde threw herself forward, still calling Massimo and Nonna, but I grabbed her by the arm.

'Stop. Stop,' I blurted out in English, because it was the first word that came to my mind. 'It's too dangerous. Don't go,' I elaborated in Italian. My mind was empty – I was running on survival instinct. Once again I lifted my torch, trying to see better, trying to decide what to do next.

Pile after pile of rubble took shape in front of our eyes, wooden beams sticking out of them, torn metal wires, broken balconies, clouds of dust in the air. People covered in blood and dirt, digging in the wreckage, screaming out for their children, their parents, their friends, buried under tons of stone and bricks. Multicoloured stars danced at the periphery of my vision, and a wave of dread and horror hit me – for a moment I thought I would pass out from breathing too hard. I was clutching at the phone with one hand and holding onto Matilde with the other, but that short, short instant when I'd almost fainted was enough to lose her.

'I need to find Massimo!' she cried and freed herself from my grasp. I tried to grab at her clothes, but it was no use. I ran after her, too shocked to even call her name, and stabs of pain shot from my feet through my whole body. All of a sudden, I realised I'd lost my sandals somewhere on Collina Cora, and I was walking on sharp, hard debris. It didn't matter. I stumbled on among the rubble, little beams of light dancing around me – other cell phones, some torches. I kept calling Matilde's name, my voice growing hoarser and hoarser as I breathed in thick, painful dust – but my calls were lost in the chaos. She didn't even have a light – I had to find her – I had to... Was that her, the dark figure running ahead of me?

'Matilde!' I called, but the woman turned, and it wasn't Matilde, but a stranger wearing a mask of terror, covered in dust, eyes big and hair matted. I kept searching in the feeble light, in that landscape of destruction.

I've lost her.

I've lost her.

'Matilde!' Dust kept filling the back of my throat and made me croak instead of cry. Voices calling for help rose and fell, but I couldn't stop and answer – I had to find my cousin. I stumbled on, my feet in agony...

And then a hand grabbed my shoulder and forced me to turn around.

'*Aiuto, ti prego, aiuto!*' Help, please, help. A man in torn pyjamas, his terrified eyes shining black through the white dust covering his face, had materialised from nowhere. 'My daughter is under there! Help, please, please!'

'Where? Where?' Voices rose from around me, shadows taking shape, torch beams shining on the wreckage.

'Here! This was her room!' the man said, pointing to a shapeless mound of bricks and stones. Tears traced marks on his cheeks, washing the dust away where they rolled. 'She's under there! I can hear her! I'm coming, Papà's coming!'

He could hear her? How could have anybody survived, there? Was he delusional, in his terrible pain? I asked myself. But then I heard a little voice calling – weak, feeble, but there.

'*Papà! Aiuto!*'

She was buried under all that, but alive.

I gazed towards the black street ahead of me – and back to the desperate father. I quickly slipped my phone in my crossbody and threw myself on the rubble, joining the other men and women who had answered the man's plea. All I knew then was digging, digging desperately. My mind went blank, there was no pain in my feet or hands, no more noise or voices – and suddenly, the tiny voice seemed close: 'Papà, I'm here, I'm here, Papà...'

'Benedetta! Benedetta!' the man cried. Benedetta? A vague memory came back to me. The girl twirling to show off her party dress in the square yesterday... A lifetime ago, when Matilde, Massimo and I sat peacefully together, with people celebrating all around us.

Before.

Tears streamed down my face and I tried to dry them, dust and saltwater mixing and making me blink. Through the veil of tears, I saw a tiny hand appearing – the man held it. 'Papà's coming, we'll get you out, Benedetta, I'm here...'

And then the top of the child's head appeared, black hair made white by dust – her face, eyes closed and mouth open, dust on her lips, ragged breathing – like a painful second birth.

Voices rose. 'We have her! We have her!'

I wiped my forehead, my skin covered in cold sweat, and crawled aside, sitting back on my heels, while the child's father and the other men tried to pull her out. But the girl screamed and cried.

'She's injured!'

'It's not safe!'

'Papà is here, Benedetta, don't worry, we'll get you out…'

I watched in horror as the girl's lips began to turn blue.

'Don't move her! Wait!' A voice came from behind us, together with beams of light and heavy footsteps on the rubble. A group of men in reflective clothing and heavy boots, holding powerful torches and carrying backpacks. Paramedics? Police? I had no idea, I didn't care. All I knew was that help was here, at last.

I was on my knees, numbed with the pain in my hands and feet, as the booted men worked on the child, digging and then gently freeing her arms, digging some more, freeing her torso, her knees, until she was finally out, covered in dust and bruises, her yellow pyjamas ragged – but she was alive.

Benedetta's father hovered around the men checking her over, crying; finally she was cleared, and father and daughter clung to each other.

'Mamma!' the girl cried.

'Mamma will be here soon. I'm sure she's fine. I'm sure she's fine…' the man said.

I shivered and wrapped my arms around me.

Was she?

Was her mother really fine?

I stood on sore feet, and the cries for help all around began flooding in again as I came out of my suspended reality. Sirens were blaring in the distance, and helicopters appeared above us, half-illuminated by the beams of torches. I had to find Matilde… I looked left and right, unsure where to go. It was such chaos. Where had she gone? Maybe to her home, looking for Massimo? Maybe to look for Nonna? I couldn't even find my bearings around the crumbled buildings, in the uneven light. My head was spinning, and I'd lost all sense of time and space.

'Luce!' One of the men called my name and brought me back to reality. I jumped out of my skin and jerked around. I didn't recognise him at first, with his helmet and covered in dust – but then he rubbed his face with a gloved hand, and I recognised Andrea, pale and wide-eyed. Beside him was Massimo; he seemed unhurt too. The relief made my knees go weak.

'Andrea! Massimo! I don't know where Matilde is… We were on Collina Cora when it happened, the ruins nearly fell on us, and then we came here and she ran off, I…'

Massimo hugged me briefly, then pulled away. 'She's safe, don't worry. We saw her and told her to go to the slope down Collina Cora.'

'We're sending people over there, in the open, away from the ruins or any other building. You need to go too. Help is coming,' Andrea said, taking me gently by the shoulders. He spoke slowly, enunciating every syllable – he knew how to deal with someone in shock. Then, he looked up to the sky, to the helicopters hovering. 'The Protezione Civile is here now. We'll be fine.' I didn't know what Protezione Civile was, exactly, but it sounded like something good – protection of civilians?

'*Grazie al cielo*,' I said. Thank goodness. Matilde was safe, in an open, grassy space where nothing could fall on her. It was like a boulder had been removed from my heart. 'I'll stay and help,' I said.

'No.' Andrea squeezed my shoulders a little harder. 'All civilians must leave. There will be aftershocks, there might be gas explosions. We need everyone away from here.' At that moment, the sound of a helicopter coming closer and closer made me look up too; it was then that I realised the village tower was still standing. It was a strange vision, darting up to the sky, over the flattened buildings.

'I can't believe it wasn't destroyed,' I murmured. I was almost in a daze, now.

'Come on, we need to go, please…' Andrea said. He took me by the hand, and I winced.

'Oh my God, Luce…' I looked at him, then followed his gaze down to my hands. They were bloodied and flayed; in seeing them, the pain hit me suddenly, like my hands had caught on fire.

'Anyone who can walk!' a megaphone shouted at us. 'Please leave the village. Meeting point at Collina Cora! Go!' Bright lights shone on us, a small sea of men and women, some in uniform and khaki helmets and some dressed in bright yellow, filled the streets.

'I'll take a group over to the Collina,' Andrea yelled. 'Follow me!'

'I'm not going anywhere! My wife is under there! Please, take my daughter and let me stay and dig…' Benedetta's father cried out, and many seemed to echo his words, though it was hard for me to fully grasp what they were saying. Of course they wanted to stay. How were they all going to leave the village and run to safety, when the people they loved were still buried under the rubble? How were they going to find it in themselves to let others take charge? And still, they had to. Andrea had mentioned aftershocks. If another tremor was to happen… Just thinking of hearing that deep, rumbling noise again made me shake all over again.

'Come on, let's go,' Massimo whispered, and began to lead me away. I followed, docile – what else could I do? And then we stopped – a familiar voice had resounded above the din.

'Massimo!' We both turned towards the voice; it was Matilde, stumbling down the now brightly lit road, beneath the shadow of the tower.

She hadn't gone to Collina Cora?

And then, it all happened in a moment.

She was running to Massimo, her hair blown back, feet pounding the ground in the sudden, eerie silence. Was there really silence? That couldn't be. It must have been me, shutting everything out, not knowing where I was or who I was any more, but looking at myself from somewhere far away – because it was starting again, now. The earth was moving underneath our feet once more; the world was trembling for the second time.

I fell on the debris and I saw Massimo sprinting towards Matilde, then stumbling and falling not much further from me. I was still submerged in silence, as if I were underwater. Andrea had disappeared.

Trying to steady myself by pinning my hands on the ground, I raised my head. Matilde wasn't running any more – she was trying to remain standing, and for a moment she was a tragic figure against the backdrop of the tower, before falling on her knees too. The tower was above her; and then, in an instant, it crumbled in a cloud of dust, like a house of cards, and swallowed Matilde.

When it finished crumbling, when the dust settled and the screams began to rise, there was nothing left to see but a pile of rubble, where Matilde had just been.

Maybe I'd been injured, somehow, or maybe my mind simply could not bear the horror of what I'd just seen; all I knew was that the ground rose to meet me, and everything went black.

CHAPTER TEN

When I opened my eyes – maybe a few minutes later, maybe hours later, who knew – the first thing I saw was a set of yellow and orange rays, searching the black sky like enormous torches. I breathed in a sweet scent, the scent of a summer night in a warm country, but it was mixed with something harsh, dry, settling in the back of my throat. Dust, a thick coating that I could taste, as well as smell. My cheek was resting on something cold and sticky. Where was I?

I wasn't in my bedroom in Seattle, that was sure... Wait... I'd flown to Italy, and...

It all came back to me, in a wave of horror and dread, and my body retched with a fit of coughing and nausea. The earthquake. Running through the woods. The village destroyed, the little girl buried alive.

The crumbling tower, swallowing Matilde.

Where was she?

Massimo, Nonna... Andrea. Where were they?

Matilde couldn't have been under that tower. It couldn't be, I must have dreamt it. It was all a nightmare...

I realised I was lying flat, looking up to the sky all lit up with the searching rays. My family needed to know that I was alive. I needed to find my phone. I tried to sit up, but I couldn't; my head was swimming. Was I hurt? I ached everywhere. My head pounded as I turned left and right: a small sea of stretchers and camp beds surrounded me. It looked like a hospital camp, set up outside so that nothing could crumble on us.

The memory of that noise in the belly of the earth, and everything shaking, covered me in a cold sweat. Never in my life had I known such primal, all-consuming fear. I closed my eyes for a moment and forced myself to breathe as deeply as I could, causing another fit of coughing. When I could breathe normally once more, I tried to sit up again – then, I noticed for the first time that the wounds on my hands were dressed. They hurt.

Leaning on them and grimacing at the pain, I managed to get into a seated position, even if the world was spinning around me. I looked around. There were people lying with their eyes closed – maybe unconscious, I wasn't sure – some bandaged and bloodied, some sitting up with blankets around their shoulders. A group of women were crying in the corner, while a man sat with his hand on his mouth, mute beside a woman lying on a stretcher. A teenager was cleaning a little girl's face, covered in dust, the girl too shocked to cry. That thick dust was everywhere, on our faces, our clothes, down our throats. The eerie yellow and orange lights passed over us and moved away, and then came back with the same trajectory. Not far from us, the blue lights of ambulances danced their intermittent rhythm.

With relief, I noticed that my crossbody was still beside me. I opened it quickly and peeked inside – *yes!* My phone was there. A lifeline. I could call Eli… As soon as I collected myself. I wondered if news of the earthquake had reached home already. Only then I saw that there was no signal. Damn! I had to speak to my family. For a moment, panic overwhelmed me, and the irrational fear that they might be hurt too – it made no sense, a part of me knew that. But the need to hold my son, my child, and make sure he was okay, was so strong that I almost burst into tears. I had to tell them I'd survived. I had to find Matilde – and Nonna, I had to find my nonna! How could I ever tell Mamma that I'd gone all the way to Italy, just to see our family decimated, or obliterated?

I covered my face with my hands for a moment and squeezed my eyes tight, trying to calm my breathing and steady my crazy heart; I had to keep it together.

'*Sta bene, signora? Signora?*' An elderly lady lying on the camp bed beside me, wrapped in what looked like a military blanket, stretched her hand towards me.

'*Sto bene,*' I said, and found it in myself to smile.

'My house has fallen down,' she said, matter-of-factly, with that abruptness that older people seem to have, sometimes. 'But we are all alive. All of us. My husband and me. And my children are in Bastia. We are blessed.'

'You are,' I said, and took the hand she was offering. The touch of that kind stranger grounded me.

'Say a prayer with me,' she said, and she murmured an Ave Maria, like an incantation of comfort and protection. I hadn't prayed since I was a little girl, when I used to recite my prayers with Mamma, every night.

When we finished the prayer, I thanked the woman and she squeezed my hand one last time before letting go. Maybe she'd been an angel sent to help me compose myself and gather the courage to move forward.

I exhaled. Slowly, slowly, I stood. A small shower of dust fell off my hair and, for a moment, I thought I would fall again – but thankfully, I didn't. My feet felt strange, icy cold and cocooned in something soft: I looked down and saw that some kind soul had slipped some socks on them. I could feel the bandages underneath. Hopefully, I would find a pair of shoes, somewhere…

There were men and women in reflective waistcoats and nitrile-gloved hands running around, fast and focused, wearing tense, set expressions. Some were seeing to the wounded, others were asking questions and taking notes on a clipboard. Maybe they were trying to make a list of survivors, of those still missing, of those who'd died. On unsteady feet, I stopped one of them – a thin man with bright blue eyes, the yellow jacket looking huge on him.

'*Mi scusi…*' My lips were dry and parched. I swallowed, and tasted dust once again.

'*Un momento,*' he said, his lips pursed, and strode on. It was only then that I saw he was carrying a syringe and what looked like a plastic bag full of a clear liquid – he ran towards an elderly man, lying immobile, his face unnaturally white.

They were treating the wounded the best they could, outside, with what looked like not much more than first aid kits. How long had passed since the earthquake? A few hours? It was amazing that they could set up a hospital camp at all. The determination to find order in chaos, and a blessing in the darkest hour, like the lady beside me – it was such a wonder to me, and a consolation of some sort.

I leaned against my bed, not wanting to lie down in case getting up again would be another struggle, and waited for the man to come back. After a short while, he did; this time, he was holding a clipboard.

'How are you feeling? Sit back down for me. Feeling sick? Double vision? We think you hit your head, obviously we couldn't ask you…'

'I don't feel sick, and I can see fine. Thank you for looking after me. How long… how long has passed? Since the earthquake?'

'Not long,' he said, and his voice betrayed distress, behind his composure. 'You need to be checked over properly when we can access the hospital, just in case. Your hands and feet are in a bad way.'

'They're not too bad, really. Can I have some water?' I asked. I didn't want to bother anyone as there were people all around in a much worse condition than me, but the dust was suffocating me, and I could barely speak.

'Of course. I'll get it to you at once. We need to register you, first, though. What's your name?'

'Matilde…' I croaked, and then a fit of coughing hit me. The man laid a hand on my back.

'Matilde. Second name?'

'No, no. My name is Luce Nardini. Matilde is my cousin, and…'

'Date and place of birth?'

'I need to know what happened to my cousin. She was just in front of the tower when it fell…'

At the mention of the tower, the man's expression morphed into grief. 'I'm so sorry.' He was sorry? Did he know something?

'Is she dead? Do you know that for sure?' My lips stuck together as I spoke, parched and caked in dust.

'No, no!' he said, and laid a hand on my arm. 'Nearly everyone here is looking for someone. They're setting up a station for the missing and the dead,' he said, pointing at somewhere beyond the car park, where I saw some soldiers pitching tents at the light of the portable spotlights. 'But if she was near the tower…' He decided not to finish the sentence, and a long, cold shiver travelled down my spine.

'I understand,' I said, as calmly as I could.

Oh, Matilde.

'Matilde Nardini?' a voice came from behind us. I turned around and saw a young woman, without a yellow jacket but with a reflective sash across her chest, carrying a stack of blankets. There were fresh, deep scratches all over her arms, parallel to each other like comet's tails. It looked like she'd dragged herself out of somewhere… And yet there she was, helping other people.

'Yes! Do you know what happened to her?' I coughed again.

'I know her,' the woman said. She blinked a few times, tears shining on her eyelashes, and cleared her voice. 'Matilde and I went to school together. She's alive. They flew her down to the hospital in Bastia, by helicopter.'

There was hope. There was still hope!

'I need to go see her,' I said, and stood straight once again, letting go of the support of the bed. This time I felt steadier, stronger.

The man with the clipboard was quick to stop me. 'Nobody is allowed to circulate, except official vehicles.'

'I could walk down.'

'You can't. The roads are blocked. We need to wait until they clear them,' the young woman intervened. 'But nobody should be wandering around anyway, at this time.'

'But…' A siren began to scream, and blue intermittent lights lit up all our faces with a strange, livid hue.

'I have to go. I'll come back to check on you. My name is Romina,' she said, and made her way towards the ambulance that had just arrived.

The man took a step forward. 'Let me finish registering you now, so if someone is looking for you, they'll know you're alive. Place and date of birth, then?'

'Yes. Of course. Sorry.' I had to focus. I had to help these people, not hinder them. I was only one of many searching for loved ones. 'I was born in Ralston, Seattle, US, June twelfth 1963.'

'Thank you. So you're a tourist? But you have family here? We'll take a note of anyone you're looking for and cross-check once we come across them. Matilde Nardini, then?'

'Yes, and Clelia Nardini, my grandmother.'

'Do you need help to contact anyone in the States? Your family… or maybe the consulate in Rome? Will you be stranded here? I'm sure there will be provisions for tourists, though nothing has come through, yet…'

'You're very kind, but I'm good.' I was lying, obviously. I wasn't good. I had nowhere to stay. But I couldn't think of anything beyond finding Matilde, Nonna and Massimo. And Andrea too… who knew what happened to him after the tower fell? Anything else would have to wait. 'I don't need to notify the consulate and I'll call my family myself.'

'Noted. We need you to stay here for now, okay? I'll get you some water. Are you cold, would you like a blanket? Some coffee to warm you up?'

Although I was cold and almost shivering, I didn't need a blanket, because I wasn't staying there. 'Just water, and a cup of coffee would be really good, thank you.'

'We need to find you shoes as well, Luce. Wait here.'

'I'll come with you,' I said. The idea of sitting still among all those injured people, being waited on like there was something wrong with me, was impossible. I followed the yellow-jacketed man through what seemed an endless line of stretchers. The most serious cases must have been carried away by helicopter, just like Romina had said, but seeing all this blood, these wounds, people attached to pumps, bandaged children in their mothers' arms, grown men crying, was shocking enough. With every step, another bit of this nightmare was revealed to me.

We came to an army tent, made of heavy-duty, khaki-coloured plastic – once again I was amazed at how much they'd managed to do in just a few hours, from setting up a camp hospital to pitching tents, from carrying supplies, to flying those who were worst off to a proper hospital. A fit of coughing hit me again and, without a word, the man handed me the promised water in a small sealed bottle he'd extracted from a box.

'If at any point you don't feel well, call out. I don't want you to end up back on a stretcher. Let me get you some coffee; come over here,' he said, and led me to a table where several stainless-steel containers were laid out, together with plastic cups.

'Thanks, I can get it myself, don't...' My words hung in the air. I couldn't finish the sentence, because I'd caught a glimpse of what was beyond the tent.

In spite of myself, and against my better judgement, I took a sideways step, and looked.

There were bodies wrapped in blankets and secured with black plastic straps. One beside the other, line after line, like a small graveyard had risen up to the surface, exposing the dead for everyone to see. Beside one of the bodies there was a kneeling man, crying alone. I recognised him at once – the father of the girl I'd helped dig out... Was that the girl's mother, lying there wrapped in plastic? I wanted to go to him but, as I took a step, the man stopped me.

'Come. No need to go there,' he said gently, and wrapped an arm around my shoulder to try to lead me away. But I couldn't move.

My chest began to rise and fall, shock and panic hitting me again – each of those bodies were a father, a daughter, a friend, a mother, crushed by their own homes as they were sleeping. It was all too tragic, too harrowing, to wrap my head around. And so, for a moment, my soul detached itself from the situation and went hiding somewhere dark and secret inside me, where it was free to cry. The panic disappeared, giving way to emptiness. I was left hollow, rigid, unable to move.

As I was staring, a medic in a bright red uniform stepped into my line of sight, holding a woman by the arm as he led her to one of the bodies. He kneeled down and gently, respectfully, slipped the cloth from the dead man. That uniform, I'd seen it before. The Bosconero voluntary ambulance service.

'Massimo,' I whispered.

It couldn't be. It couldn't be. It was too cruel.

But the woman who was kneeling beside him called another name among her tears. 'Giacomo!'

Relief and sorrow filled me at the same time. It wasn't Massimo, thank God! But lying there was the man who just yesterday had passed around his phone, with the picture of his new baby. That little girl was never going to see her papà again.

*

Dawn was breaking on the devastation, and the searching beams in the sky were fading against the daybreak. Thankfully, I'd been allowed to help. For a few hours, I'd handed out coffee, bottles of water and blankets, wearing a pair of borrowed trainers – I didn't want to think where they could have found them. I kept checking my phone, but there was still no signal, and I had no idea how long the battery would last. Not much longer, probably.

I couldn't stay there any more, blocked roads or not. With every hour that passed, I grew more and more frantic. And with the phones down, I couldn't let Eli know I was fine: to put them through this, when surely news of the earthquake would have reached home by now, was a kind of torture. To my shame, warm tears began to roll down my cheeks. I glanced over towards Romina, working a few beds away from where I stood. If she saw me crying, she would make me stop and take a rest. But I couldn't.

I looked around, trying to hatch a plan. I was almost sure they couldn't force me to stay there if I wanted to leave, but I didn't want to chance it. Maybe I could find a way down through the woods? But what if I got lost, exhausted and confused as I was?

The military trucks were my best bet; apart from the ambulances, they were the only vehicles allowed to circulate. I made my way towards the trucks parked at the edge of the camp, and approached a young soldier. I took a breath before explaining my situation. Anxiety was rising inside me, and I was struggling to keep it together any longer.

I'd flown over from America to solve the mystery that was my family. I was drinking wine on a warm summer night, watching the fireflies, against the backdrop of ancient ruins – then, the world had turned upside down. Everything had been strange and new before, yes, but not like this. Not like seeing a tower collapse over my cousin, not like digging in rubble to save a little girl buried under her own house, not like giving out blankets to people who'd lost everything, not like seeing row after row of corpses wrapped in plastic.

I was imploding. But I had to make sense, if I wanted help.

'My family is at the hospital in…' What was the name of the place? 'Bastia. I need to go see them. I need to go down the hill,' I said, as composedly as I could.

'*Signora*, we're dismantling the camp and taking everyone down, anyway.'

'Can I just jump in one of the trucks leaving now? My cousin is in a bad way. I worry about not getting there… in time,' I explained, and swallowed a knot of anxiety. The young soldier exchanged glances with another, who shook his head. Oh, no. It wasn't going to work…

'Fine. Fine. Come up,' the older soldier said, and my knees nearly gave way in relief. I turned around once again, catching one last glimpse of the camp. They helped me to lift myself up, and I kneeled on the metal floor, my arms around myself. I wasn't alone in the truck: two people, a man and a woman, were lying on stretchers. This could only mean they were still digging the dead and injured out of the ruins. I tried not to look at them, and kept my eyes out on the winding road, in the cold, grey light of dawn.

Would the sun come out?

Would the golden Italian morning shine again?

It didn't seem possible.

We drove through two small hills made of rubble – former homes, somebody's homes – and bend after bend, to the bottom of the hill. At every turn I felt more relieved and more afraid. I was desperate to get to the hospital, and yet I was terrified of what I was going to see, what I was going to find.

Finally, we were there. The vehicle stopped and a soldier helped me down, in front of a large, yellow building. Over the door, in stolid, steely letters, was the sign Ospedale Sant'Anna di Bastia. The casualties on the stretchers were wheeled past me, and they disappeared inside the automatic doors. Slowly, step after step, I followed them, unsteady with dread and exhaustion.

All of a sudden, a noise came from my crossbody. It was my phone – finally, there was a signal! I scrambled as quickly as I could, and almost burst into sobs when I saw Eli's number flashing on the screen.

'Eli! I'm fine. I'm not hurt. I tried to call you…' I swallowed back tears and tried to steady my voice…But it wasn't Eli who replied.

'Luce! Thank goodness! I've been trying to call you since last night… I saw it on the news, I couldn't believe it when they mentioned Bosconero…'

'Ethan?'

'Yes. Yes, I'm here with Eli. He drove home as soon as he heard; we're at my house.'

'What? He should be in school. He—'

'Mom!' Eli was on the call too. Hearing his voice brought tears to my eyes again. 'I couldn't be there on my own when this happened! I came to Dad's house. We're coming to get you at the airport, okay? Just get there and catch the first flight back.'

'Eli, sweetheart, you're making too big a deal out of this,' I said, trying to sound like I believed it. Like I wasn't horrified and scared to death. 'I'm okay, please don't worry about me. It's not as bad as they probably said on the news, you know, they always exaggerate,' I added. There was no way I would tell him about the state I was in, the things I'd seen since the earth shook, my bandaged hands, maybe a dead person's shoes on my ruined feet.

'Stop it, Luce. I know how bad it is, I'm out of my mind with worry,' Ethan again. 'Please, come home.'

Come home? Was my ex-husband really telling me that?

For a moment, the concern in his voice touched me in a way that went beyond the circumstances; for so long, I'd felt he didn't even see me. He'd travelled around the world without even checking in for days at an end. I remembered trying to get a hold of him in Nigeria, the day a bomb had gone off in the same airport he had to travel from, and how blasé he'd been about it – *We're all adults, here*, he'd said, when I'd complained about him not contacting me at all. Now the roles were reversed, and although I hated for him to go through all that worry, a part of me was melting in relief.

'Ethan—'

'Luce, listen to me. You need to make your way to the consulate, in Rome. They're organising flights for American citizens. Let me know at once when you have the flight details... we just want you back here safe.'

Oh, me too. I wanted to see Eli. I wanted to get away from all this destruction...

'I can't come back yet,' I forced myself to say.

'I know it'll be difficult to find transport, but I'm sure the consulate—'

'No, Ethan, I can't come back now. Matilde is in the hospital. I don't know what happened to my grandmother and my uncle yet. I haven't found out—'

'What? Mom, are you crazy?' Eli sounded so upset. I was overcome with guilt.

'I need to do what I came out here for. And I need to make myself useful. They need extra hands, there's so much to do...'

'You can't be serious. Luce, please...'

'Mom! Come home!'

My stomach churned at hearing the fear in their voices. This was torture for them and for me. I didn't know if Mamma knew about the earthquake – she wasn't an avid news watcher like Ethan – but if she did, she'd be terrified. Was I doing the right thing in staying there? I was afraid too, just as much as they were. Afraid of aftershocks, afraid of seeing all this destruction, and the wounded, and the dead... It was tempting to imagine sitting on my sofa back home, reading a book, with a candle burning beside me – to imagine normal life, no rubble, no corpses, no tears and pain all around me...

But just thinking of getting on a plane and leaving this all behind, like it was none of my business, was impossible.

'Ethan, I—' I began, but a sudden rumble made me jump out of my skin – an aftershock?

I turned around to see truck after truck making their way into the hospital parking lot and the streets beyond. It wasn't another earthquake. The phone felt slippery in my hand; I was covered in cold sweat.

'What's happening?' Ethan called.

'Nothing, it's all fine... I'm at the hospital—'

'So you are hurt!' he interrupted me.

'No, I'm not, I promise! I'm not a patient, I'm here for Matilde...'

'Make your way to Rome at once. I beg you, Luce... If something should happen to you...'

I didn't hear the rest, because the noises and voices coming from the trucks, disgorging their cargo of hurt and injured people, of stretchers and helpers, swallowed his voice. My stomach churned.

'I'll think about it for a bit and then decide, okay?'

'I can't hear you! Luce. You need to come back. They're bracing themselves for aftershocks. It said so on the news. Eli is beside himself, I haven't told Angelina yet…' I managed to hear, before the noise was too much again.

'Let me call you back. I won't be long. I promise!'

'I can't hear you… God, what's happening there?'

'It's just… traffic…' I hastened to find non-loaded words and avoid mentioning military trucks. 'Ethan? Eli?'

Silence.

'Ethan?'

I kept my phone to my ear for a bit, thinking Ethan was just pausing – but a beep told me that the line had gone dead.

For a moment I stood there, in the early morning breeze, surrounded by chaos, fighting the impulse to call them back and say: *I'm coming home, I'm coming home to you – where I can be safe, and never feel the ground shaking under my feet again, and never see buildings tumbling down in front of my eyes and row after row of dead people lying in a hospital camp. Back to my normal life, my son, my run-of-the-mill job, my comfortable home…*

But I couldn't give in.

I turned around and went looking for my family.

I slipped inside the automatic door alongside a paramedic supporting an elderly woman leaning on him, a foil blanket on her shoulders. I had to squeeze myself against the wall, arms flat by my sides and sucking my stomach in, to avoid being run over by someone on a stretcher. When I made my way into the hospital lobby, I couldn't believe what I saw. It was like a scene from Dante's *Inferno*.

The hospital was overflowing. The sterile scent I would have expected was obliterated by the ever-present smell of dust and crumbled stone, of blood, of fear. It resembled a refugee camp in a war-torn country rather than a hospital in a first-world one. A small group of women, some in yellow jackets, some in nurses' uniforms, stood at reception trying to direct people to the right places. An exhausted-looking doctor ran through the lobby, towards an incoming batch of casualties. At that moment I was sure, without a doubt, that the earthquake had hit many more villages, beyond Bosconero. The hamlets I had seen on the hills on the way here – were they all gone? Frassino, and the abandoned homes and frescoed church Andrea had showed me, was it dust, now? And with the flashback of my car journey to Bosconero came another image: Matilde's profile, smiling, her hair flowing in the breeze coming in from the open window…

I was about to try and approach one of the nurses at the reception when another flood of casualties came rushing in, like a wave crashing on the shore. Soldiers kept the automatic doors open as the first cluster arrived, then another, and another, in a sorrowful blur of bloodied sheets, an arm falling out on the side of a stretcher, bare feet covered in cuts and dust, children crying or wide-eyed with fear. I scoured faces, trying to recognise my grandmother, or my uncle, as though I'd never seen them – every elderly woman could be Clelia, every middle-aged man could be Carlo… My eyes flickered around looking for a resemblance…

There was no way now to ask anyone – the makeshift reception was in a frenzy. They gently took relatives away from stretchers, checked registers and files, flagged the most urgent cases to the frantic doctors; they disappeared inside the hospital corridors only to re-emerge a little paler, lips a little more pursed, eyes a little wider. After standing aside for a while, I saw that some volunteers had set up a station in the opposite corner of the lobby. They had warm drinks, diapers and formula milk for babies, wet wipes for those covered in dust and other basic necessities.

I walked across to them and gratefully accepted a cup of hot sugary coffee. I sat on the floor beneath a window, not wanting to take a chair from someone who might need it more. I waited and waited, hoping the right moment would come to ask for news of my relatives…

My coffee shone golden all of a sudden, and my arms too; I turned around towards the window behind me. A bright, sunny, warm day was preparing itself, golden rays seeping from the glass and making everything shine. I closed my eyes, and almost felt unable to open them again, as sheer prostration weighed on my shoulders. I felt myself drifting away, quickly falling into a haze that was somewhere between wakefulness and sleep. And then someone called my name.

'Luce!'

The call reached me through the lobby, and I jerked my eyes open to see a familiar figure, a tall young man in a yellow jacket and heavy boots, running towards me. Massimo! He strode towards me and offered me his hand, helping me up. I threw my arms around him – the relief to see him alive!

'Thank God you're safe!' I could only say.

'And you, Luce!'

'Matilde? And Nonna?'

'I don't know anything about Clelia. Matilde is alive, and believe me, it's a miracle; almost everyone there when the tower collapsed is gone. We dug her out ourselves,' he said, and ran a hand through his matted hair. His eyes were sunken and circled with blue. 'She's still unconscious. They don't know if she'll make it,' he added. He seemed close to tears – and this gave me the strength to hold back mine. If Massimo was trying to keep it together when his fiancée lay in a coma, I owed it to him to show the same determination. Even if I couldn't breathe for terror and grief, because I knew that Matilde was badly hurt, of course she was: I'd seen it happening with my own eyes. But hearing it spelled out was like a stab in the heart.

'Massimo, I'm so sorry.'

'I couldn't fly here with her. On the helicopter, I mean. I just arrived. I spent all night digging people out. Almost all of the village is gone…'

'Andrea?'

'He's been working with me all night. He's not hurt, apart a few scratches. And his daughter is okay too.'

'Thank goodness. Can I see Matilde?'

'We can try. Come,' he said, and took me by the hand. We zigzagged through the lobby in between people, away from the golden rays coming in from the windows and into the dim belly of the hospital. We left behind those with minor injuries, those waiting for relatives and friends, and found the ones who were badly hurt, sorted out of the lobby when they'd come in. There were camp beds everywhere, and so many elderly people. For a moment I wondered: when they recovered, if they did, would they have a home to go back to? If their homes were among those destroyed, would they be destitute? Had it not been for the thought of seeing Matilde's face, leading me on like a beacon, I would have let go of Massimo's hand and turned away. Every part of me wanted to escape, run far away and forget about all this. Forget I even knew about Bosconero, return to the time when my Italian family was a mystery and when such destruction was something I saw on the news in some faraway country, something that could never happen to me…

Nobody stopped us as we made our slow way, stunted at every step, into the crowded corridor; they saw Massimo's uniform and let us pass. We came to a door with a sign that said Terapia Intensiva: Intensive Care Unit. In normal times there would have been no way we could have just wandered in – but now nurses and doctors were stepping in and out everywhere, trying to sort out the chaos and put out fires wherever they were arising. My heart was trying to jump out of my chest. Everything seemed hushed now, except for the stranger's shoes on my feet, making a squeaky sound on the lino floor.

We came to a room with a wide glass panel, allowing us to see inside. Massimo stopped, and laid a hand on the glass. At first, I could see only the ghost of my reflection, and the tiny cloud of my breath on the glass…

And then, there she was.

Matilde looked tiny, white-faced on the white sheets. Her head was bandaged and so were her arms, rigid and immobile within bright white casts. Tubes came out of her and linked to a machine that beeped, and beeped, and beeped. Was every beep a beat of her heart?

I laid my fingers against the glass, beside Massimo's.

Why was Matilde in that bed, so young and about to start her life, when I was twice her age and standing on my own two feet?

'She should have listened to me. She should have gone to Collina Cora. That's Matilde, though. She never does what she's told,' he said and gave a low, heartbreaking laugh. 'She came looking for me. Giacomo told me. She ran away from the group and came looking for me.'

Giacomo. The new father, the young man who'd shown us his daughter's photograph. The one I'd seen lying lifeless, wrapped in a blanket. I swallowed.

Did Massimo know? I opened my mouth… and then I found I couldn't tell him. Not then, while his fiancée was lying unconscious on a hospital bed.

'Did you speak to a doctor already?'

He nodded. 'Head trauma. Several fractures. They put her in a coma…' He cleared his throat, an accumulation of dust and grief.

'That will give her a better chance to recover. Her body will rest and heal,' I said, tentatively, and laid a hand on his back. 'We must keep the faith. We must believe she'll pull through.'

'It doesn't look good, Luce. The doctor told me.'

It was as if his words had sucked all air out of our space.

Once again, an image flashed in my mind: Matilde laughing beside me on the ancient stony steps, her wedding dress shining on the phone screen as we sat in darkness… All that loveliness, all that promise. It couldn't end this way. No. She had to pull through. She was much the same age as Eli; if something should happen to him, I…

I knew it was completely irrational to think of that now. But once again I was swept by an overwhelming desire to speak to my son, to see his face. He was safe far, far away, I had to remind myself that. But oh, how I needed to see him with my own eyes, hear him with my own ears, be with him…

'What happened after… after the tower crumbled?' I asked. I remembered seeing Matilde swallowed by the wreckage – I would never, never forget that moment – and then waking up in the field hospital. In between, there was almost nothing. Distant voices, out-of-focus hands and faces: that was all.

'I dug,' Massimo said simply, and folded his hands in front of him, like a prayer. He took a breath, and I realised that I'd never seen anyone in my life so close to breaking down and holding it together, so bravely. 'When I saw that she was still breathing, I couldn't believe it. It's a miracle she's here. I'm so sorry I lost sight of you,' he repeated. 'I saw you falling, but I was trying to get Matilde out. By the time we made it, you were gone. Next thing I knew, I saw you here…'

'I was fine. It was just shock. They took me to that kind of camp hospital they had up in Bosconero… Just scratches, really.'

'Everyone has been taken down from Bosconero, now. While we keep digging up in the village.'

The implications of those words chilled me. There were people under the wreckage, and rescue squads were trying to dig them out. What if there was another aftershock? Both the people buried alive and the rescue services would be decimated. I blinked, trying to push that thought away. No point in thinking what might happen; things were bad enough in the present moment.

'We lost Giacomo,' he said suddenly.

He knew; I nodded. 'I saw him up at the camp. For a second, I thought it was you… with that uniform…' I shuddered at the thought.

'Maybe it should have been me. If Matilde goes…'

'Stop it. Don't speak like that.'

We stood for a moment side by side, in a silence broken only by the beeping of the machines.

'I have to go,' Massimo said, and took a step backwards from the glass. I could see how hard it was for him to leave Matilde. 'The Protezione Civile are organising us volunteers, I must be there…'

I was confused as to who was who within the Italian rescue services – the army, the paramedics, the volunteers – but I just knew that many people were coming together to help, in this bubble of destruction we'd found ourselves in. I wanted to be one of them. I had no idea how far and wide the earthquake had struck, no idea about the surrounding villages, or how many people had died… all I could see was what in front of me. But I needed to be here for Matilde and Massimo. To look for my grandmother and my uncle. And then, to help in any way I could, even if it meant just handing out blankets and water like I had at the camp.

'Can I come? I'd like to help.'

'No, no civilians, for now. Also, you need some rest. They're putting people up in hotels, gyms, wherever they can… You can try and get some sleep. Oh, what am I thinking? Go to my father's,' he offered. 'His home is minutes from here. I'll call him and let him know you're on your way. Do you have a phone?'

'Yes. For now. I don't know if…' I rummaged in my crossbody. 'Yes, still charged. Barely.'

'I'll punch the address in,' he said, taking the phone from me. "Do you have a map?"

"Yes, I picked one up yesterday," I said, and patted my crossbody.

'There. Now you can go and recuperate a little.'

'I need to look for my grandmother first. Then I'll go.'

'Okay. Look after yourself, Luce,' he said, and hugged me briefly. When he let go, his face was set in determination.

I wanted to say something encouraging, positive… anything. But Matilde was there, broken and bandaged and silent, and all I could say was: 'You take care too.'

After Massimo left, I stood with my hands against the glass and murmured a prayer. I imagined sitting on Matilde's bed, stroking her face like Mamma used to do with me, sending her off to sleep with a kiss on her forehead. Eventually I went back into the lobby. I was looking out over the sea of people, some wounded, some assisting relatives, some nurses with masks on and exhausted eyes, when I heard my mother's name being called. 'Angelina!'

Nonna! She'd called me by my mother's name. Maybe she was confused, in shock… I scanned the small crowd.

'Angelina!'

Finally! There she was, lying on a camp bed, a foil blanket on her. She was in her nightie, her grey hair loose and not in its usual tidy bun. She must have been caught out by the earthquake when she was asleep already.

'Nonna! It's me, Luce!'

'Oh, Luce! Of course! I'm sorry. I don't know why I called you Angelina…'

'You're a bit upset, that's all. With all this happening. You'll be fine…'

'Yes, I will be. The house can't crumble, you know. Rosa Bianca can't fall. It's still standing.'

'Of course it is,' I said soothingly. 'I'm sure it's all good. But how are you, have you been seen by a doctor…'

'No, but Carlo…'

'I told you to stay away.' My uncle was towering over me all of a sudden, as I crouched beside Nonna. He was safe, thank goodness – but as hostile as before.

'You don't tell me what to do, Carlo,' I said, just as cold. But the petulant statement made me feel slightly ashamed. I shouldn't have risen to the bait.

'I don't have time for this now. I need to find Matilde,' he said.

'Oh, dear God, Matilde!' Nonna shook her head and clasped at the cross she had around her neck.

'Zio Carlo…' I got back on my feet, still holding Nonna Clelia's hand.

'Don't call me that.' His words were like a whip.

I composed myself quickly. 'Fine.' It wasn't the moment to think about my feelings, my claims. Matilde needed her dad. And her dad needed her. 'Matilde is here. Did Massimo tell you…' I began. I wanted to gauge how much he knew, so that if he was in the dark, I could break the situation to him gently. But he ignored me, too frantic and frightened to listen. I couldn't blame him. He seemed torn between wanting to protect Nonna from me, for some reason, and needing to find his daughter. His daughter won, and I watched him approach a harassed, exhausted-looking nurse. I couldn't hear what they were saying, but the expression on Carlo's face gave everything away. He threw a glance towards us, and I could feel what that look meant – how was he going to break the news to Nonna Clelia? And then he made a gesture towards Nonna, as if to say just wait for me, and disappeared, following the doctor.

'Nonna…' I crouched down once again. I looked for her eyes and held her hands in mine. 'Matilde is poorly now. She was injured in the earthquake.'

Nonna nodded. I could see her trying to wrap her mind around what was happening. 'I understand.' she whispered, calm and collected. The Nardini genes Matilde had mentioned, I supposed. We were strong women, for sure.

'I'm sure the doctors—' I began.

'Excuse me… sorry to interrupt you. Has she been checked over?' a nurse asked me.

Nonna was calm, but put the nurse right at once. 'I can speak for myself, *cara*. I'm old, not deaf. I've had all the checks I needed. I'd like to go home now.'

The nurse's expression softened. 'Sorry. We must make sure that you're okay, first. I'm also sorry it's taken so long. I'll get someone to check you over at once. We're trying to see to the most vulnerable categories first, children and the elderly, but…' She looked at me and made a sweeping gesture, encompassing the small sea of people in need, inside the lobby and out in the parking lot. I nodded in understanding.

'You're doing all you can,' Nonna said, and she sounded softer too, now.

'Doesn't seem enough,' the nurse replied with a gentle pat on Nonna's shoulder, and disappeared for a moment, only to come back with a colleague pushing a hospital bed.

'Let's get you on here, *va bene?* Don't worry, we won't let you fall…'

'I can stand on my feet, thank you, *cara*,' Nonna said, but she leaned on the nurses anyway.

'Can I stay with her?' I asked.

'No need, you can come home with me.' Nonna was adamant, but she still lay down on the bed. Her mind was saying one thing, her body was saying the opposite.

The nurse caught my eye. 'Of course you can go with her. Any previous health conditions?'

'Not at all. Just a little trouble with my heart,' Nonna was quick to say. 'Otherwise, I'm healthier than you, *cara*. I really don't think this is necessary. I just need to make sure Matilde recovers. And maybe sleep a little…'

'She takes medication for her heart; she sees a cardiologist regularly.'

'We'll have a doctor see you as soon as possible,' the nurse decided, and began filling in a form. Nonna squeezed my hand. 'Let's go, *signora*,' the nurse said, and began rolling the bed inside.

'I don't need to be taken in!' Nonna protested. 'My grand-daughter needs help, my son…'

'Maybe that's how you can help, by being here,' I said softly, trying to placate her. 'You can be in with Matilde for a little while. And Carlo will come back in a moment.'

This seemed to convince her – or, most likely, she realised she had no choice – and she was quiet, eyes closed, as we travelled the corridors, stopping many times because people, chairs or other beds were in the way. The place was overflowing. We were led into what seemed more like a storeroom than a hospital room, with metal shelves full of medical equipment: boxes of gloves, rolls of paper, folded gowns.

'I'm so sorry,' the nurse pushing the bed said. 'We don't have any proper rooms left. But it's nice and clean here, and cooler than the wards.' Behind him, from a little window lined with boxes, the sun was shining brighter than ever.

'This room is perfectly fine. Thank you,' Nonna said.

'The doctor will be in soon. Is there anything I can get you in the meanwhile?'

'I'm fine. Please, you try and get some rest, if you can,' my grandmother said, and both nurses smiled at her concern and shook their heads, as if to say *no rest for us, not for a long time.*

'*Grazie,*' I called after them as they left us, then helped Nonna settle on her pillow, tucking in her sheets. Her hands were so cold, even with the warmth in the air. I unfolded the blanket at her feet and covered her with it.

'I think this is a dream,' Nonna said. She closed her eyes for an instant, as if to process everything that was happening. There was a heartbeat of silence during which I held my breath – and then: 'I'm so happy you're here. I've been waiting, and hoping, for years. To make amends. I'm so glad I'm alive, so I can finish my story…' She had closed her eyes again, and all of a sudden her strength seemed gone, and she looked small and frail. 'I'm sorry about Carlo.'

'Oh, Nonna, it's not your fault,' I replied, but it was like someone else was talking for me. I was beginning to lose sense of my own body. I let myself fall on the chair beside her and rubbed my face with my hands. The pain and exhaustion were too much to bear. Maybe they'd given me some kind of painkiller when I was asleep, and it was beginning to wear off now.

'*Tesoro,* you need to rest!' Nonna said, and the irony wasn't lost on me. An elderly woman on a hospital bed, in a storeroom, having survived an earthquake and waiting to be seen by one of the harassed, exhausted doctors who were slowly making their way through the wounded, the sick, the elderly – telling me that I needed to rest.

I nodded. 'Yes.' I leaned over and held her in my arms. I was gentle, as she seemed even thinner and frailer now, in that bed – but she held me tight, almost forcefully.

'Goodbye, Nonna. I'll come back real soon.' When she lay down again, her eyes were closed and her breathing deep and regular.

I stepped outside the room, on my way to Massimo's father's house. Now that sleep and rest were on the horizon, I felt even heavier. I had truly reached my limit.

*

I made my way through the crowded lobby once again, in a daze; the sun blinded me as I stepped outside. I took out the phone from my bag to check the address, and I noticed that my hands were now shaking uncontrollably. I was close to collapsing. Thankfully, according to the map, Massimo's father's home wasn't far. I put one foot in front of the other, almost in a daydream, as the sun kissed my skin and the warmth of the day enveloped me. I was now in a bubble, thinking only of one thing: *keep going.*

I'd barely stepped out of the hospital when I saw a figure waving his arms in the distance – as he came nearer, I could make out a small, grey-haired man. He wore glasses and sported a tidy, short beard; he must have been in his sixties. He ran to me, and I thought he was about to hug me – but he stopped, his arms in mid-air, and stared at me, mute. I couldn't read his face. He seemed in shock too.

'Luce,' he said. He brought his hand to his forehead, to see me better in spite of the glare. 'I'm Giuseppe, Massimo's father. I thought I'd come to get you. Massimo sent me a picture of you, but… you look very different.'

'I'm sure I do, after all this,' I said, and found it in myself to smile a little. 'Thank you for putting me up, it's very kind of you.'

'No problem at all. You are… Angelina's daughter.'

'Yes. Do you know my mom?' He blinked behind his glasses. I noticed that his eyes were blue and very clear. Most people here had brown eyes, like my family and me. He was a handsome man, serious-looking – almost solemn.

'I did, yes. Come,' he said after a few seconds, and we walked in silence. After a few steps, he offered me his arm, in an old-fashioned, almost timid way; I took it gratefully, and leaned on him. It was a relief, to be supported this way, after having walked on aching feet for so long.

We came to a row of small terraced villas – *newly built: safe*, I thought, and then marvelled at how quickly I had adopted that way of looking at buildings: susceptible to crumbling, or not. In Seattle, I would have never thought that.

Giuseppe opened the door for me, with a few words of welcome. After the chaos of the hospital, being in this cool, fresh, orderly home was heavenly. I took a deep breath and, as I coughed it out, I realised I still had dust in my lungs. Giuseppe soon had me sitting at the kitchen table and offered me water and food, but I could only gulp the water down. I was too tired to eat, even if my empty stomach hurt. All the while, as I drank, he was looking at me. Almost studying me. In other circumstances I would have been a bit uncertain about his stare, but I was beyond anything like that. All I wanted was to sleep. And anyway, he had kind, warm eyes, just like Massimo.

'Come upstairs, Luce,' he offered, and I followed him. He showed me the bathroom and led me to a guest room.

'Matilde left these here, for whenever she stayed over,' he said, showing me some clothes he'd laid out on the fresh bed.

I was so grateful. I managed to ask for a charger for my phone – the lifeline with my family – and, thankfully, he was able to fish an old one from Massimo's room that was the same make as mine. The whole conversation since we'd met must have been less than twenty words; either Giuseppe was a very quiet man, or I looked worse than I thought. He was about to step out and close the door, when he hovered on the doorstep for a moment, giving me another long look. Then he shook himself and murmured a few words to wish me a good rest. He closed the door and left me alone with myself and all the memories.

Under the shower, my tears mixed with the warm water. I could still feel Nonna's arms around me; I could still see Matilde lying unconscious, the despair in Massimo's eyes, the wrath in my uncle's expression. And that terrible moment, when the church had swallowed Matilde, and spat her out broken... And before then, that noise, that terrible noise coming up from deep inside the earth. It took me a while to stop crying and shaking. When I finally did, I was shivering, in spite of the hot day. I dried myself and slipped on Matilde's clothes – a pair of trousers and a long t-shirt. Though I was wearing my cousin's clothes, I had no tears left to cry.

I put the phone to charge, slipped under the blankets and closed my eyes. The strongest, warmest sunlight was seeping from the shutters, but I felt like it was the middle of the night. I would rest a little, now. My last conscious thought as I lay in the clean, fresh bed laid out for me was for Matilde: *please, be well...*

And then my body took over from my feverish mind, and forced me to fall into a deep, black, dreamless sleep.

CHAPTER ELEVEN

On my way back to the hospital, I almost ran – Matilde and Nonna needed me, and I was desperate to hear the rest of Nonna's story. I couldn't wait.

I'd slept for a long time, and it was now late afternoon; the blue of the sky was deepening, darkening, and the temperature was beginning to drop. I wrapped myself in Matilde's cardigan.

With every step I took, I felt grateful for things I'd always taken for granted: being alive, for a start. But also walking in soft socks and shoes, my wounded feet having been washed and disinfected once again; being clean, and not covered in dust any more; wearing fresh, comfortable clothes. Giuseppe had wrapped my hands in gauze, and they hurt a lot less. He had also fed me a plate of pasta, giving me no choice as to whether to eat or not, like a mother hen. Even if my stomach hurt from the long fast, the meal had given me energy and allowed me to swallow some painkillers. The absence of searing pain, the cleanliness, the clothes, a full stomach – all that seemed normal, before, obvious. And now all these things were a gift.

Before.

I slowed down a little to send a text to Eli, Ethan and Mamma – I just didn't have the heart to speak to them yet; I wouldn't even have had the words to explain what was happening. I just needed to make sure they knew I was fine, and that they were well too.

Mom, please come home. Eli's reply came in at once, and broke my heart.

Soon, I promise, I texted back, trying to steel myself. Mamma's reply came after a minute or so, another plea to go home… a plea I longed to listen to, but had to ignore.

I'd barely pressed the red button when the phone lit up again. Ethan.

Before I could stop myself, I'd answered.

'Ethan,' I called to him, while rogue tears gathered in my eyes, and once again I blinked them away, trying to stop them from seeping into my voice.

'Luce… Any news on your flight?'

'I can't come back yet. I…' Breaking down and promising I was on my way home, back into their arms, was not an option. 'Ethan. I'm fine. Seriously. I will come home soon. But not yet.'

'This is madness.' He was cross, I could hear it in his voice. And maybe he wasn't wrong. Had I been in his place, I would have been cross too, I supposed, out of fear.

'It's not as bad as you think…' I began, dishing the same lie again.

It is bad. It's very, very bad. In fact, I'm desperate for you to hold me and tell me it's all going to be fine.

'Don't. Luce, just don't. I know you're lying.' He took a breath. 'I don't want to speak any more. I just… don't.'

'I understand,' I said, but the silence at the other end of the line told me that he'd hung up. I cried for a long time, then my gaze returned to the Bosconero hill once again.

There was no way to see, from here, what still stood and what was destroyed. The irony wasn't lost on me; so many years not even considering coming back here, then the overwhelming need and desire to do so – only to see the place crumble.

Well, I could take it. If all that was left of my life was debris, I would own that debris, and call it mine.

*

My shoes, a pair of Matilde's – I had thankfully shed the trainers they'd given me, and their sinister implications – made no noise as I walked. The small town of Bastia was enveloped in an eerie silence: the only vehicles allowed in the streets were rescue ones, Giuseppe had explained while I was eating. When I awoke, he'd seemed a little less in a haze and more talkative, like the shock had subsided a little while I was sleeping. He'd filled me in on what he'd learned from the news, painting a fuller picture for me – one that I hadn't been able to paint myself, having been in the eye of the storm.

Bosconero had been almost in the centre of the earthquake, and about a third of it had been destroyed. Many were back in their home villages for the holidays; in the summer, Bosconero's population almost doubled, just like Matilde had told me. Six hundred lives had been lost. They were still digging under the rubble by hand, as using machines could endanger those who were still trapped underneath. Many villages and hamlets in Umbria and the surrounding regions were gone. Thousands of people were displaced, their homes destroyed or declared unsafe, especially because the risk of aftershocks was high. Bastia and its modern buildings had been almost spared, but the town was in lockdown, and holding its breath. Rescue services from all over Italy were on their way or had arrived already, and even some from abroad. An army of people ready to help…

It was hard to wrap my mind around all that, hard to believe that such disaster had happened, because nature seemed to have forgotten already.

The afternoon light was golden, the air laden with beautiful scents, the Italian summer shone in all its splendour… The only signs of the aftermath pertained to us humans: the near-empty streets, the army vehicles and ambulances making their way up the surrounding hills and coming back with the dead, the wounded, the homeless.

Finally, I came in sight of the squat yellow building that was the Bastia hospital, and it took all my willpower not to run.

The work that had been carried out at the hospital had me in awe. The parking lot had been cleared of waiting people; only rescue vehicles came and went now. I made my way inside through the automatic doors and saw that the lobby was still full, but there were no more stretchers around, only camp beds, carefully arranged in rows. There were more nursing personnel walking around, scrubs of different colours – white, blue, aqua. Clearly, they had been deployed from all over to come and help. The stereotype of Italians said that they were chaotic; the hospital in Bastia said otherwise.

There was still a sense of sorrow all around, but greater calm.

The reception was staffed again. I asked them if I could see Matilde, and because I was a blood relation I was allowed to do so, with a nurse by my side. The day before I'd been able to walk into the ICU by myself, but only a few hours later the normal protocols had been reinstated. Almost normal, because I still had to zigzag between the beds set up in corridors, to get to Matilde. I tried not to look anyone in the eye, to keep focused – but the sight of so many children and elderly people lying hurt broke my heart. Gone was the peace of summer, the storm was here again.

I stepped, slowly, through the door and onto the linoleum floor. The ICU corridor was about to open in front of me.

Would my uncle be there?

Would he send me away?

I followed the nurse, as the beeping of the machines seemed to be in tune with our steps. 'Here we are,' the nurse said, and her voice made me startle. She stepped back against the corridor wall, and finally, through the glass, I could see Matilde... but there was someone else there too. Silhouetted against the window, just outside the room, was a diminutive figure in a wheelchair.

'Nonna?' I said, tentatively. I hesitated for a moment – but Carlo wasn't there, thank goodness.

'Luce! I was hoping you'd be back soon,' she whispered, and offered me her hand – I took it, and crouched beside her, still holding her hand. She brought my fingers to her face.

'Is there any change? How is she doing?'

'No change,' Nonna said and shook her head sadly.

'We must have faith,' I said, for the second time while in that horrible, silent place where Matilde lay.

'Yes. My poor Matilde. She didn't deserve this.'

'Nobody does...'

'No. None of us deserved all that happened. We built our homes on shaky grounds,' Nonna said, and I suspected she meant more than just the earthquake.

'You can go in, you know,' the nurse said from behind us. 'Go and sit with her, it will help, I'm sure,' she said, and I was so grateful that this weary-looking woman had found time and energy for a kind word, in the middle of all this.

I pushed my grandmother's wheelchair in, and we sat one beside the other, close to Matilde's bed. The machines kept beeping, and Matilde's hands were white and still on the sheets, her arms rigid in their casts. Her face looked peaceful, in a state of being that was lighter than death and deeper than sleep.

Nonna began her story once again.

CHAPTER TWELVE

Bosconero, 1939, Clelia

Time passed, and Carlo grew to be a handsome, kind little boy, who adored his parents, and us too – Zia Clelia and Zio Arturo. We had everything. We loved each other, we had enough to eat and a roof over our heads. Mamma could finally rest in her older years, after the backbreaking work of her youth.

She still wore the apron with my papà's letters in it.

I had a thorn in my side, though – my barren belly – and we had not stopped trying. There were more losses. I was consoled by Carlo's presence but, underneath it all, I couldn't find peace. Only Arturo knew, because, on the outside, I smiled and worked hard and didn't show anyone my sorrow.

Those days brought more grief with them. My mother died suddenly, in her sleep. I consoled myself thinking it had been a peaceful death, and she'd had many years of happiness after the poverty of her childhood and her youth, especially with little Carlo.

A man called Mussolini has been in power for years now, but at the beginning, his regime didn't change our lives much. To most of us, it was just another government, ruling over our heads, far away from common people's lives. And then, the balance tipped. Mussolini's voice through the radio became more and more aggressive, more and more frightening. Some men and women in the village were awed by him. They wanted some sort of power over their fellow men, and being an ardent fascist gave them the chance.

Almost overnight, Bosconero was controlled by Mussolini's Black-shirts, a few sent from Rome, but most from the village. Men I'd known all my life had donned a uniform and wanted to rule over everybody. I hated them. They walked around like they owned the place.

We'd all had to become members of the Party, or we couldn't work, own land, not even buy things in shops. Without those little Party cards, our life would have been impossible. Oh, how I hated mine. It was like being a slave. No: we were slaves.

I knew that our predicament was affecting Arturo greatly. He grew more and more silent, brooding. And then, one day, he didn't go to the fields to work – he disappeared altogether. He came home at night, from Bastia, he said; he was wearing a Blackshirt uniform.

He was one of them, and he began telling me over and over again how convinced he was of his decision, how there was no other choice.

And what about all that he used to tell me, about history and philosophy and literature? He had a brilliant mind, even if he was just a labourer. Now, it seemed like his mind had been blown out, like a candle. All that was left was someone else's ideas.

But not everyone in the village was on their side. There was a small group of people who called themselves Partigiani, and they had joined the wider net of the Resistance.

How did I know, being the wife of a Blackshirt?

Because my sister was one of them, and so was Mauro. I have no idea how Arturo didn't find out and denounce them. Someone was watching them from above, for sure, Luce!

A family from the city, some said Rome, some Milan – far away from our woods, anyway – came to live in a farm above our village, in a place so isolated, barely anyone knew about them. People from the village brought them food and supplies. They said they'd come because the eldest daughter had tuberculosis, and she needed mountain air. But Nora told me the truth: they were Jewish, and in great danger. One of the members of the family who owned the farm had worked *for them, and now was hiding them away. You see, many Jewish people were being arrested, or even made to disappear. Mussolini had decided that they weren't Italian, that they were our enemy. He was creating enemies, that's what he was doing! He was making enemies so that we could all feel like we were fighting a good cause, to free our country from 'inferior races'. I could only see one race, Luce, human beings, but it seemed like everyone was under a strange spell; they followed Mussolini into slaughter.*

I wanted to visit the Jewish family. Especially their mother, who I'd been told was called Miriam. My heart went out to her, in hiding with three young children. She must have been so afraid. But I couldn't go to her, because it would have been too dangerous for them, Arturo being who he was, so I sent them food through Nora and Mauro. Food was scarce, but I had plenty: Arturo had become quite the leader among the local Blackshirts, and even if we were a humble household, we hosted important members of the Party coming from the cities. Or should I say we used to be a humble household, because now we received many gifts: good food – impossible to find even on the black market – money, clothes, even jewellery and artwork. Things that might once have belonged to someone.

Someone who had been made to disappear.

I was disgusted, Luce. I couldn't even sleep in the same bed as Arturo any more. To think how much I loved him before! And now, my gentle husband had become a bully. He knew I despised him, so he hardly ever spoke to me at all. Sometimes I caught him looking at me with a strange expression on his face – almost… longing, like he wanted me back. But he couldn't have my heart and soul back, ever.

One day news came that Miriam and her children had been spirited away. I cried. I didn't know where they'd been taken, I could have never… What we discovered after the war, Luce, none of us could have imagined! But I knew they'd been sent to their death. Strangely, the family who'd hosted them weren't arrested. Arturo told everybody that he'd taken it upon himself to punish them and, because he had become this great authority among them, among those monsters, they didn't ask him questions.

At night, I lay awake thinking of Miriam and her children, these people I never got to meet and who had 'disappeared', swallowed by the unknown.

I'd been a shepherdess for a long time, and I thought it was just like with the sheep and the wolves: we were all sheep, and some of us took on the role of wolves.

I couldn't bear to be with Arturo any longer.

But oh, what a moment to leave him. I was pregnant, my desire of a child having been stronger than my hostility towards him. And this time, the first time after so many losses, a baby of mine had quickened! Part of me wanted to stay in our house, safe and hidden... but I couldn't. I had to save my baby and save my soul too.

The partisans in the village were now in constant danger – it was only family ties and friendships that stopped people like my own husband rounding them up and arresting them, or worse. It was impossible to hide who was who, now. News from the rest of Italy and the world came to us distorted, in little pieces that made it impossible to see what was really happening. It seemed to us that the Fascist Party ruled us, and Italy, and the world – it was only afterwards I found that Italy was being defeated, that the Americans were on their way...

*

A knock at the door interrupted us; a nurse in blue scrubs stepped in. I did a double take when I recognised her... It was Romina, from the hospital camp.

'Signora Nardini, you weren't in your room, I got a bit of a fright! But I guessed where to find you.' She smiled, her bright blue eyes shadowed by tiredness. The scratches on her arms, telltale signs of having been hurt in the earthquake, were now only red marks, thankfully.

'Romina!'

For a moment, she didn't recognise me, then she smiled. 'Luce! You disappeared,' she replied, and for a moment I thought she might be angry at my impromptu escape from the camp. 'Your hands look much better. Are your feet still painful?' she asked kindly.

'Not really, I'm fine. How are you?' I asked, which seemed a bit of a silly question, given the circumstances.

'Trying to stay awake. And what about us?' Romina asked Nonna as brightly as she could, in spite of her evident fatigue. 'How have we been?'

'I have been fine. You?' Nonna said, cheeky as always. Romina and I exchanged a glance – this lady would not be defeated by a mere earthquake.

'Oh, not a care in the world! I think it's probably better we take you back to your room and see how you're doing, *va bene?*'

I was expecting Nonna to protest, but she didn't. Instead, she nodded softly, and leaned over to touch Matilde's white, still hand.

'I'm so sorry about your granddaughter,' Romina said, and laid a gentle hand on Matilde's forehead. 'She's in good hands, I promise you.'

'I'm sure,' I agreed – there was no doubt of that. It was incredible, what these people had done already and were still doing: the nurses and doctors and rescue services, finding their way through the chaos and turning it into order, ignoring their own physical and emotional bruises, the trauma and lack of sleep and weariness, to serve these wounded people.

I said a silent goodbye to my cousin and stood to push Nonna out. We rolled down the corridors and, together, Romina and I settled Nonna in her bed again, Romina's movements quick and gentle. She took Nonna's vitals and scribbled the results on the clipboard attached to the bed. Then, she gave her some drops from a medication tray she'd left in the room. Nonna's eyelids were heavier, now.

'Nothing new to report,' Romina said, straightening the blanket folded at the end of the bed. Even if it was scorching hot outside, Nonna seemed to be always cold. My radar went off. There was something in Romina's tone that made me think all was not right. My eyes went from Romina to Nonna, trying to read the nurse's hidden meaning, trying to gauge any indication from Nonna's face.

'When can I go home?' Nonna asked, and her voice was feeble.

'The doctor will decide that. I think we'll probably keep you in for just a little longer. Just to see what that heartbeat is doing. Yes?' she said to me.

Nonna seemed crestfallen. 'I suppose that's wise,' I said, trying to conciliate. The idea of Nonna going home was fraught with problems. We still had no idea if Rosa Bianca was standing and, even if it was, Bosconero was still off limits – so she couldn't be granted her wish to go there anyway. Carlo would take her in, for sure; but then, how would I be able to see her? Maybe it was selfish, but I'd had her in my life for such a short time and I was desperate to spend time with her. On the other hand, I knew that staying in the hospital wouldn't do any good for her morale.

I wished Carlo would speak to me, so that he'd tell me what was going on, what Nonna's doctor had said. If Carlo and I were on the same page, we'd know what to tell Nonna, especially about Rosa Bianca and how it might not be there any longer. I could help him, now that he had both his mother and his daughter in the hospital… I had to set my pride aside; I had to try again.

'Maybe you could bring in some fresh nightgowns and underwear? If you can. Otherwise, we have plenty of donations, you know, for people who can't access their homes,' Romina said before waving us goodbye. When I looked back at Nonna Clelia, her eyes were closed. Telling her story and bringing to light all the emotions connected with it had worn her out, and I suspected the medicine she'd taken had done its share.

'I'm not going to sleep. I need to tell you more...' she whispered.

'Of course. You will. But you need to rest now,' I said, in spite of my desire to hear more, there and then.

'*Va bene.* But if I need to stay here for longer, you must go home for me... I need you to get me something.'

'From Rosa Bianca?'

'*Sì.*'

For a moment, an image of the blue door torn and crumbled, the roses scattered on the ground and mangled by the debris, flashed inside my mind. I rejected it with all my might. It couldn't be. But still, it was possible – even likely – that the image I'd conjured was real. Even if our family home was still standing, I wasn't sure when it would be possible to reach Bosconero. Certainly not now. And even if I did manage to find my way up, and the house was still there... what about aftershocks? The whole place was in danger of falling on my head, all that hadn't crumbled already. My heart began beating harder, and a cold sweat covered my forehead – just thinking of it terrified me. Flashes of the night of the earthquake came back to me. I knew that I would never forget everything I'd seen – never. The scene was imprinted in my mind and it would be there for the rest of my life. Houses ripped apart, rooms broken in two, so that you could see inside – as if an enormous claw had carved away half of the buildings, or pushed the roofs in. Hills of debris, with everyday objects thrown in them – a lamp, a doll, a stack of books, all covered in dust...

In fact, I didn't even know how Nonna had made it out of Bosconero. It was a miracle in itself. And now, I was being asked to go back there…

'Luce?'

'*Sì*, Nonna. I…' I desperately looked for the right words, but I was at a loss. I couldn't put all my fears in words, not then. I couldn't upset her. She wasn't to know the full extent of this disaster until she was ready to get out of the hospital – and then Carlo or I would prepare her, as gently as we could. She had enough worry and heartache with Matilde being so hurt; I couldn't tell her that her home might have been razed to the ground. And anyway, what was the point in saying anything, when I didn't know for sure? 'Don't worry about nighties or underwear, or food… Anything you need, just ask. I'll find a way.'

'No, it's none of that. What I need is at my house. Upstairs, in my bedroom… Will you go get it for me?' she pleaded again.

My attempts to distract her from Rosa Bianca had failed. 'I will. Of course. I'll go and check on the house as soon as I can, Nonna. As soon as it's allowed again. And I'll get whatever you need.'

All colour had left her face. She was falling asleep – now I was sure that the medication that Romina had given her had something to do with that. I held her hand above the sheet, which was cold again. I tucked the blanket higher, to warm her a little.

'Luce. On my dressing table, there's a box. A wooden box. Oak wood, nice and strong. Arturo carved it for me. He was so good at making little wooden trinkets… Please can you bring it to me?'

She seemed so tiny, in that hospital bed, talking with her eyes closed. Small and fragile, and at the mercy of the people around her. She was beginning to drift away. I took a breath. I had to do this for her. 'Don't worry. Don't worry about a thing… I will bring you what you need.'

'Will you?' She opened her eyes for a moment, anxious.

'Yes,' I said, with more confidence than I felt. 'I'll go to the family home and find the box. I'll bring it to you.'

'*Grazie, tesoro…*' And with that, Nonna had fallen asleep, almost suddenly, the way toddlers and elderly people do. I sat back on the chair beside her bed, surrounded by boxes, in this tiny storeroom converted to a hospital room, and rubbed my face with my hands.

I was overwhelmed, between the undertaking that Nonna had laid on me and the revelations to digest. Nonna was sleeping soundly, now, her chest rising and falling a little too fast; once again, she seemed to me like a little bird.

I stood, claustrophobic with unanswered questions and heavy thoughts. I needed out of the hospital and into the light, into the summer sun that shone unawares of our troubles. I would look up into the sky, stand in the fresh air and soak up the light, I thought as I made my way out quickly, almost running, and unravel my thoughts. But as I passed room after room of injured people, and came to the lobby where even more men and women and children were waiting, I was reminded that my own quest was a piece of a bigger jigsaw. Whatever secrets were there to be discovered in my family, whatever thoughts weighed heavy on me, I was uninjured, and strong, and there was a lot of work to be done. Along with accomplishing what I was here for, I had to find a way to be of service to these people, the best I could.

*

For a moment, the glare of sunset blinded me as I stepped through the automatic doors, and I couldn't see where I was going. I walked straight into someone, almost bouncing off him.

I heard his voice, first, and then, when my eyes adjusted to the light, I saw who it was.

Carlo.

'Why are you still here? Go home,' he murmured, standing very, very close to me, so that I had to look up to find his face. I couldn't help but take a step back, and I needed a moment to find my bearings. My heart was running away, and I laid a hand on my chest, as if this could calm it.

'Zio... I mean, Carlo.' I swallowed. 'Yes, I'm still here. In fact, I'm not going anywhere, at least for a while.' I looked into his face, hoping that my fury would stay hidden and not antagonise him further: I was determined to try again, to find a way through to him, for Mamma, for Nonna, for Matilde.

What I saw in his eyes surprised me.

It was dread. As if my presence daunted him, for reasons I couldn't understand.

No. I must have misunderstood. I couldn't possibly be the *object* of his fear – he was frightened for Matilde, for his mamma. I had nothing to do with this.

'Carlo, please, let me help. I'm so sorry about Matilde, and...'

'Listen,' he said, and his tone was softer, almost pleading. 'You being here is not good for anyone, can you not see?'

'That is not true. Matilde was happy to meet me, she has no idea why there's been this rift between us! She asked me and Mamma to be at her wedding! And Nonna wants me here...'

'You have no idea what you're talking about!'

For a moment, I was silenced. I had no idea what I was talking about? Was he deranged? Of course Nonna wanted me here. It was clear to see.

Patience.

Patience.

'Carlo. You'll just end up upsetting your mother. More than anyone else.'

'Like I said, you have no idea what you're talking about.'

'You can't come between me and Nonna, or between Nonna and her daughter. Your sister Angelina, remember?' Adopted sister, apparently, but now was not the time to be so specific. 'The sister you threw out of all your lives.'

'Do we not have enough trouble, Luce? Look around you! You had to choose this time to—'

'I didn't choose the timing! The earthquake happened all by itself, Carlo,' I said, still trying to keep calm, and failing.

'Well, maybe this is the time to think of other people, Luce. My daughter is in a coma. My mother – your nonna – has a weak heart. She's—'

'Actually, it was me in there with Nonna, just a minute ago!'

'I look after my mother and my daughter!'

I stared at him, but I couldn't speak. All of a sudden, I felt my rage deflate, just like that. It dissolved around me, like steam, rising in dragon-like curves and disappearing.

This man should have been my uncle. He should have been there for me when I was growing up, he should have been at my birthdays, at my graduation, at my wedding. He should have cared for me, and I could have cared for him; but for some reason, he wanted nothing to do with me… I blinked away tears of rage and disappointment. He took a step towards me, and once again he wanted to tower over me and intimidate me with his physical presence, but I wouldn't let him. He was about to open his mouth to speak again but I simply turned around and left.

I was shaking. I had hoped – against all hope – for a little love. A little love for Mamma, who'd been so alone for so long, and for me… but it would not happen. I walked until I was around the corner and out of sight, and then stopped, leaning my back against a stony wall. I brought my arms around myself and breathed deeply.

Why?

Why did Carlo hate me, and my mother too?

I looked up to the sky. It was drenched in orange light from the setting sun, and tinged lilac at its edges. The day had passed like the beat of a butterfly's wings, and night was falling on the hill where Bosconero stood – or used to stand. Would they keep digging, at night? Would they still try to lift people out of the rubble? Or was it too late, now, to hope for more survivors...

Grief washed over me and, for a moment, I was too dismayed to even move. I leaned my back against the wall and felt a tiredness that was bone-deep.

But this was my quest. I couldn't afford to stop now. Not even if nature had decided to throw a spanner in the works; not even if members of my own family, my people by blood, seemed to hate me and my mother, for reasons known only to them.

I was so lost in my thoughts that at first I didn't hear it – and then the sound of the ringing phone reached me and jolted me out of my thoughts.

Of course, it was Mamma.

Weird how many times in my life, ever since I was a little girl, my mother seemed to materialise when I needed her the most. My mother's intuition seemed almost telepathic. The desire to tell her all, to hear her voice, was overwhelming. I couldn't wait any longer – she had to know I was fine, and she had to hear it from me, not third parties. I put the phone to my ear and closed my eyes, so I could hear her more deeply.

'Mamma!'

'Luce, *tesoro! O mio Dio*, I can't believe what happened...'

'It's not as bad as they make it look on the news, I promise.' I repeated the same lie I'd told Ethan. 'I'm fine, and there are so many people helping—'

'Are you well, *tesoro*? Tell me you're well...'

'I am, I promise!'

'Did you meet my mother? Is she alive?' I could detect the effort she was making to keep her voice steady.

'I met her, she's fine. She regrets all that happened, and—'

'Did she tell you *what* happened?'

'Not yet.'

Silence. 'Luce, come home. Please. I can't lose you too.'

'You won't lose me, of course you won't! Try not to worry.'

'*Tesoro*, there's more for you to fear than the earthquake…'

More cryptic statements about danger and fear. I'd had enough with secrets and half-truths, I really had. 'Mamma, could you please not sound like a horoscope in a magazine? Could you please be a little bit clearer?'

But she ignored me. 'Matilde? My niece?'

I swallowed. 'She's injured, but she'll be fine.'

'Injured…'

'Yes.' I prayed for my mother's radar to blip for a moment, but I had little hope she wouldn't pick up on the anxiety in my voice.

More silence. 'I suppose there's no point in asking you to come home. Again.'

'No, Mamma. Sorry.'

A long, long sigh. 'Please call me soon.'

'Yes, of course. I said I will. I'll call you tomorrow… whatever time it is there now, I can't even remember. My tomorrow, anyway. Bye, Mamma.'

CHAPTER THIRTEEN

Once again, Giuseppe's house was a haven of peace. He welcomed me in, in his quiet, warm way, as if welcoming me home. Massimo was there too, wearing jeans and a t-shirt, having finally shed his uniform. When he saw me, he opened his arms, almost apologetic. 'They sent me home. I didn't want to go, but apparently I need rest.'

I agreed with his friends; he looked ghastly, and no wonder. 'You *do* need rest.'

'What I need is to go and see Matilde.'

'Please, son,' Giuseppe pleaded. 'Matilde needs you healthy and strong when she wakes up. You must look after yourself. You haven't slept in two days, I don't know when you last ate… Tell him, Luce.' He made a very Italian gesture, throwing up his arms in frustration.

'He's right,' I replied, and put on my mom voice. I spoke to him like I would Eli. 'And I won't let you go out again tonight if you don't get a good meal inside you, and at least try to sleep for a few hours.'

Massimo nodded, defeated, and twenty minutes later we were sitting around the small table, like a makeshift family.

Strange, I know, but that meal marked the happiest, lightest time I'd had since it all happened. Even with such worry and pain on our shoulders, Massimo, Giuseppe and I sat there and ate together, grateful to be safe, grateful to have a roof over our heads, and each other. It's amazing what a plate of tomato pasta and some coffee can do to battered bodies and souls.

When we finished, Massimo's colour had returned a little and, in the same way I'd seen with Nonna, his eyes were almost closing of their own accord.

'Go get some sleep, now, *figlio mio*,' Giuseppe said, when Massimo began to clear up the table.

'We'll sort this. Come on, off you go,' I insisted, and followed him with my gaze up the stairs, my heart full of affection for him, full of hope that his tomorrow would be better than today had been.

I helped Giuseppe clear up, and once again I had the impression that he was watching me whenever I wasn't looking. I didn't feel uneasy – Giuseppe gave me nothing but positive, respectful vibes – just curious.

'So, you knew my mamma?' I asked while drying a plate he'd just washed.

His hands were suspended in mid-air for a moment. 'Oh, yes. And you look just like her, you know.' His words seemed to echo in the cool, silent house. The light of a long summer evening seeped through the windows and made everything look a little dream-like, like thoughts drifting between sleep and wake. Twilight waited, suspended, over us.

'Yes. I've been told before,' I said and, once again, Giuseppe gave me one of those intense looks – like I was an apparition of some kind. He gave me the plate to dry, and then rested both his hands on the sink for a moment, letting the water run. He said nothing more.

*

My phone chirped just as I was laying my head on the pillow – I left it on all night, just in case there was an emergency. Andrea's number popped up, and I grabbed it at once. I'd been in a constant state of alarm since the earthquake, and everything felt like a disaster soon-to-happen.

'Andrea... Where are you?'

'I'm home, at this moment. Trying to recuperate a little before I go back out.' The sound of a deep, broken sigh. 'The things we're seeing, Luce. It's... oh, it's just awful. Awful.'

'Oh, Andrea! I struggle to believe it's really happening... it's like a nightmare. Like I should wake up any moment and...'

'And we'd all be fine, waking up after the Summer Festival to a normal, sunny day. I know.'

'Thank God you and your daughter are fine.' Suddenly, I remembered how he had mentioned that his daughter had been having nightmares. Was it Nin's gift, having been passed down the line?

'Thank God, yes. I'm so sorry for Matilde. I'm not much of a religious guy, but I promise you I'm praying and praying. Never did that since I was a little boy.'

'Me too...'

A short silence, and then – 'Luce, I just wanted to ask you... will you be flying home?'

'No, not yet. Not until I sort out my family business.'

'I'm so glad. You see, it'll be impossible to see you alone in the next few days, there's too much work to do, but...'

'I can imagine! Please, don't worry, really...'

'...but I don't want you to think I've forgotten you! That day in Frassino, and then our picnic... you know, that memory kept me going. It was so weird to go from meeting you, feeling... well, happy. Excited, for the first time in a long time... to all this. I'm just holding on, you know, doing all I need to do. But I've not forgotten you... I just wanted to tell you that.'

I was so touched, my eyes filled with absurd tears. Absurd, because it was simply self-indulgent to cry over a demonstration of affection, with all that had happened. That he could be so sweet to call me and make me feel... *important*, when so much more was going on.

'Don't worry about me. Just do what you need to do. I'll be here when it all gets a little easier, okay?'

'Okay. Goodnight, Luce.'

'Goodnight.'

*

Sleep was hard to come by that night, and it was full of laboured dreams. I awoke with a startle, convinced that everything was shaking, and that a deep rumble was coming from beneath me. I switched on the torch on my phone – thank goodness for that torch – and stared at the lampshade on the ceiling. Giuseppe had mentioned that's what you do, you look at the lampshades for imperceptible oscillations, to see if something was happening; but it was still. I had imagined it all, but it'd been enough to drench me in cold sweat.

The aftershocks everyone mentioned – the ones that were to come after the first earthquake, and the second that destroyed the tower – hadn't manifested yet. It felt like the night itself was holding its breath, waiting for the inevitable. I glanced at the phone. Two in the morning. There was no point in trying to sleep. My throat was dry and achy, even if the dust we'd all breathed after the quake was just a memory; I made my way downstairs for a glass of water. I tiptoed, careful not to wake anyone.

But the light was on in the hall, and someone was awake already.

It was Giuseppe, sitting at the kitchen table with his hands folded, staring out of the window. A waning moon hung in the sky, limpid and free of clouds, and the orange glow of a street light illuminated the scene. Of course, with everything that had happened and was still happening, I wasn't the only one who couldn't sleep. For a moment I hesitated; he seemed so deep in thought that walking in on him felt like interrupting a private moment. But he cut such a lonely figure, alone in the night…

Suddenly, out of nowhere, I wondered if there had been anyone in his life after Massimo's mother had died, or if he'd been alone all this time.

'Giuseppe?' I whispered, to announce my presence; I didn't want to startle him. I took a few quiet steps through the hall and went to sit beside him. He didn't turn around, he didn't answer.

Now I was worried.

'Giuseppe… *tutto bene?* Can I make you some tea, maybe?'

He shook his grey head, and at that time, in the half-light, he seemed much older, and tired. 'I must have done something wrong,' he said and opened his hands, like he was helpless, defeated. 'I don't know what.'

He was in a daze – it was like he'd opened his mouth, and his thoughts had come out without context, without explanation.

I wasn't sure what he meant, but something was torturing him. I gazed at him – shoulders hunched, a handsome, Mediterranean face now turned down in grief. He was dressed; he hadn't gone to sleep at all. I looked for the right words, but in spite of the circumstances that had thrown us together and made us feel close, so quickly, I didn't know him – I'd just met him, after all. The best I could do was some sweeping words of comfort and encouragement, even if I didn't know exactly what was troubling him.

'We all make mistakes, at some point in life. Whatever it is, it probably looks a lot worse in the middle of the night. Everything does, when we're sleep-deprived and it's dark outside. Why don't you try and get some sleep? I'm sure everything will seem easier in the morning…'

Giuseppe seemed to come out of his reverie and back to himself. His eyes widened and he shook his head, looking embarrassed at having been caught in such a delicate, helpless moment. Maybe I should have just gone back upstairs without making myself known; but he'd seemed so desolate, sitting there on his own…

'Yes. Of course,' he said. 'It's all in the past, I suppose. And it's wonderful to have you here. *Meraviglioso.*' He nodded.

'Thank you. It's wonderful for me too. Even with all this happening, you know… It's still amazing to be here.'

'*Amazing* is the right word, yes. I am amazed for sure.'

Now, those were strange words. He was very kind, but I hadn't realised my presence was making such a difference to him.

To my surprise, he leaned over and touched my cheek gently, the sort of gesture you'd make with a little girl, not a middle-aged woman. '*Buonanotte*, Luce,' he said simply, and got up, disappearing out of the room.

CHAPTER FOURTEEN

The next morning I was awoken by the phone. Still half asleep, I felt the bedside table with my hand until I found it, half hoping, to my shame, that it was Andrea calling. But it was a text message. From Ethan.

I'm sorry I put the phone down. I'm just so worried about you.

I rolled my eyes. Okay. And putting the phone down on me was the way to show it? I took a deep breath. No, I couldn't be angry at him. Not in those circumstances. Not when he was so worried about me.

It's okay.

Is it, though?

Ethan, what's all this interest in me all of a sudden?

My heart was in my throat as I waited for the reply. Wait – why was my heart in my throat? It was all over, with Ethan. The only bond we had was our son, but our relationship had been over for a long time. I'd been unhappy in our marriage for years. I'd steeled my heart against him, and it had to stay that way.

I'm sorry. You've moved on… I'm sorry for everything xxx

What? Yes, I had moved on. A long time before. And *sorry for everything*?

What was all this about? Putting the phone down on me, sentimental texts… This wasn't like him; he was never one for dramatic gestures. The primal instinct to worry for him no matter what, having been his partner for almost thirty years between dating and marriage, made me call him immediately. I could feel in my bones that something was wrong, that he wasn't himself. Had something happened to him, while I was away? Would he have told me? Would Eli have told me?

The line was busy; I tried once again, but the busy signal was still there.

I was probably being silly, and overreacting, and too anxious – all the things us women tell ourselves when we get a hunch, a gut feeling that something is not quite right. We dismiss our instincts like they are there to deceive us, instead of being there to guide us.

No. I knew something was up with Ethan, beyond what had happened here in Bosconero and the situation I'd found myself in, and I'd learned through the years that with Ethan there was no use in trying to force answers or explanations. I just had to wait until he was ready to talk – if he ever would be.

*

Once again, I was in Nonna's improvised hospital room, lined with metal shelves full of boxes, and filled with golden light. I'd just been to see Matilde, still asleep and being kept alive by machines, while Massimo and Nonna and Carlo and all those who loved her waited and waited.

Yes, it was a waiting game all around, now – with everybody doing all we could until every loose end would be tied up again.

'Where was I, *tesoro*?' Nonna asked, as we settled with a cup of warm tea from the vending machines. Visiting time had just begun, and the hospital was teeming with people, but the storeroom where Nonna had been put up was tucked away, and always quiet.

'You were planning to leave my grandfather...' I said, and took a sip of tea. Part of me was drinking in every bit of the story; part of me couldn't wait until Nonna got to the bit that involved Mamma. The fact that Nonna had begun from her own childhood and was telling me so much about war times made me realise that whatever had happened to Mamma, or around her, had deep, deep roots in the past.

'Yes. Yes. Oh, it was horrendous. Luce, I loved him so much... But I couldn't stand what he was doing. And Nora and Mauro were now working with the Resistance! I was petrified that Arturo might cause them harm... as unbelievable as it was to me, that my beloved, kind husband could sink so low. And so...'

CHAPTER FIFTEEN

Bosconero, 1944, Clelia

Nora, Mauro and I escaped one night, into the woods, with our partisan comrades. We were the Brigata Autonoma Patria, ranging in age from eighteen to thirty-two years old, three men and three women only. We'd taken aliases, like all partisans did: Nora was Granda, Mauro was Capitano, and I was Bianca, like my old shepherd dog. The other men went by the names of Libero and Tritolo, while the third woman, who was barely eighteen and came from a farm just outside Bosconero, was Pietra. We'd known each other from the cradle – apart from Mauro, we'd all grown up in the village.

Back then, the woods were thicker and darker than they are now; you could still disappear in them. There were places so remote that it seemed like no human being had ever set foot under those canopies, that only wolves and hogs and foxes lived there. Arturo knew the woods, yes, but not as well as we did.

We left little Carlo with friends. We knew for sure that Arturo would not let him be put in danger, that he would be way safer in the village than with us. But how he cried, that night! He clung to his mother and didn't want to let her go. It was terrible to see. I had to extricate him from Nora and carry him, kicking and screaming, to our friends. I could guess that Nora was wavering, seeing her son so upset, but she couldn't afford to waver. We had to go.

'*Mamma! Mamma! Papà!*' *he was calling. As night had fallen, and the time for our rendezvous with our comrades came near, Carlo's little voice had resounded all around. If he started screaming, somebody would notice the racket and wonder what was happening.*

'*Nora, we need to go!*' *I said and turned away. Though I wanted to cry for Carlo too, I dragged my sister with me and tried to placate her, because her sobbing would attract attention.*

The last time I saw Carlo, that night, our friend had her hand on his mouth, to keep him quiet; I could see his desperate eyes above her fingers.

Arturo and his squadra – *so they were called – weren't around, that night. It was an incredible coincidence, that they should be called away on the night two of the comrades who were in hiding already were due to come and get us. It gave us the chance to run without being caught – Arturo would come back and find us gone.*

We marched through the night, until we arrived at the camp. It was hard for Nora and me, because we were both heavily pregnant. Yes, Luce, finally, after so many losses, this pregnancy was going well! And my due date was coming near. I felt like I brought all the hope of the world in my womb. In the midst of all that despair, I was happy.

Life in the camp was hard – we were always cold, and food was scarce – but with the childhood I'd had, I was more used to hardship than easy living. Our lives in the house Mauro had built for us, and then the privileges that had come with being Arturo's wife, were less familiar to me than poverty. The encampment was organised around an abandoned shepherd's hut; it was half ruined, but at least it had a roof and four walls. Because Nora and I were pregnant, it was us who slept in there, on top of bundles of clothes and blankets, and every time a rabbit or a bird was caught, they were given to us to eat. Everyone did their best, for us. It was with the comrades of our Brigata that I learned to shoot, and I was good at it.

It wasn't the scarcity that wore me down, no; it was the constant fear. Our comrades, together with Mauro, went on raids from which we were always afraid they would not come back. I think the word for it is guerriglia *– many little battles fought on the land, without armies but only isolated bands of partisans and squads of Blackshirts and Germans. Every valley, every hill, even every village, was a battleground. News had come that the Americans were coming from the south, and chasing the Germans up, and as they went, the Germans burnt and killed as much as they could in the time they had left. The woods around us had never looked blacker, Luce, when every shuddering leaf, every shadow, could have been an enemy's ambush.*

I was petrified for Arturo, and that he would be hurt; I still bled for him. The heart wears many contradictions, doesn't it?

Nora's thoughts were always with Carlo; she couldn't find peace. One night when Mauro was away, she was crying, bundled into the blankets and turned towards the stone wall.

'Nora!' I called her. 'Are you well? Is the baby coming?'

'I'm well. The baby is not coming, yet. My little Carlo. Clelia, I shouldn't have left him!'

'We didn't have a choice, did we?'

'I should have stayed behind with him.'

'They know that you're with the Resistance. They would have sent you to prison.'

'Do you really think Arturo would have sent me to prison?' She gestured at her belly.

'I didn't think Arturo would be a Blackshirt. And that Jewish woman, remember? She disappeared! And her children! Did you ever think Arturo would be capable of that?'

'I just cannot believe he would have harmed us, Clelia! But I didn't want to leave Mauro… so I left my Carlo! Oh, how wrong I was!'

'You're not thinking clearly.'

'Oh, Clelia, maybe…'

'No. No. You're not thinking of going back, are you?' I took her by the arm, shook her, and forced her to turn around. 'If you went back, they would torture you, and you'd have to take them to us! Maybe they would kill Carlo too!'

'Stop it!' she wailed, trying to turn towards the wall again.

'No, you stop it. Be quiet and get on with it,' I said, and left her to cry. I know that my words sounded hard, but you have no idea of the danger we were in. Every day Mauro – Capitano – and our comrades risked their lives. My sister and I were left behind during the raids because we were pregnant, not because we were women. I was seriously worried that Nora's misgivings about leaving Carlo behind would get us killed.

She went into labour a few days later, and it was long and hard, as it had been with Carlo; her daughter, Neve, was sickly and couldn't breathe properly. As for me, it was easy and quick, and my daughter – your mamma, Angelina! – was healthy, fat and beautiful. I had a daughter, at last! How could I not be happy, even in that situation? Surrounded by fear and danger – I was the happiest I'd been in all those years. Finally, I was a mother too.

My happiness was endless… but it was not to last.

*

The fateful night came. Nobody is left alive to say things didn't really go that way – there is only me, to remember what happened to all of us, to remember how the Brigata Autonoma Patria was destroyed.

I'll never forget a moment of that night. I was twenty-nine years old, and now I'm ninety, and there is never a day I don't think about what happened.

The fourteenth of April 1945, I was asleep in the hut. There was a bright, white, full moon in the sky. I was sore from the birth, but at least I wasn't cold or hungry – and my baby Angelina was asleep in my arms. I would have done anything to protect her. We both slept, Nora and I, and our babies, watched over by our comrades.

A shot woke me. The camp stirred at once, screams of alarm at first, and more shots; then just moaning and crying and foreign voices, their language as hard as their guns. The Nazis had found us somehow, or maybe they'd just tripped over us by chance while trying to find their way north in these dark woods. Still clutching Angelina, I crawled to my sister before she could make a noise, and held her tight. I laid a hand on Neve's little face to stop her from crying, and squeezed both of them, so they would be still and quiet. I had to make Nora stay put, even if she was terrified and wanted to run. I could feel it, I could feel her body rippling, wanting to spring up and move. But I'd always been the wise sister, the older sister who protected her and looked after her since she was a baby, and so I continued to hold her, almost crushing her, and prayed that neither Nora nor the babies would make a noise.

And she didn't; she was silent, shaking hard against me.

I wanted to live, so, so much. I was so young. I wanted to live! But more than anything, I wanted my sister and our daughters to survive.

Maybe, if we hold on long enough, still and quiet inside the hut, they won't come in.

Maybe, even if they come in, they won't see us.

Maybe, if they see us, they'll think we're dead already.

Maybe. If we are very still and very quiet…

But holding a hand over a baby's mouth will only work for so long before you have to let go. I moved my fingers so that Neve could breathe, and with the breath came a squeal, and then a cry, the way babies cry so hard and loud even if they're so small – and after the cry came the light of a torch.

They'd found us.

I rolled above my sister and my niece, keeping Angelina tucked behind me as well; I wanted my body to be a shield between them and the German bullets. I moved my hand over Nora's eyes, so she wouldn't see when death would come, and I squeezed my eyes hard too, hoping it would be quick.

When the shots were over, when they'd finished with their rifles, they kicked me to make sure I was dead, and even then I didn't move or make a sound, even if their heavy boots hurt. Like those tiny creatures that roll up and play dead if you touch them, only to unfurl and run away when they think you're gone. I waited until their hard voices disappeared in the distance. Only then I opened my eyes.

Shots had been fired, so I had to be wounded. I had to be. Cautiously, I moved my body, just a little. Hands and feet. Arms and legs. Apart from the ache where they'd kicked me, there was no pain. I was unhurt!

They had missed – the bullets must have hit the stones or the ground, because I wasn't wounded – and I had lain on my sister and the babies to be their shield. I was sure the bullets couldn't have reached them, because they would have hit my body first. We were saved! We'd survived!

'Nora, Nora,' I called. 'They've gone! We're saved! Nora!'
I shook her, and my fingers felt something wet and sticky.
'Nora!' I called again.
But only silence answered.

*

One day, when I was just a little girl, so little that my head barely reached that of a grown sheep, I was in the field with our herd. Mamma was home with Nora, who was just a baby then, Papà had gone already, away to America. Bianco, my shepherd dog, sat beside me. He was faithful and fearless, and I loved him so!

That day, Bianco was restless; he smelled something in the air. I became anxious too and looked around, trying to see as far as I could; it was spring, and we had a few lambs with us. All of a sudden a wolf came out of the woods, a grey shadow materialising in front of us so quick, I couldn't even scream. Bianco ran at it, ready to fight. Just one wolf could have killed our whole herd, and me. I was so scared I wet myself, while the wolf and Bianco growled and jumped at each other and bit each other, and I knew that if Bianco was killed, our sheep would be lost, and I would be lost too. I should have run, but you must remember, the sheep were all we had. Starvation doesn't happen here now, you know, but when I was a little girl it did. And so I didn't run, but I shouted and ran to the wolf with my wet legs and my shepherdess's stick and hit it with all I had. And then there was fighting and everything happened so fast. All of a sudden, the wolf was lying on the ground with its throat open, and Bianco's white coat was covered in red, but he was standing! I fell on my knees and prayed all the prayers I knew. I prayed and cried in relief, because we were all safe.

But I couldn't allow myself to be on my knees and cry for long; I had to run down to the village and tell Mamma we were fine, we were saved, we had survived. I called for Bianco to get our sheep together, and he looked at me, his black eyes telling me he really, really wanted to do it, but he couldn't. His legs gave way and he fell, and I remember those sweet eyes looking at me, before they closed and never opened again.

That day came back to me then, when I was on my knees again, just like the little girl I'd been once, after having survived the wolf.

'Nora, Nora,' I called again and again, and I held her in my arms, but she was quiet, and the babies were quiet. I don't know how it had happened, that a bullet had nestled itself into her head, and killed her while she lay beneath me. And the weight of her body had smothered Neve, it seemed, because her tiny body bore no wounds. My sister and Neve were dead, and I've had their ghosts at my shoulder since then. Why did you not save us, Clelia? Over and over I hear those words late at night, when sleep can't find me.

But my daughter, my precious daughter Angelina, she was alive, and she was crying, strong and clear! I held her to my heart – I'd saved her, I'd kept her safe. I needed her to be silent, so I lifted my sweater and let her nurse until she fell asleep. I sat there with Angelina at my breast, and Nora and her baby lying dead before me. I crawled across the hut and looked out of the glassless window: I saw all of them under the moonlight, my comrades, lying around like broken dolls. Mauro's head was just below the window, as he sat with his back to the hut, his chin on his chest; and Pietra, so small, the youngest of us all, curled up under a tree with her back to me.

Finally, when Angelina was asleep, I stood. My legs were soft and, just like when the wolf had come out of the woods all those years ago, I had wet myself. I went for the door, and there I turned to fill my eyes with Nora and my niece, fill my eyes with them, because I loved them so, and they were dead, and I had to leave them just like that, alone and cold in that Godforsaken hut, and take my daughter to safety.

I folded Angelina into me and stepped out. At that moment, howls came from all around.

They had come to get me, after all these years, I realised. After my lucky escape as a child, they were back for me! The Germans haven't killed me, I thought – but the wolves will.

CHAPTER SIXTEEN

'Luce! Luce!' Massimo was calling my name. My eyes jerked open. He was crouching beside my bed and shaking me awake.

'Nora!' I called out.

That night, I dreamt of them, Nonna and Nora and the babies, and the men and women of the Brigata. In the dream, I stood under a tree, in front of the hut, Pietra lying by my side, Mauro flopped against the wall; and then, Nonna appeared on the doorstep of the hut. She had Angelina in her arms, and she began to walk towards me – she wasn't the Clelia I knew, but a young woman, her eyes dark, fiery, like my mom's sometimes could be. She stepped out just as the howls began – and then I saw Nora, her arms empty, walking behind her. I woke with a startle, terrified. Nora's face was white, and where her eyes should have been were two black pools. She was dead, and yet she walked, arms outstretched, as if she wanted to take Angelina back from Nonna's arms…

'It was a nightmare, Luce!'

I was confused, and sweat covered my forehead. 'What?'

'You screamed. I came to see if you were okay. You were dreaming.'

'Oh. Oh, I'm sorry.' I breathed deeply. Nora walking on with that uneven gait, her eyes hollowed out… I blinked many times, trying to erase the image from my mind. 'Yes, it was a nightmare. I'm sorry I woke you…'

'No, I was awake already. I just called the hospital.'

'Matilde? Any news?'

He stood. 'She's just the same. No changes,' he replied. I spared him the 'no news is better than bad news' clichés, and sat up, feeling slightly queasy after my nightmare. I was slowly coming back into the here and now.

'Would you like to come with me to the camp?' Massimo asked. 'They need all the help they can get. Or would you rather rest…'

'No! I mean, no, I don't want to rest, and yes, I want to help!' I rubbed my face and swept back strands of unruly hair behind my ears. Only then did I notice that Massimo didn't have his uniform on, with the boots and heavy trousers, and the bright reflective jacket – he was wearing a light orange waistcoat over jeans and t-shirt. 'So you're not going up to Bosconero, today?'

'No. They've stopped… you know, looking for survivors. They need less hands now. They can use the machines.' I swallowed. Just an early morning conversation about digging people out of their homes. The new normal. 'Andrea thought I'd be better off staying away from where… you know, where it all happened.'

'I understand.'

'I don't, really. It doesn't change anything for me, to be here, or up there. . Will you come to the hospital with me, later?'

'Yes. Certainly. I have to run some errands for Nonna, and…' I hesitated. Should I tell him that I was planning to go up to the village, and enrol his help? If I did, would he stop me from going, for my own safety, and watch me like a hawk in case I tried to – with the risk of aftershocks still high? 'I… I need to bring her some changes of clothes. She'll be staying in the hospital a little longer.'

'Oh, I'm sorry. I thought she was okay?'

'Apparently not. But I probably don't know the whole picture. Carlo won't speak to me.'

'Yeah, that's Carlo for you. Anyway, there have been a lot of donations, thankfully, so you can look through those and put together something for Clelia… The shops are still closed, but they'll probably open tomorrow or the day after. In the meanwhile, my dad can get some toiletries.'

'Sure, thanks. Obviously it won't be her own things, and you know how elderly people are…' I was chancing it. 'It'll be strange for her to wear other people's clothes…'

'Yes, I can imagine,' Massimo said. He was sympathetic, but made no mention of retrieving something from Rosa Bianca. 'See you downstairs, then?'

'I'll join you in five minutes.' I quickly got washed and dressed – still Matilde's clothes, a pair of jeans and a simple cotton t-shirt. Wearing her clothes was somewhere between poignant and, as strange as it might seem, comforting. She was always there, in the back of my mind – so brave and so foolish, wanting to stay with her fiancé, running to him instead of keeping herself safe…

Yes. Brave and foolish.

And maybe I was being foolish too, because I'd made up my mind. I would try and walk up to Rosa Bianca, to retrieve the keepsake my grandmother had asked for, whatever it took.

*

Shortly after, hot sugared coffee having perked us up, we were on our way to the camp, in Giuseppe's car – Massimo's car was somewhere under the ruins of the village square. When we left, Giuseppe had been still asleep, to my relief – after having seen him so dazed, sitting there in the middle of the night talking about past mistakes, I felt we'd both be embarrassed to make small talk over coffee.

'I was thinking. Why is Carlo not taking care of all that? Taking a bag to the hospital for his mother?' Massimo said.

'I'm sure he will. But he refuses to speak to me, like I said. So, to be on the safe side, I'll be bringing her a few things too.'

'I'll speak to Carlo anyway. To test the waters. So at least you know what Nonna needs and doesn't need. Oh, this is absurd, that I should be some kind of mediator between the two of you! On the other hand… he's… very upset now, as you can imagine.' He winced at the thought, and I touched his arm, lightly. 'Carlo has always sabotaged himself. He drove his own wife away, because she just could not live with him. She disappeared; nobody knows where she is. The only people he hasn't alienated in his life are Clelia and Matilde.'

'But why did Matilde's mother disappear? Did she not want to stay in touch with Matilde, or even take her along…'

'I have no idea, and Matilde doesn't either. All I know is that Matilde's mamma couldn't stand Clelia. Which is strange – I don't know anyone who doesn't like Clelia.'

Nin didn't, I thought – or so Andrea had told me.

'I understand Carlo is distraught, of course – who wouldn't be? But this goes beyond… you know, beyond what happened to Matilde. He hates my mother and me, for some reason.'

'I don't really understand what's going through his mind. Matilde's family are… complicated. To say the least.'

'Carlo might even think I'm not who I say I am. An American impostor!' I laughed, though there was a bitter edge to my laughter.

'You're definitely who you say you are! You look so much like Matilde, and like Nonna. The same eyes, the same height…'

'As in, pocket-sized…' Massimo laughed too. 'I'm also my mamma's twin, like your dad noticed last night.'

'Mmm. I suspect your mamma was the one who got away, for my father.'

'Really?' That would explain why he'd been looking at me so strangely. Perhaps I reminded him of Mamma?

'Oh, yes. You know, I'm his stepson. He married my mother when she had me already. She passed away when I was young, and he brought me up. I couldn't have asked for a better father.'

We were at the foot of the hill already, and, if my sense of orientation was to be trusted, we weren't far from the hospital as well. They called Bastia a town, but it was probably just in comparison to the tiny places all around, because it was a small place. I could see the evacuee camp already, blue tents having risen like mushrooms in the space of a few hours. It was so different from the field hospital I'd been in, just after the earthquake. There were solid-looking tents pitched in tidy lines: clean, comfortable, shaded from the sun. It looked like the practical needs of the women, men and children who'd lost their homes were being addressed as thoroughly as possible…

And yet, there was an air of desolation all around – like the bodies were being looked after but the souls were hurting, catapulted into an unknown place, without anything they could call truly theirs.

My stomach churned as we stepped inside, afraid of what I would see. We walked between two rows of tents, towards a bigger white canopy; on one side there were tables and benches, protected by tarps; on the other, a grassy space where a few trucks were parked, with boxes piled all around. Step after step, the sense of alienation seemed to lift a little, as small signs of life beyond pure survival were appearing already.

Two older women were knitting side by side on plastic chairs, heads covered by scarves tied under the chin, dressed in long skirts as if they'd come from another century. A small mongrel dog lay at their feet.

A little boy blew soap bubbles under the watchful eye of his mother, who was sitting in the shade just inside the tent. Her face was resting on her hand and betraying her exhaustion.

Two men stood one in front of the other. One was holding a mirror, the other was shaving, his chin covered in foam.

Scenes of daily life, normal life, in circumstances that were anything but normal.

I was desperate to take pictures, but I didn't want to do it without official permission – it wouldn't have been respectful. I wondered if the world knew, beyond the generic news of an earthquake in central Italy, what was really happening here. But then, how many camps like this rose and disappeared all over the world, because of natural disasters or war? How many people, right now at this moment, were in a refugee camp, doing their best to look after their children like the mom I'd seen; trying to keep clean and dignified, like the man shaving; passing time and making themselves useful, like the knitting women?

We reached the canopy, and I saw that a young priest, wearing his embroidered ceremonial robe over jeans, was saying Mass where the benches and tables were. Under the canopy, volunteers were quietly peeling mountains of vegetables. More volunteers were going up and down between the boxes on the grass and some metal shelves inside the canopy, carrying donated goods.

Once again, I was awed by how generous the relief help had been. I could see soldiers, paramedics, civilians like me, Scouts, uniforms I couldn't identify – some even speaking foreign languages, Eastern European, maybe? Just like Giuseppe had told me when I'd first met him, when he was trying to help me realise what had happened and look at the bigger picture – help had come from all over the world. When I'd first stepped into the camp, watching those impersonal, tidy square tents, I'd felt desolation; now that I was in it and I saw the people, their willpower, their zest for life, I felt hope. If it hadn't been for the community coming together, all those people would have been lost.

When I'd helped dig little Benedetta out of the rubble, all we could see was fear and destruction, and it seemed time would stop forever. Instead, there was an after. Life did continue, as impossible as it seemed at the time.

A familiar figure stepped out from behind the line of cooking volunteers – tall, with salt and pepper hair, a handsome face now lined with exhaustion and stressed, his lips in a thin line.

'Andrea?' I called in a low voice, as to not disturb the religious function going on not far from us.

'Luce, at last!' Andrea came to embrace me, giving me the customary two kisses on the cheeks. 'It's so good to see you safe… I knew you were, but it's a lot better seeing it with my own eyes!'

'Same here, Andrea!'

Andrea and Massimo embraced quickly too. 'How's Giacomo's family?' Massimo asked sombrely, and I felt cold as I recalled seeing Giacomo, the new father, lying dead on that stretcher. It was an image I would never forget.

'Anna and the baby are staying with her sister, here in Bastia. They'll let us know about the funeral,' Andrea replied. There was a moment of silence, then: 'How is Matilde?' he asked, and I was touched to see his eyes fill with tears. Andrea and Matilde were good friends too – so many people were rooting for her.

'Still the same. The machines breathe for her,' Massimo replied.

Andrea's eyes widened a little, and I could feel him sucking his breath in. 'Do you not want to be at the hospital, now?'

'I spoke to her doctor this morning. Matilde would want me to make myself useful. But yes, I'll go, as soon as we're finished here.'

'Massimo—' Andrea began. I knew he was going to advise him to go and be with Matilde, or to rest, to spare himself a little. And I also knew Massimo would have none of it.

I was right. 'How can I help, now?' Massimo said curtly. He needed to be busy; he needed to be where the action was. I thought he was right – in times of anxiety and pain, being busy is the preferable option, for me.

Andrea nodded slightly, as if to recognise Massimo's choice. 'Provisions have arrived overnight. They have to be divided up and delivered to the tents. Come,' he said, and led us to the mountain of boxes lying on the grass, some official-looking, some that seemed improvised, held together with Sellotape. Those were probably people's donations. One of them was half-open, revealing its contents: toys, colouring books and felt tips... I wondered how many kids had been displaced now... How many had lost their lives...

The young priest gave the final blessing – 'Go in peace' – and those who'd attended the improvised church began to make their way back to the tents. Old and young, a woman with a baby, a family with two young boys who skipped away like they didn't have a care in the world, passed in front of us and walked on. Andrea's eyes met mine, and he touched my arm.

'Can I have a word with you, Luce?'

'Sure...'

'Andrea! Over here!' someone called him.

His face fell, but he didn't complain. 'I'm sorry, I have to go... but can I catch you later?'

'Of course. You do your thing... they need you.'

'I'm so sorry. I can't wait to see you alone, Luce... I...'

I smiled, but said nothing. I was overwhelmed as it was – I couldn't think of *that* now, not there, not then. The butterfly day of driving in Andrea's car with the sunroof down, discovering Frassino, sitting in the shade chatting like we'd known each other for years. It seemed like another life.

*

I made myself busy. It was a whirl of opening boxes, stocking shelves, delivering bags of toiletries and water to the tents, and then helping cook a pasta dish in enormous pots.

We all sat together for lunch, Andrea beside me; I smiled to myself thinking how Italian it was, this need to sit down for a proper meal even in the middle of an emergency. No plastic-wrapped sandwiches for them, then, not even in an evacuees' camp. Such an attitude felt familiar. When I was growing up, Mamma was religious about meals, even when I was in school. I was the only kid in kindergarten who had a Tupperware full of pasta instead of PB and J sandwiches, which at the time, I found terribly embarrassing.

'We need to get to the hospital,' I said to Massimo as soon as we finished. 'We'll miss visiting time. I know they're flexible, these days, but…'

'Yes. Let's go.' We stepped over the benches we'd sat on, plates in hand, to be given back to the kitchen. I felt bad about not helping clean up, but Nonna and Matilde came first – I was sure the other volunteers would understand. We waved at Andrea – but he followed me.

'Luce… Do you have a minute now? I won't keep you long.'

I looked at Massimo. 'I'll wait for you at the car,' he said.

I followed Andrea to the patch of grass where we'd worked on the donation boxes. 'I know I told you on the phone, but… Well, I really would like to see you again. The next few days are impossible, but as soon as things calm down a little… I had such a great time in Frassino, I couldn't wait to see you again… and then all this happened!' He took my hand, and I held his hands in mine and squeezed them – but, I realised, I meant it as a gesture of affection, of friendship.

Nothing else. Not any more.

I didn't quite understand the change in me – everything that had happened seemed to have brought me back to earth with a thump.

'Luce… I was waiting for someone like you. I was waiting for you.'

'Andrea…'

'I'm sorry, have I been too forward?'

My jaw dropped open.

I couldn't speak; I couldn't move.

'Luce?'

'Ethan,' was the word that came out of my lips.

Because there, at the edge of the camp, all blond and foreign and looking like an American tourist lost in deepest, darkest Europe, was my ex-husband.

CHAPTER SEVENTEEN

'I'm looking for Luce Nardini. I was told she was here…' Ethan was trying to explain. Except he was speaking Spanish, trying to make it sound Italian. For a well-travelled person, he looked incredibly conspicuous. The only things missing were a Hawaiian shirt and the sandals-and-socks combo, and then he'd have been the perfect American tourist. Instead, he looked so good, in his jeans and simple shirt with the sleeves rolled up, his blond hair making him look exotic among the mostly brown-haired and brown-eyed Italians. He seemed so familiar, standing there in that evacuee camp, where everything was strange, that I nearly burst into tears there and then.

Wait. I was probably dreaming. He couldn't *possibly* be here. Maybe I'd cracked under the stress?

That was entirely possible. Even probable.

'Ethan?'

'Luce, here you are! I tried to call you, but weren't picking up, and… *Gracias, gracias!*' he said to the people who'd been trying to direct him, and ran towards me. I expected a formal embrace – we'd hardly spoken in three years – but he enveloped me in his arms and held me tight, and then he pulled back a little to touch my forehead with his, his eyes closed. He was trembling.

He seemed pretty real. I wasn't dreaming, then. He *was* here, in all his Ethan-ness. He'd flown all the way from the US to Italy, to be here with me, now.

'It's *grazie*. Not *gracias*,' I said, dazed.

'Excuse-mo,' he said, and I laughed from the heart for the first time in days. People looked at us, my laughter being so out of place, considering the circumstances. I covered my mouth with my hand.

'Has something happened to Eli?' I cried out at once.

'No, no. He's perfectly fine.'

I could breathe again. Now Ethan looked at me for a moment, studying my face, looking up and down my body as if to check I really was unhurt. 'Hi,' he said.

'Hi,' I responded, and we both sounded bewildered. We looked at each other for a moment, taking each other in. I was reminded of the beginning of when we'd fallen in love, and how we used to stay on the phone without speaking, just being together. Here we were, many, many years later…

'No, no, don't cry!'

'I'm not crying! It's just dust in my eyes. That's all. I'm not crying.'

Again, he drew me against his chest, and we clung to each other.

'I can't believe you're here,' I said, pushing him away enough to look at him in the eye.

'What did you expect? That I'd leave you alone in this situation? With the earthquake, and your family, and everything…'

You left me alone for years, I wanted to say, but this wasn't the time nor place for recriminations.

'Will you introduce me to…' He made a gesture, and I realised that Massimo had come back and was looking on, eyes wide – and… Andrea was there too. I couldn't read his expression, but I was pretty sure he wasn't happy. I felt terribly, terribly guilty.

'Oh. Of course. Yes. This is Massimo, my cousin's fiancé. And this is Andrea, a… friend of ours. This is Ethan, my ex-husband.'

'Hello, Massimo…' He shook Massimo's hand. 'And yes, Andrea. I saw you in a photograph Luce sent over,' Ethan said in English.

Good God. The look between them.

'Sorry, I don't understand English.' Andrea shrugged his shoulders. '*Devo andare*,' he added towards me – I have to go.

'Sure. Sorry, I…' But I couldn't finish the sentence, because I had no idea what to say.

The first time in three years that I went out with someone was also the time that Ethan came back into my life. Coincidence?

Then again, I'd never been in an earthquake before – never even been abroad without Ethan. He'd never been in a position to worry about me, the way I had about him all those years. No wonder he was distressed.

'*Ciao*, Andrea,' Ethan said, and I glared at him.

'Sorry, Luce, but we need to go… visiting time, remember?' Massimo said. 'I'll go back to the car. Don't be long.'

'One minute, I promise!' I said, and dragged Ethan away, towards the parking lot opposite the camp. 'You came because I went out with Andrea? You really took a plane to the other side of the world because of him?' I blurted out.

'Of course not! Don't be silly. I just couldn't take this…to have you so far away, maybe in danger!' Ethan opened his hands.

'Now you know how it was for me all these years.'

'I was never in an earthquake!'

'I can recall quite a few incidents in your travels.'

'Yes, well, I'm here now.'

'You are, yes.' I glared again, but in seeing his face, all irritation went out of me. 'And I'm happy to see you. I really am,' I said, looking down.

'Oh, God, so am I, Luce! You have no idea. Your hands! What happened?' He held my hands in his, gently, like he was afraid to touch them, still bandaged as they were.

'I'm fine. Just a few scratches.'

'Were you seen to? Properly, I mean?'

'Of course I was. Stop fussing, I told you, it's just a few scratches, it's nothing. People were crushed, and I was unhurt, and…'

'Luce…' he said, and held me to him again, one hand holding my sore wrists, one around my back, pressing my face to his chest. I closed my eyes, and thought I could stay like that forever.

And then berated myself for that thought.

'Where are you staying?' I said, trying to be pragmatic. 'Where is Eli, Seattle or New York? How's Mamma? I have so many questions, but I have to go to the hospital.'

'I'm staying in a fancy hotel. *Really* fancy. There was no room anywhere else, everything is full of displaced people, but they were refurbishing when the earthquake happened so they couldn't allow any evacuees there. Eli is back in New York.'

'Thank goodness, he's not missing lessons. Mamma?'

'She's okay, given the situation… I'll tell you all after a shower, if it's okay with you? I'm dead on my feet. Will you come with me?'

'I can't, Ethan, I'll miss visiting time, and Nonna…'

'I understand. Can you come to the hotel, after? It's called… wait…' He handed me a crinkled piece of paper he'd retrieved from his jeans.

'Spa e Resort Cascata D'oro,' I read. 'Sounds grand. Okay, I'll take a taxi there.' I turned away, but spun around again. He was still standing there, looking at me, still taking me in, like he couldn't believe I was really there. It was entirely reciprocal. 'Ethan… thank you for being here.'

'Yes.'

'I'm going, then…' I took a step backwards.

'I'll make it up to you, Luce,' he blurted out. I was taken aback by those words, and had no idea how to reply. In the short silence that followed, he rubbed his forehead – he often did that when he was embarrassed – and I noticed he was wearing our wedding ring, a simple gold band.

I wasn't. My hand was bare.

Just add another surreal moment to a mountain of surreal moments.

'See you later, then,' I said. We were beginning to speak like teens in a romcom. All awkwardness and monosyllables. *Luce, get a grip!*

'Bye,' he replied, and then mumbled something.

'What did you say?'

'I said, *ciao*, Andrea.' He gave me a roguish look, and I was left fuming – half impressed, half annoyed at Ethan's eternal self-confidence.

Only he, it seemed, had the ability to made me laugh in the direst of situations.

A memory came back to me: of when Eli was born, two months premature, and I'd been worried out of my mind, flooded with hormones and in shock from the sudden labour and birth. There, in the special care baby unit, in spite of his own distress, Ethan had whispered in my ear: *His name was E-li, he was a ba-by,* to the tune of 'Copacabana'. The nurses must have thought we were crazy, because even then, as I'd looked at my beloved tiny baby in a plastic cot and was a mess of worry and hormones, Ethan had made me smile.

*

'Have you been to the house, *cara*?' was the first thing Nonna said when she saw me.

'Oh, Nonna, I'm sorry. I couldn't, yet. It's tricky, you see, to get to the village. But I'm going this afternoon… You see, there are so many people in need. I had to help. Distributing meals, giving a hand to people with young children…' I changed the subject quickly, not wanting her to dwell on the fact that many people were homeless, now.

'Distributing meals? Like… an outdoor kitchen?'

'Yes. Yes, like an outdoor kitchen. Because lots of people have no electricity, or gas.'

She seemed to think for a moment. 'Many houses must have been destroyed,' she said, thoughtful.

I held my breath. 'Yes. But don't concern yourself with this now; you need to concentrate on getting better…'

'But not Rosa Bianca.'

'Nonna…' I searched for the words, but none seemed adequate to prepare her and yet not alarm her. It was an impossible fear.

'You don't need to hide things from me, sweetheart. And you don't need to worry about Rosa Bianca. It's not destroyed. I know that.'

I smiled and squeezed her hand. 'Of course. Of course.' A pause. 'You know, my ex-husband… he's here. He flew over because he was worried about me.'

'That's nice! So everything is fine between you now?'

'No, it isn't, Nonna. Not after all that happened… It's a long story.'

'I'm sure you'll find the way back to each other.' I wasn't sure at all, and in fact, that was not in my plans, but I didn't reply.

I had to call Andrea and clear things up. But how could I clear up something that wasn't clear at all? I just wanted him to know I hadn't taken him for a fool, or used him. That I'd had no idea Ethan would come, that we weren't even in touch, apart from formal contact regarding our son…

My thoughts came back to Nonna, as she inhaled as deeply as she could. My heart tightened as I realised what a shallow breath it was.

'And now, let me get on with our story. I don't know why, but I'm so drowsy these days. Maybe it's all those medicines they're giving me…'

'Yes. Of course, it's the medicines, Nonna,' I said, not wanting her to make the connection between her drowsiness and her ill-health. But she was already lost in memory.

'…So there I was, holding my baby as tight as I could.' She wrapped her thin arms around herself. 'And the howling was everywhere…'

I shuddered as a flashback of my nightmare returned to me – Nora, dead and still walking on behind Nonna, like she was haunting her…

CHAPTER EIGHTEEN

Bosconero, 1945, Clelia

You can't hide from wolves, because they smell you.
You can't run from them, because they're faster.
All I knew was that I had to keep my daughter alive. And to keep
her alive, I had to keep myself alive. I couldn't let her die like I had
with my Nora and my niece.
I couldn't stay in the hut; the wolves would smell my sister's blood.
I couldn't go into the woods either, because there we would be prey.
I was lost.
My thoughts were a tangled mess, but my instinct was sharper
than ever. There was howling, there was a baby in my arms, there
was wind rising towards me, carrying our scent. I had to move, I had
to do something, anything *that would give us a chance!*
I stepped back inside. Loose flat stones lay all around the hut.
I laid Angelina gently in a corner – two walls to protect her were
there already. I would make another two tiny walls, and a roof for
her, like a tiny home where she could be safe from the wolves. Then
they would come and kill me, but they wouldn't be able to get to
Angelina, not if I did a good job. My baby would be left alone there
in the cold, but at least she would have a chance. I would buy her
some time. Angelina's only hope would be to be found by someone,
anyone – even a German soldier, if he had pity in his heart. Or
maybe Arturo! How I longed for his presence, now.

The howling was coming closer, a chilly wind blowing through the glassless windows over Nora's and Neve's bodies. Nobody would come to help. We were alone.

'Ave Maria, gratia plena, dominus tecum, benedicta tu in mulieribus…' *I prayed. I kept praying and the wolves kept howling.*

Angelina was sleeping like she had not a care in the world, full of my milk. I began to build a wall around her, but the flat stones were damp and slippery, and it wasn't working the way I had imagined. The wolves would be able to paw the stones away and get to her. Were those tears on my face? Yes, but snow as well. Snowflakes were dancing over us, falling from the sky through the rotten roof. My sister would catch cold. My niece would be drenched. My poor Nora, my poor niece – my poor daughter! We would all die, and the snow would be tainted red…

And then, I heard a noise that was not wind, it was not howling. It was the barking of a dog.

Sometimes both deer and boars almost bark; they might sound like dogs – but when the next bark came, I was sure: it was a dog.

I turned around, and back on the doorstep, but there was no dog nor wolf nor man there. I was alone.

Another bark resounded in the night, and my mind went blank. I had no other thought except that where there's a dog, there are no wolves, because the wolves would silence it at once. And so I grabbed my Angelina once more, leaving the mess of stones on the wet ground, and she woke and started crying. I stepped out with her in my arms, and I swear, I swear, through the blizzard, as real as you are right now, Bianco was there, with his kind, brave, black eyes, calling me to follow.

I knew Bianco had been killed years before, and some part of me knew that this could only be an illusion, a vision, maybe feverish delirium; but I followed, because it was the only thing I could do.

I followed Bianco through the woods, his white coat flashing between the trees, showing me the way every time I lost it. I slipped and fell on the snowy ground, but kept Angelina safe, and when I got up, my dog, the dog that had been killed long ago, was there, waiting for us to find our footing again.

And when I finally arrived in Bosconero, when I finally saw a little light shining in the distance, and tears of relief and mourning and terror and disbelief began pouring from my eyes again – Bianco was gone.

*

I stepped out of the snow and inside Rosa Bianca, cold and dark and deserted. I just wanted to crawl somewhere and sleep, but I had to change Angelina and myself into dry clothes, or we would catch pneumonia. That was all I could think of, for now, the next move: get the baby dry and warm, get myself dry and warm. I would think of the rest later. Nobody knew I was back anyway; nobody had seen me. My friends were dead, up on the mountain.

I took off my daughter's wet clothes at once and wrapped her in the first thing I could find in a drawer – a tablecloth. I hunted for a match – I had to scrape it against the box again and again because my hands were shaking too much – and lifted it to the candle in its brass holder that we always kept on the kitchen table. With Angelina in my arms, I changed her by candlelight into warm, cosy clothes, and laid her under the blankets. Oh, how she looked like Nora! Now that she was warm and dry, I took off my own clothes – I was sore all over, from giving birth and from terror and from the long walk across the woods.

Round and round my mind went, back to the same, wordless thought: keep Angelina alive, stay alive. Like Bianco's white coat among the trees, it was what kept me going. I lay on the bed and held Angelina to me, eyes dry and not even a prayer on my lips, I was so weary!

It was then that in the deep, deep silence of the night, I heard the door downstairs open. Someone had walked in and was coming up the steps. I sprang up and blew the candle out, and crouched on the *other side of the bed, on the freezing floor. Nobody could save me now. A light danced on the landing and filled the room.*

Little Carlo, standing there with his eyes wide. He threw himself into my arms and clung to me.

'I came to find you, but I got lost,' he said.

A chill ran down my spine. 'You came to find us?'

'Yes. I missed my mamma and papà. So I came. I watched you from afar, but then I thought you'd be all angry at me, and I went back.'

They hadn't stumbled upon us.

It had been Carlo, in his innocence, guiding the soldiers to us.

I couldn't ask him if someone followed him to the camp. I couldn't lay this on his shoulders. 'I'm here now. And here's your baby cousin, see? Angelina. We are together now, tesoro...' I said and held him tight against me. I loved him so much!

'Where are my parents?' he asked, his voice muffled against my shoulder.

I couldn't answer, not yet – I held back my tears and simply held him, held Angelina and Carlo both, and I promised on my sister's life, on Neve's life, that he would never know what he'd done...

*

Both Nonna and I were in tears when there was a knock at the door – we dried our faces hastily, as a doctor peered in. I was embarrassed to have been caught by a stranger in such an intimate moment, and tried to compose myself quickly.

'Oh, I'm so sorry. Clearly it's not a good moment. I'll come back...'

How sensitive, I thought, for someone so busy to offer to come back. I followed him out of the room and closed the door behind me. I did my best to put Nonna's story away in a corner of my mind, until I could go over it and digest it all.

'I'm so sorry, doctor. My grandmother and I were sharing some memories and… we were a bit overwhelmed.'

'I understand. I'm Doctor Meinardi, I don't think we've met. I've been looking after your grandmother, but I always spoke to your… well, Signora Nardini's son?'

'Yes.'

'Well, Signora Nardini is going home anyway,' he announced, leaning towards me slightly.

I was surprised. Had they not said she was to stay for a little longer, that I was to bring her some changes of clothes?

'Oh, that's great!' I smiled between the tears that lingered. I was so happy to hear that Nonna could leave the hospital that I decided to set aside the thought that she couldn't go back to her home, not for a while, anyway. But Doctor Meinardi seemed taken aback by my reaction.

'Did your father not tell you?'

I guessed he was talking about Carlo. 'He's not my father, he's my uncle.' *Well, he's not that either, but no point in elaborating about my soap-opera family now.* 'Tell me what?'

Doctor Meinardi laid a hand on my back, and led me further away from Nonna's room, to make sure we were completely out of earshot. The smell of disinfectant and medicine that lingered everywhere was beginning to make me feel nauseous. I knew I was about to receive bad news, and all my being was braced for it.

'Her heart. It already wasn't in a good way before… all this. But now…' He made a gesture to signify something was gone. 'She's an elderly lady,' he said, as if I didn't know that. 'There's only so much we can do with medication. And an operation would just be too much for her. Now we must focus on giving her the best quality of life we can, in the time she has left.'

I couldn't reply. I clasped a hand on my mouth, desperately trying, and failing, not to cry some more.

'I'm sorry. I hope you draw comfort in the fact that she's lived a long life… though of course that doesn't take your upset away. If you need anything, if you have any questions once she's gone home, do call me here.'

'Thank you.' I refrained from saying that although yes, she'd lived a long life, I'd only had a few days with her.

'Maybe I can see how she's doing now,' Doctor Meinardi said, and lightly knocked at Nonna's door. He opened it just enough to see that she was sleeping. She lay supine, her head turned on one side, in complete abandon.

'Better let her sleep,' he whispered, and closed the door. My eyes were on her as she disappeared from view – maybe it was just my impression, but I thought I saw her eyelids fluttering. Had she heard what had been said? Did she know? Was Nonna aware of her health declining? Most likely they'd told her she was better, and that was why she was going home…

Doctor Meinardi left me with one last kindly pat on the shoulder, and I leaned against the door for a moment. I'd just found her, and I was about to lose her?

Was Mamma never to see her mother again?

Carlo knew. Of course he knew, and he hadn't told me. But I couldn't be angry with him, not now – not when both his mother and his daughter were in such desperate condition. Also, if my uncle was to take Nonna to his house, he would not allow me there. He wouldn't let me see her. And maybe Nonna would be too ill to argue, and that would be the end of our reunion – maybe I would never know the rest of the story. We'd be deprived of each other once again, and forever. And Mamma would never meet her own mother again.

I couldn't let that happen.

*

Ethan opened the door onto the most luxurious hotel room I'd ever seen. Not a room, actually – a small apartment.

'Wow!' I exclaimed, not very imaginatively – but I was speechless. The hotel was a little further away from Bastia, in a wooded area, and I'd reached it via a taxi. It was an ancient convent that had been converted to a hotel and spa, and a modern outbuilding, harmonious with the surroundings, had been added. We were now on its top floor.

An enormous glass window ran the length of three walls and opened onto the woods – and on one side, it faced a mossy opening with a natural waterfall. I could hear the water rippling down, the sweetest, most healing sound I could imagine, after all I'd seen.

I stepped inside and walked across the room, furnished like a living room. In front of the waterfall, separated from the water only by the transparent wall, I laid my hands on the glass and closed my eyes for a moment.

'I know. Wow is the word. Literally everywhere else was busy, and I know they couldn't accommodate people here because this is the only room which actually has *floors*, right now – they were closed already when the earthquake happened… but I feel bad anyway. This place is huge. It could host one or even two families. It's just red tape.'

'Yes. I'm also looking at the glass walls in an entirely different way, now. I mean, earthquake-wise.'

'Good God,' Ethan said.

'Don't worry, apparently Bastia sits on solid rock or something…'

'Or something. You've become very fatalistic!'

'After seeing a tower collapse in front of your eyes, you become that way, I suppose. By the way, I don't want to think how much you're paying for this,' I said, and took off my shoes, letting my still-sore feet sink into the soft, terracotta-coloured carpet.

'I don't care. I just had to see you,' he said, suddenly serious. 'I would have slept in the station quite happily.'

I nodded, touched. He'd changed into fresh jeans and a t-shirt, and he was barefoot too, his hair still damp after the shower.

'Are you okay?' he asked. 'You don't look so good.'

'I had more bad news.'

'Oh, no… Look, come, sit down… I'll make you tea, or coffee? There's a whole kitchen here! And they have cakes as well, they left a whole tray of pastries. And I brought you some clothes, your own clothes… I didn't know what you had left, after the earthquake…'

He was fussing over me like a mother hen. I wanted to be strong and proud, and show him once again I could hold my own, and I could manage all this craziness, and I didn't need anyone…

Instead, I burst into tears.

*

Twenty minutes later, having had a shower in a marble bathroom that made me feel like a Hollywood star, we were sitting opposite each another, cross-legged on the carpet. I was wearing one of the t-shirts and a pair of shorts that Ethan had brought from Seattle. It was good to wear my own clothes again. My feet were bare, and I was vaguely embarrassed of the chipped mother-of-pearl nail polish on my toes. I probably looked a sight, from my hair to my feet, covered in scratches. Grooming hadn't been exactly high on my list.

'I've got to go,' I said, unconvincingly. I was leaning against the glass right beside the waterfall, letting the silvery sound seep into my bones and slowly, slowly unknot me. I couldn't even get up. It had all caught up with me, all of a sudden.

'You need to rest.'

And to my surprise, he lifted a hand and caressed my cheek.

There had been no sweet gestures like this one for years. I allowed myself to close my eyes and lean against his hand.

'I have to go up to the village, I have to get something for Nonna.' I wrapped my arms around my bare legs.

'What? You want to go to a place which is, apparently, razed to the ground? The people of your village…'

'Bosconero.'

'…Bosconero, are in that camp for a reason! You can't go there! You're not going, Luce. And that's it.'

I raised my eyebrows at him. Surely he knew better than to lay down the law with me. To be fair, he'd never done it – he knew there was no point.

'Luce, please, be reasonable,' he continued. 'You've always had common sense; you've gone crazy all of a sudden!'

'We're leaning against a glass wall, Ethan. Rock bed or not. Nowhere around here is safe at the moment.'

'Don't remind me.'

'I have to go, Ethan! Nonna asked me to get a keepsake from her house. A box that my grandfather made for her.'

'How important is a box, compared with your life!'

'Nonna is dying!'

'What?'

'She's dying. The doctor told me today.'

'Oh… I'm so sorry…'

'Yeah. And I only just met her.'

'Oh, Luce. It's terrible. Angelina…' Mamma and Ethan had always been close and, even after we'd broken up, Ethan still called and checked on her. 'Angelina needs to see her own mother, before it's too late…'

I leaned my head against the glass again. Ethan had dragged the coffee table beside us, on which he'd laid out the cakes and fruit they'd left for him in the kitchen, together with a cup of herbal tea for me and one of coffee for him. I was hungry, but I couldn't eat. However, I could have drunk and drunk – days after, I still had dust in my system.

'She does, yes. I'm worried about her flying here, for many different reasons. But she must. Or that chapter will never be closed.'

Ethan looked down. 'The choice, after all, is hers. To risk coming here, or never see her mother again.'

'I'm pretty sure she's more scared of her brother than of the earthquake,' I said, and filled him in on everything that had happened.

'If the guy upsets you again in any way…' Ethan growled.

'We'll ignore him.'

'I won't. Listen, I'll call Eli and ask him to organise things for her… I should have taken her, but I had no idea… I'm sorry.'

'Don't be silly! It means so much that you're here.'

'Thank you. And now, to business. You must eat!'

'You've turned Italian in the space of a day?' I smiled, and I was rewarded with laughter.

'Have some of these… look, they're mini masterpieces! So cute. Look at this one, a mini fruit tart. You'll love those. Please, it'll give you some strength…'

I took it from Ethan's hand and bit into it. I must have been hungrier than I thought, because it went down beautifully with my tea.

'A chocolate one. You love white chocolate, don't you? Come on, do it for me.'

'You sound like when Eli was a toddler and we had to convince him to eat!'

'I'm *this* far from doing a choo-choo train. So if you don't want to be submitted to that, eat!'

'I'll eat this, then I'll go.'

'Look, if you really, really want to go to Bosconero, as crazy as it is, I'll go with you. But *tomorrow*. Stay here, we can have dinner together. There are a gazillion rooms in this suite; just choose a bed.'

'Okay. I'll eat,' I conceded. 'We need to call Eli. I want to try and have Mamma's situation sorted.'

'There's my phone,' Ethan said, and grabbed it from the enormous couch against the blind wall. It was the middle of the night in Seattle, but we called anyway, putting the conversation on speakerphone.

'Dad?' Eli sounded sleepy and anxious at the same time.

'Eli! I'm so sorry to wake you up…' I began.

'Mom! Are you okay? Are you and Dad coming home?'

'Soon! We're in Dad's hotel, now…'

'You're together?'

'Hello, son,' Ethan said.

I ignored the question about us being together. 'Eli, my grandmother is not good. Her doctor just told me… There isn't much they can do. It's her heart.'

'Oh, Mom. I'm so sorry. I can only imagine what you're going through, with all this…' he said, and his voice was so soft, so *Eli*; I was desperate to see him.

'Eli, please… your nonna,' Ethan intervened. 'We'll call and do our best to convince her to come, but please can you help us? Can you get her a ticket? She can arrange a taxi ride herself, but she's not practical with plane bookings and all that. I know it's a lot to ask, with your school and everything…'

'That's not a problem. I can make up for lost time. But Nonna? It's not safe, you know that! You and Dad are gone, both in a place that looks half-destroyed, from the look of it, and now I should put Nonna on a plane too?'

'Only my home village is destroyed… and a few others…'
Oh, God. It didn't sound convincing at all.

'We know it's not safe,' Ethan said. 'And that it's a lot to ask.
But I'm staying in a hotel that wasn't damaged at all, and your
mom is going to stay here with me…'

'Am I?' I mouthed.

Ethan lifted his hand up, as if to tell me to wait. '…Nothing
is going to happen to us. It's Angelina's last chance to see her
mother,' he finished.

'Please, Eli. I'll call her and do my best to convince her. Please,
help her to organise everything. It's now or never,' I pleaded.

'Look, I'll speak to her,' Eli said. 'I'll try my best, okay?'

'Thank you. Thank you, sweetheart…' I touched the phone
with my fingers, longing to see my son again, to hug all six feet
of him and make sure he was good, and safe…

'Thank you, son,' Ethan said.

'So, you and Mom… you're there together? Staying together?'

'I'll still send you pictures!' I exclaimed, without answering
his question.

'Good, okay. Mom, Dad?'

'Yes?'

'Please, take care.'

'We will.'

'You too, *tesoro mio*,' I said, a bit teary.

Ethan put the phone down, and miles and miles of distance,
miles and miles of ocean, were stretched again between my son
and me. Hearing his voice was bittersweet, when my desire to
see him was so strong; it made my heart ache.

I had to take a moment, then I composed myself. 'And now,
to convince Mamma.'

'I'll help you,' Ethan said, and squeezed my hand. 'I'll speak
to her too.'

I allowed myself to exhale and leaned against the glass wall once again. Even that simple statement – I'll help you – was such a relief. I could stand on my own two feet, for sure. I could take care of myself. But to have someone beside me, to share this burden put upon my shoulders by my messed-up family, was such comfort.

'Drink your tea,' he said, and I smiled.

'Shall we call now, do you think? I don't want to alarm her, but if we phone in the middle of the night she'll fully get the urgency of it all.'

'Yes. Good idea. Can I try?'

'Sure.'

I sat cross-legged, biting my nails, as Ethan made the call. The little waterfall outside the window was so close, I felt like I could touch it. They'd built the suite so that there would be no barrier between the inside and the outside, except an invisible wall, and being in this idyllic place while sitting on a soft, soft carpet, in a fresh room, having the chance to stop for a moment, was heavenly. Even if it made me feel selfish, and self-indulgent – there, in a luxurious place, when so many people were suffering. But I was so, so very tired.

'Angelina? It's Ethan.'

I could hear Mamma's voice, hazy with sleep, but Ethan didn't put the call on speakerphone. As much as many times during the conversation I wanted to shout out and grab the phone from Ethan, I stopped myself. Mamma was speaking so low, I could hear only a word here and there; finally, it seemed to me that she'd agreed, but I wasn't sure…

'She's coming,' Ethan said, ending the call. I closed my eyes, letting relief sweep over me at last. 'And now, you're going to pick a bed somewhere… I think there are three or four… and go to sleep. We'll have room service tonight and you'll eat a proper meal. And then, tomorrow, we'll go to Bosconero. Somehow.'

I wanted to protest. I wanted to say he couldn't tell me what to do; I wanted to get up and go now, in case Nonna was being sent home and I didn't know; I wanted to call Massimo and make sure I'd be given the chance to actually *make* it to the village, tomorrow.

But I did none of that. I had no energy left to summon, from anywhere. Ethan's presence had allowed a part of me that had been alarmed and frightened and traumatised for what seemed like forever to relax now. And with the adrenaline leaving me, I found that my strength had gone too.

I got up and wandered to the next room, followed by Ethan. It was a bedroom, with a king-sized bed covered in an aqua-coloured spread that made it look like a pool of fabric. I saw Ethan's things scattered on it, so I moved on. Another, smaller room, with a pure, white bedspread, crisp and clean and fresh. I lay there, without a word. I curled up over the quilt, but Ethan slipped it from under me and covered me with it, and I allowed myself to fall into the first peaceful sleep I'd had for a long, long time.

CHAPTER NINETEEN

I woke up without the slightest idea of where I was, who I was, and who was the man beside me. It was the most surreal feeling, like waking up in a dream. 'Ethan?'

'That's me.' He was sitting beside me, a brochure in his hand.

'What are we doing?'

'I was reading. You were sleeping. Don't worry, I slept in my own bed. I just settled here this morning, waiting for you to wake up.'

I sat up. 'I need to go to the village. And to see Nonna at the hospital. Oh, my God... is that... evening?' I looked out to the enormous window, filling the entire wall. It made me feel like I'd been sleeping suspended in the sky.

'Just dusk. I called the hospital and asked for the visiting times...'

'But you don't speak Italian!'

'I speak Spanish-*o*, I adapted. Cringy, but it works. And we have time. We'll take a taxi. I mean, I'm saying we, but I don't want to intrude, if you want to be alone with your grandmother...'

'No. No, of course not. You're welcome to come. Oh...'

'What?'

'I just remembered that Mamma is coming!' I sat up and kneeled on the sheets, my hair a tangled mess.

'Yes. Eli texted me what time she'll arrive...'

'Already? Oh, that's amazing!'

'I'll go get her at the airport. Don't worry about a thing.'

'Thank you, Ethan, I…'

'It's the least I could do…'

'That's not true. It's a lot *more* than I asked or expected. And I'm… well, I'm so grateful,' I said, and began scouring the floor.

'If you're looking for shoes, I brought you a pair from home,' he said and disappeared next door, coming back with a pair of old trainers of mine, as soft as slippers. 'And socks.'

'Oh my God… these are so comfy. Oh, thank you!'

'Where's Massimo's house?'

'The centre of Bastia, twenty minutes from here. It's his dad's house. You know that he was an old friend of Mamma?'

'The plot thickens,' he said, ominously.

*

Ethan was silent and sombre as we stepped into the hospital lobby, still lined with beds, and through the back corridors. The place was still overflowing.

'If I think how much you tried to sell me that this earthquake had been no big deal…' he murmured.

Nonna was awake, with a rosary in her hand. 'Nonna… I brought you a visitor…'

'Oh, *tesoro mio*, that's nice. I guess this is your husband?'

'Ex-husband. This is Ethan.'

'E-tan,' Nonna said, unable, like most Italians, to pronounce the sound *th*.

'*Piacere*,' Ethan said – and I looked at him, impressed. He'd managed one word that wasn't English or Spanish with an *o* at the end.

'He's so blond!' Nonna said and laughed like a mischievous little girl. 'Oh, Luce, he can help you go to Rosa Bianca, no? To get my box?'

'She says you can help me get to her home and retrieve the box,' I translated for Ethan.

'I don't think that's very wise…' Ethan began.

'He says it's a good idea, that he will help me, and we'll bring you the box back.'

'Oh, bless you! *Grazie, grazie!*' Nonna said towards him. Ethan looked confused.

'Wait, what did you tell her?'

'Shhhhh, now. Nonna is recounting our family history.'

Ethan eyed me suspiciously, but he was too much of a gentleman to argue in front of Nonna. 'I hope to see you again soon,' he said in English, and I translated. 'I'll be outside.'

'What a nice man!' Nonna commented. 'Why on earth did you break up?'

'One story at a time,' I said, smiling, and settled down as Nonna began.

CHAPTER TWENTY

Bosconero, 1945–46, Clelia

Everybody was celebrating. There was dancing in the square, people were waving handkerchiefs from the windows, singing partisan songs.

It was finished.

Mussolini had been shot and then his corpse hung in a petrol station in Milan, for everyone to see. A pitiful end for the man who ruled our country for twenty years, who had believed himself all-powerful. The Germans were gone. We were free.

I felt hopeful for the future, in spite of everything. Carlo and I went out to join in, with me carrying Angelina in my arms, but not everyone was happy to see us.

'Is Arturo dead? Or in prison?' some men called out to me. A woman spat on the ground in front of me, and it took all my strength not to scratch her eyes out – I had my children with me; that was the only thing that stopped me.

'I don't know!' I shouted, and held their gaze. Did they not remember I'd been a partisan myself? That my nephew had lost his parents, that I had lost my sister?

I was dismayed. There was no fear in my heart for myself – I've always been one to fight, not to retreat – but I was responsible for two children, and I was all they had in the world. After the horrors I'd seen in the war, and even before then, after what Felice had almost done to me, I knew what people were capable of. Yes, Luce, people are capable of the most horrific things, given the chance: this I know.

We went home in a hurry, although I hated every step I took, like I was hiding instead of defending myself like I was accustomed to. But it seemed like that celebration wasn't for us. Carlo wasn't a child for festivities, anyway. He was quiet, solemn. The loss of his parents had taken a huge toll on him.

But we loved each other, the three of us, and we kept going.

I didn't see Arturo at all, for a long time. Word came that he'd been taken away by the partisans. I knew he'd probably been killed. My heart was shattered. In a way, I still loved him, in spite of what he'd done. Some of his own comrades returned, while others, many, had died by the hands of the partisans or the Americans.

Everyone remembered what each of us had done during the war; the former Blackshirts were shunned. People spat when they saw them, just like that woman had done. The village was never the same again, but forever after divided in two.

I looked after Angelina and Carlo, and lived by myself, the best I could. I took such joy in my children. Even after all that had happened, I woke up in the morning and thought: I'm a mother. And that was enough.

And then, one day, Arturo turned up at the door. He wasn't thin or ragged, like the others who'd returned, whatever side they'd been on. He was in good shape, shaved, healthy. I wanted to turn him away. But I couldn't.

When he saw him, Carlo screamed and went into a rage that horrified us both – he was only six, and full of an anger we couldn't begin to fathom. He ran out of the door, screaming he would never come back; but I reached him, and convinced him to stay. I told him that, after all, if he ran away, he would probably starve. He seemed terrified enough to give up on his plan.

I said I would sleep in the kitchen with Angelina, but Arturo offered me the bed and went downstairs alone, to sleep by the light of the smouldering fire.

I lay awake in the darkness. I was aware of my husband's presence downstairs, and I couldn't make sense of my feelings. I wanted him gone, but I longed for him at the same time. I needed an explanation. I needed him to tell me why, why he had joined the Blackshirts, what it was he believed in. I needed him to explain why a man with such a mind and heart would go down such a wicked, wicked way.

When the night was at its darkest, the door opened slowly, and Arturo came in. I didn't say a word when he lay beside me, because I didn't want him there, and yet I did, and I was rigid with my own confusion. Angelina was sleeping in her cot and Carlo was next door, in the room that had been my mother's.

'Please, listen, Clelia,' he whispered. I waited. 'I wanted to tell you many times, but I knew what was coming and I was afraid to put you in danger. I'm not who you think I am.'

'No, you aren't,' I said, trying to keep my voice low. 'I thought you were a good man. But you—'

'I was never a fascist at all. And my name is not Arturo Riva.'

When he said that, I began to cry – just like that.

It seems like a crazy thing to say – to go up to your wife and say you were not what she thought you were – I should have thrown him out of bed, called the doctor, told them that the war had made my husband crazy.

But I believed him straight away.

Because what he'd said made sense to me. There was always something in him that I couldn't understand, I couldn't reach. There was always a side of him that did not make sense, parts of his story of how he'd come to be in Bosconero, of his past, that didn't hang together at all. His education, the way he spoke – everything was out of kilter. And his time as a Blackshirt had been out of kilter too.

Looking back, my love for him had been the only thing I was sure of – everything else about him was a mystery. I'd never met a relative of his, he'd never mentioned family or friends, or his past.

I knew nothing about him.

'Who are you?' I asked in between sobs.

He said nothing, but took out some papers from his pocket, and gave them to me.

It was a foreign document, with Arturo's photograph and a name printed underneath: David Zevi, born the twentieth of October 1915, in Lugano, Switzerland.

I got up, on my knees on the bed, and my tears wet the paper.

He explained that he belonged to a wealthy Jewish family in Lugano, and that when he was at university he'd been recruited by the English. He was meant to be sent to Rome, but someone there recognised him as David. He didn't want to give up on the work he'd been recruited to do, so he came to Bosconero, and stayed in touch with a net of anti-fascist agents from England and America.

He didn't plan to fall in love with me, and he knew he shouldn't have – but he couldn't help it.

'I tried to tell you. Over and over and over again. But if something had happened to you… They said I should have never married you. To leave you, and go somewhere else. I couldn't do that.'

'But I was in danger anyway. I gave birth in the woods… I was almost killed.'

'I didn't know you were going, Clelia! Had I known, I would have come clean! I thought only Nora and Mauro would go. When you disappeared, I couldn't come find you without bringing the Blackshirts on you all. I made up some business to be conducted in Bastia, so that we wouldn't be there, the night Nora and Mauro left. I did it so they wouldn't be caught.'

I was speechless. But I'd always wondered how, that night, we could have been so lucky.

'What about Miriam and her children? What happened to them?'

'That was my work, Clelia. It wasn't just Miriam, it was many more. They weren't taken away, to the concentration camps.' I knew about those camps now – although such brutality was almost impossible to believe. *'They sailed to Israel, through Naples. I didn't condemn them. I helped to save them.'*

I remember I took his face in my hands and gazed at him. I looked deep into his eyes, trying to come to terms with all he'd said.

His name was David Zevi.

Arturo Riva, my husband, did not exist.

*

Nonna's voice trailed away – I realised I'd been holding my breath. My head was spinning.

Arturo Riva didn't exist. My grandfather was a Jewish man called David Zevi.

And he was a spy.

It was too much for me to take in.

Whether it was the medication or the intensity of her emotions, Nonna was drained. I'd intended to ask if she knew when she would go home, if she could ask Carlo to speak to me at last, so I would know – but she was just too weary for such a conversation.

'I'll leave you to rest, Nonna,' I said, and kissed her forehead. She didn't hear me; she was asleep already.

*

Ethan was waiting for me outside, in the gathering shadows. He was leaning against the wall beside the automatic door, his phone in his hand. He looked tired, in the light of the street lamp – tired, and familiar, and so very Ethan. I'd seen his face changing from that of a high school boy, to a young man, to middle aged – and he'd seen mine. For a moment, I was overwhelmed by the desire to hold him again, and to feel his arms around me – but I stopped myself.

'Hey.'

'Hey. Any news?' he asked.

At that moment, the image of a six-year-old Carlo wanting to run away from home, and being told that if he did he would probably starve, came back to me and gave me a lump in my throat. 'Can I change my mind?'

'About what?'

'Can I stay with you tonight?'

CHAPTER TWENTY-ONE

Once again I was on the winding road to Bosconero; not in an army truck this time, but in Giuseppe's car. We were following the red truck of the Protezione Civile, driven by Andrea – if anyone stopped us, we were with them. Massimo was in full gear, and Andrea had found a yellow hard hat for me and one for Ethan.

I was beyond anxious, and the sense of dread grew with every bend; Ethan looked gloomy and uncertain. 'I can't believe we're doing this,' he said.

'Me neither.' I felt his hand find mine, and I didn't pull away.

The night before we'd spent hours chatting. I'd filled him in with my family history, and we'd talked about these three years apart, making up for all the silence we'd shut ourselves in. Before wading into our hours-long conversation, though, I'd called Giuseppe to let him know I would not come back that night. And then I'd spoken to Massimo, and convinced him to take Ethan and me to Bosconero, just long enough to find what Nonna wanted and needed so desperately.

'Tell me about Andrea,' Ethan had asked while we ate, and I'd nearly choked on my risotto. This time there was no sarcastic inflexion to his words – he really wanted to know.

'Andrea and I… we went out once. Not that I owe you an explanation, of course. You didn't let me know when you got together with Vicky, did you?'

'No. So… you're together? You and this Italian man?' He turned his eyes away from me and to the window, trying to seem nonchalant – but I knew him better than that.

'No, of course not!' I laughed. 'I've only known him a few days. No. I liked him, but after the earthquake… I don't know. It's just impossible to think of that kind of thing now.'

'Yes,' he conceded. 'Just, when I saw those pictures…'

'Is that why you came? Those photographs? Be honest.'

'No. It's been… well, it's been on my mind for a while. I made changes to my life, and…'

What changes? 'Are you seeing someone, after Vicky?' I had to ask the question. I had the feeling that he wanted to come close to me again, but… I needed things to be clear. Everything else was nebulous enough.

'Nobody. And if you want to know, I've been miserable, these three years. Lonely.'

'With all your travelling, you don't have time to be lonely.'

'You can be lonely while travelling.' He shrugged.

I looked down. 'And Vicky?'

'It didn't work out. It just didn't. I couldn't… I just couldn't commit the way she wanted. Because of… Well, because of you.'

'Then *why*, Ethan? Why did you choose to keep things as they were, instead of staying home some more, being with me? Being a family, you and me? You know I was never clingy… but you were always away. You were possessed by your work.'

'You think I *chose* my work. But I didn't. I tried my best… I couldn't do it. I didn't know how to be any other way, Luce. I've always lived like that, since my twenties. But you have no idea how much my life has changed now.'

'Has it?' I was suspicious. Not about whether he was seeing someone else. Ethan had always been straightforward with me; I never had to worry about interpreting what he said or wondering what he thought. But this statement, about his life being different – I would believe it only when I saw it. But I'd had enough for one day – all I wanted was to shut down my brain and my heart, and just be. Ethan knew me well enough to guess that.

'I'll prove it to you, Luce. I'll make it up to you,' he repeated, like he'd said in the camp.

When neither of us could keep our eyes open any more, Ethan had taken me by the hand and led me to the snow-white bed I'd chosen. I'd woken up after just a few hours and contemplated the dawn through the glass wall; all the beauty of the sky changing from dark blue to a hundred hues of purple, lilac and pink, with stray orange clouds over the wooded hills, soothed my heart and soul and prepared me for the day ahead. Because I knew it would not be easy.

Now things felt more and more ominous as we got closer to the village, and yet everything up to then had looked fairly normal, like the first time I'd driven up that road with Matilde, full of excitement and expectation. It wasn't about what I saw – it was about how I felt. The memories of that night were more vivid than I could describe, imprinted in my brain in bright colours, never to disappear. Even recounting it all to Ethan, I'd trembled and shook like it was all happening again...

Silence fell between us for the rest of the way, until we arrived in Bosconero, and all I could do was cover my face with my hands and cry.

*

We stepped along the streets, our feet making crunching noises on the flattened debris.

Every single house, every single building, had been razed or broken to the point that it looked like it was about to crumble.

All that beauty – those ancient homes, and the cheerful, lively community around them – was destroyed.

Would people ever be able to come back here? Would the ties of families related to each other for hundreds of years, friendships that had lasted generations, be broken, and the people scattered around?

I walked slowly, looking left and right, holding my breath. Heavy machinery was at work, its constant noise filling the air, and yellow hats were dotted everywhere. A group of men stood at the edge of the square, talking animatedly and pointing upwards; I was too dazed to make out what they were saying. It was like walking on the bottom of the sea, everything muffled, while only the intensity of my trauma and dread could make themselves heard. Ethan was holding my hand.

'I'll stop here. Go with them,' Andrea said to Massimo, unnecessarily, because Massimo wasn't letting me out of his sight. Andrea wasn't looking at me in the eye, and I could feel he was upset, but he was still doing his duty and protecting us.

'I can't wait to take you back to Bastia,' Massimo said as we were walking, very close to each other, towards Rosa Bianca. 'I'm sorry I let you convince me, to be honest, Luce.'

'I won't be long, I promise,' I said, and my voice was raspy already – the machines at work were lifting more dust in the air, almost as much as the night of the earthquake. I rubbed my forehead with my hand, feeling sweat gather on my brow, because of the heat and the fear – and my fingers came away brown with the dust that had settled on my skin, even with the hard hat on.

'We signed up for all this; you didn't,' Massimo said. 'You're not supposed to be here.'

'Yes, well,' I said, still having to concentrate to put one foot in front of the other. At every mound of rubble I felt more and more like bursting into tears again, which was, of course, out of the question. Everyone was cool and collected, concentrating on the job in hand; I couldn't be some kind of wailing banshee, letting my feelings flow free when everyone was just as affected by the destruction as I was, and some certainly a lot more.

I won't say what I saw. I won't talk about what was in the rubble, the signs of daily lives now destroyed. I will never, never say what I saw because I must keep it buried deep down, only to come back to me in the middle of the night, unchecked, terrifying.

We passed the townhouse where Matilde's attic had been, and Ethan squeezed my hand tighter; I stepped on a mangled string of fairy lights, and an image of them hanging between buildings, shining in the dark, with people in summer clothes walking underneath unaware of what was about to happen, cut my mind. I couldn't help closing my eyes tight for a moment.

And then, up the cobbled street towards Rosa Bianca – the buildings on both sides of the alley weren't there any more. I tried to control my steps, because I wanted to run on and turn around forever, at the same time.

Suddenly, I realised that a pair of green eyes were watching me. It was the cat I'd seen the first day I was here, sitting in the alley when I was about to step towards Rosa Bianca, now perched comfortably on a low, dusty mound. He looked unconcerned and quite calm, and followed us with those clear eyes without moving a muscle. His fur, snow-white when I'd first seen him, was now reddish-grey with dust, but he seemed unharmed.

'Ethan…' I said, pointing at the cat, an uncanny sight among the ruins.

'Poor thing.'

I kept turning my head backwards, looking at the cat, as I walked on. Step after step, I was coming nearer to the opening where Rosa Bianca stood, or used to stand…

Everything around there had been flattened; Rosa Bianca had to be gone too. I steeled myself, ready to see the family home turned into a mound of rubble. Step after step I walked in dread, lifting my legs was a huge effort…

And there we were.

'Luce…' Massimo called, his voice full of wonder.

But I couldn't answer.

It took me a few seconds to take in what I saw, for it to sink in – between the sunlight burning in my eyes, and the sense of foreboding and confusion I'd carried in my heart until then, I had to blink over and over again… Because in front of me was the blue door, with its trailing roses around it like a garland; in between two houses broken open, their roofs caved in, Rosa Bianca stood whole.

Nonna was right; Rosa Bianca did not fall.

It had to be a miracle.

'Let's hurry,' Massimo said, and shook me out of my thoughts. He had to force the door; Nonna didn't have anything with her, let alone her house keys, and I couldn't have asked Carlo, of course.

We stepped into the hall, cool and shaded after the heat outside. It was absurd that I should have a feeling of familiarity with a place I'd seen only twice, and that had been mentioned so seldom by my mother. But I did. I could almost see my mother running through the hall right now, like in the picture I'd found, as Mamma's memories overlapped with the few I'd made in my visits to Nonna. But the moment was interrupted by Massimo, who hurried before me, and positioned himself on the first step of the staircase.

'Come,' he said. 'I'll go before you.'

Massimo, Ethan and I made our way upstairs slowly, Massimo and I looking up and around, for different reasons. I was entranced by the miracle of my family home still standing, while Massimo was checking it was safe. I was desperate to linger, but he rushed me, and for good reason. Nonna's bedroom was in semi-darkness, as she'd had to leave in the middle of the night, so the blinds were still closed. The ever-present dust danced in the thin rays of sunshine that entered through the shutters.

'Look,' Massimo said, pointing to the ceiling. Even in the gloom, I could see a crack that divided the ceiling in two – it ran down both walls. Was the crack running through the plaster only, or through the very walls of the house?

There was no time to think of anything. I had to be quick. The dressing table was beside the window, on the other side of the bed; I scoured the toiletries and medications scattered on it, and there it was, the little wooden box Nonna had talked about. I was quick to slip it into Ethan's backpack. I'd done it!

I was so relieved, my legs almost gave way, and I started to shake, the weight of fear on me. What if the crack began to yawn wider, what if I looked up and saw the lamp oscillating back and forth…

'Luce,' Ethan called me. I realised I was standing, frozen. I shook myself and made my way across the room to where Massimo was holding the antique wardrobe's door open. I grabbed what seemed most practical to me – cotton dresses – and ransacked the chest of drawers for underwear. Among Nonna's things, I saw a faded paper folder with the name Arturo written in old-fashioned handwriting, and I grabbed that too, thinking that Nonna might want it. Massimo was already waiting on the doorstep; as I was poised to go, I caught a glimpse of a framed photograph on Nonna's bedside table. A man dressed in a checked shirt and corduroy trousers, smiling broadly against the backdrop of a wooded hill. It had to be my grandfather. For a moment, I looked for a resemblance between us, but couldn't find any – he was red-headed, like Nonna had said. Clearly, Mamma and I had taken after Nonna's side of the family…

'Luce!' Massimo called me again, and I followed him downstairs. I was on my way out when, in passing the living room, I saw the little sacred image of Saint Emidio leaning against a vase. The saint protector against earthquakes. He had protected the house, I thought right at that moment, one of those moments when what you know and what you imagine and what you want to believe melt together. I grabbed the image, and then Ethan and I followed Massimo out in the sunshine.

I made my way out of the canopy of roses, and took a breath. Massimo hurried us away from the house.

'Did you see the crack? Come away, this place is not safe.'

Beads of sweat had gathered on my forehead, and I closed my eyes briefly, clutching Ethan's backpack and the sacred image, trying to gather myself. When I opened them, the cat I'd seen earlier was looking at me, sitting seraphically on a low stony wall.

'Come away!' Massimo was rushing us. I couldn't possibly leave the cat there, among the rubble and the heavy machinery prowling around – even though he looked like the kind of creature that could look after himself. I went to see if I could pick him up, while Ethan took the backpack from me.

'Careful, Luce,' he said in a low voice. But the cat didn't scratch me, neither did he run away – he simply let me hold him, as calm as he'd been before. He raised his little dusty head to look up at me, red and brown where it had been white, and I put my nose against his. He was unhurt, and he didn't even seem scared.

'Do you think your father will mind, if…' I asked Massimo.

'He won't mind. I'm pretty sure.' Massimo smiled. 'Let's go, now. I really want you down and safe.'

'We rushed away, debris grinding the soles of my shoes. Once again, we made our way through what was left of the village, as I held the cat close. I stepped over a geranium box smashed on the ground, and remembered how colourful and lovely the balconies had looked, along the road… It was all gone forever, and nothing would ever be the same again.

But in that moment of hopelessness, I felt the presence of my grandfather's box in my rucksack, and it was a tiny radiance in a dark place. I'd done this for Nonna. I was bringing her a piece of home.

The moment we stepped out of the village walls the cat freed himself, to my disappointment, and jumped down, disappearing among the debris.

'Oh! Ethan, we can't leave him…'

But Ethan took my arm and shook his head.

He was right. It would be foolish to go looking for the cat – also, he could clearly look after himself.

'Be safe,' I whispered to myself.

*

On the way out, we saw Andrea, his face now covered in dust, his eyes big and white, surveying the scene. I called him and waved; I wouldn't distract him for long, but I had to show him the image I'd taken from Frassino – I had to tell him!

'The house was standing, Andrea! And look, I'd forgotten this was there. Matilde and I were supposed to return it to you – you know the way nobody can take anything from Frassino, and I felt so bad about forgetting…' I shouted over the noise of the machines.

'The house is standing?' Andrea yelled back, taking the image from me and slipping it in a pocket of his orange waistcoat. 'How is that possible?'

'It's the only house still there!' another man in a yellow hat shouted.

'I had no idea! It's incredible!' Andrea shook his head. 'Frassino is also untouched, Luce. Intact.'

'Seriously?'

'Believe what you will, but they say it was Saint Emidio who saved it. We'll never know, will we?'

'No. We'll never know.'

'Luce!' This was Ethan calling – of course.

'Please stay safe,' I said to Andrea.

'You too! And E-tan,' he said, pronouncing it the Italian way, and laying a gloved hand on my shoulder. His eyes were kind and there was almost a smile in them – *almost*. It sounded like a goodbye, with me returning something I'd taken away during our one and only date, and the sad, yet gracious look he'd given me.

*

'Shouldn't we already have had aftershocks? How long can they happen for?' I asked Massimo, in between bouts of coughing, as he drove us down. He would then go back by himself to work with Andrea and his team.

'A long time. There is no way to know.'

'Are there no warnings that an earthquake is coming?' I was holding onto my loot like it meant the world. And, to Nonna, it did.

'Yes and no. We're in a highly seismic area, so the place is monitored, of course. But we never thought…' He shook his head. 'It's strange. We know that it can happen, we know it did happen in the past. But it doesn't seem real. We took earthquake training with the ambulance service, you know. And it was useful, of course. But nothing can prepare you.'

I coughed some more. I was desperate for water. 'That's for sure.'

'Bosconero's homes were hundreds of years old. Nothing like this has happened here before, nothing so powerful as to wipe out the place. You know, there are laws, in Italy, on how houses should be built or strengthened in highly seismic areas. They're often ignored. As you can see.'

'It can't be!'

'This is Italy, Luce. Things are never straightforward, here. And it's the common people who pay the price, as always. There will be an investigation on why the tower fell, for example, after having been refurbished according to the law. Too late for those who were under it.'

I had no answer to that. I proceeded to translate the whole thing to Ethan, who was as shocked as me.

'Also, if there were tremors just before… why was there no alarm given?' Ethan asked.

'Maybe it was all too quick,' I replied in English, but I also translated the question for Massimo.

'Another Italian mystery,' Massimo replied cryptically.

He left us at the bottom of the hill. 'I'll see you later at the hospital,' I said, and a flash of pain clouded his face once again. I hugged him, murmuring all the words of hope I could find, and followed him with my eyes until his car disappeared.

*

'I'm off to the airport to get Angelina. Will you be okay?' Ethan said as I gulped from a bottle I'd bought.

'Yes. Of course.'

'You don't seem okay…'

'No, no, I'm fine. It was just a little… shocking. To see Bosconero like that.'

'You can say that again.'

'Oh, Ethan. I was threading together loose ends. Threads that had been cut years ago. And then, the earthquake came and ripped it all apart again.'

'I'm here to help you hold the threads in place, Luce. I will help you tie them. I promise.' Ethan took a breath, like he was about to say something that had been heavy on his heart. 'I don't want to upset you but… You need to speak to Carlo, sooner or later.'

'Yes. I know.' I knew I had to face him, but the more Nonna told me, the more I dreaded it.

'You need to know when your grandmother is getting out of hospital, where she's going... I'll be back with Angelina in a few short hours.'

'I know, but... I'm so sure that if I tell him Angelina is on her way, he'll do anything to avoid her meeting Nonna.'

'Then don't tell him... but we still need to find out where your Nonna is going, and when. Do you want me to speak to him?'

'Maybe. If you can get something more than yelling out of him. But not yet.'

'Lulu... I mean, Luce! Sorry...' *Lulu?* That was his nickname for me when we were in high school. He'd stopped calling me that when Ethan was born. 'I'm so sorry, I don't know where that came from!'

'Lulu is fine, Ethan,' I said. 'Actually, Lulu is great.'

A small light in the darkness, like one of the fireflies Matilde and I had seen, was suddenly shining in front of me.

*

I left Ethan waving down a taxi and dashed back to the hospital, turning a few heads along the way – I was covered in dust. Romina was just coming out of Nonna's room.

'Oh, it's good that you're here,' she whispered. 'Signora Nardini is quite low, today. It's unlike her... but I think she knows she's not getting better.'

'Maybe having some of her belongings with her will cheer her up a little,' I said, lifting Ethan's backpack.

Romina looked at me with wide eyes. 'Did you go up to the village? That's why you're so...'

'Dirty? Between us, yes. But only for half an hour or so, time to get inside the house and out again...'

'But the whole place is rubble. How did you…'

'Rosa Bianca is the only house still standing. I have no idea how this is possible. My grandmother seemed to be sure it would not crumble.'

'Maybe it's a miracle, who knows?' Romina smiled. 'I have to go. Don't be long, though. We don't want to tire her out too much.'

'No,' I said, feeling like it'd been a day of people rushing me along. Almost like the universe was sending me a message: *hurry, time is running out, these people and places are not going to be here forever…* 'Sorry, Romina, one last thing. Where are you and your family staying? Is everyone in your family okay? I feel so bad that I never asked you…'

'Oh, you had enough worries of your own! We are all okay, just a few scratches when we ran out. You can say that was a miracle of our own. We're staying with my sister here in Bastia, so it's all good. We lost everything, but hey, it's all just stuff, isn't it? We are alive. See you later, Luce,' she said with a smile.

True. Losing all your belongings, mementos, your home, is horrific – but after all, life is the only thing that truly matters… And still, I was overjoyed that I carried some keepsakes for Nonna.

I knocked and went in with a smile, holding the box like a trophy.

'Nonna! Rosa Bianca is still there! It's still standing. And I got you the box.' I broke off, my joy cut short – more than pale, Nonna looked grey.

'I knew it… I told you that the house would not be destroyed.'

'You did, actually, yes.' I almost shivered, thinking of the crack running through the ceiling – and of the destruction on both sides of the house.

Nonna held the box with both hands, close to her heart, and then she opened it slowly, like she was handling a treasure. She took out a pendant – a locket.

'Would you like to put it on, Nonna?'

'Oh, yes, please,' she said, and I clasped it around her neck.

'My Arturo had this made this for me. With what I'd done to him…'

With what she'd done to him? I thought it was the opposite?

'I also found this when I got your underwear and nighties… I thought you might want to have it…' I handed her the folder, yellowed with time.

'Oh, thank you, *tesoro mio*…' She took it with uncertain hands, and I thought it would be better if I put it in on her bedside table. 'Luce, I never sent your mamma away. Carlo did. Oh, I love him with all my heart. But I'm afraid of him. And you should be afraid too…'

I felt cold. Nonna's eyes closed, and she dozed off – as she always seemed to do after the medication. I was disappointed I would not find out anything more today, but she needed her rest. Next time I saw her, I would bring her her daughter, at last…

I stood to tuck her in, as she was always chilly in spite of the heat – and as I did so, the folder fell on the floor, with papers and photographs being scattered around. My eye fell on some documents – what seemed like a Party card with the fascist symbols on it, and Arturo Riva's name – and another one, thinner and folded in two, with David Zevi typed on it, and a photo of my grandfather. I was handling the documents of a spy, I thought. Some story I would have to tell Eli…

I was crouching to pick everything up when a postcard caught my eye, with its colourful stamp… Australia. Maybe we had family there too, I thought, and smiled a little. The back was written in a tight, small, spidery handwriting.

*

Clelia, or like you called yourself when we were at war, Bianca,

Finally I can use your fighting name without fear! This is a new life and a new world. Of course I don't blame you for not taking me with you, you couldn't know I was alive, I remember the dark and the snow… It's a miracle you and me survived. I'm so sorry you had to endure the death of poor Nora, just after you lost your own daughter in childbirth…

What?

She didn't lose her daughter in childbirth! Angelina survived! It had been Neve who died…

I hope whoever gave us away burns in hell. Although we'll never know! Oh, my dearest friend Bianca, I'll never return to Bosconero, what for? My whole family is gone. I just hope you will be happy and healthy all the days of your life. I think of the tiny grave where we buried your baby, and pray for her every day.

Stai bene sempre.
Pietra

The postcard slipped from my hand.

I looked at Nonna sleeping, and the first word that came in my mind was: *liar.*

CHAPTER TWENTY-TWO

I left the room and the hospital, feeling like I was looking at myself from somewhere far, far away. It had to be a mistake. It just wasn't possible.

And still, it was like connecting the dots.

The lie about Carlo being her son.

Neve being smothered by their bodies, but Angelina surviving.

The way she'd said *trust me* to Carlo…

The way Nin, for some reason, stopped talking to her. How Andrea had said that Nin loved Nora but didn't like Clelia.

How she'd ripped Carlo from Nora, how she'd told him that if he ran away, he would starve…

How Matilde's mother loathed Clelia too.

But no, it was all too far-fetched. Maybe it was that woman, Pietra, lying?

But why would she?

Something Nonna had said came back to me: *Nobody is left alive to say things didn't really go that way – there is only me, to remember what happened to all of us…*

A strange laugh came out of my lips. It was all too absurd.

My thoughts were too jumbled to make sense – in a haze, all I could think of was going to see Giuseppe, to check on him and tell him Mamma was on her way. His house had felt like a haven since the first time I'd been there, and I was looking forward to his quiet, warm ways. As I walked, I counted down the hours, the minutes, even. Soon Mamma would be here.

I was desperate to see her, to hold her in my arms, to ask her, finally, for the truth. To tell whatever she didn't know, and had the right to know. Anything that had been kept from us.

I never sent your mamma away. Carlo did. Oh, I love him with all my heart. But I'm afraid of him. And you should be afraid too…

Truth or lie?

*

Giuseppe welcomed me with a hug and his usual quiet kindness.

'Oh, Luce, you seem so upset! Come, sit down…' he said, leading me to the kitchen where only a few days before – or an eternity, if I thought of all that had happened – we'd sat like a family of three, him, Massimo and myself. That kitchen table was a place of peace, kept by Giuseppe's warmth and gentle nature.

'Thank you. How are you, Giuseppe? Are you looking after yourself?'

'It doesn't really matter how I am! It's my poor son. He's going through hell. And I can't help him…'

I held both his hands as we sat at the kitchen table.

'But you are helping him. With your support and your love.' It sounded like a cliché, but I felt these weren't just empty words. As difficult as things could be, if you're surrounded by love everything is a bit easier, or anyway less terrible, than if you were all alone. Ethan had proved that to me, for sure.

'I know, but… I just want Matilde to wake up.'

'She's in the best hands,' I said. I would have given anything to be able to reassure him more than that, but what else could I say? The truth was – we didn't know if she would come through this. 'We must keep hope. We must believe, Giuseppe.'

'Yes. I'm so sorry. Here I am, whining when there's nothing to be done. You said your husband is here?' He smiled.

'Ex-hus… Yes, my husband is here.' My thought went to my wedding ring, in a silver box kept in the bathroom back in Seattle, where I wouldn't see it every day. 'That's where I stayed, last night – in his hotel. I mean, we're separated, but…'

'You don't owe me an explanation!' Giuseppe laughed, and it was good to see him a little bit lighter.

'Giuseppe, you're about to meet a very old friend,' I said, and laid my hands on his again. I was so comfortable with him.

'What do you mean? Who?'

'My mamma. Angelina.'

Giuseppe looked like I'd told him he was about to see a ghost. He didn't seem happy at all.

'Don't worry, we won't all pile up at your house!' I added quickly. 'We'll stay with Ethan; you see, he found this hotel outside Bastia, it's being refurbished, so they couldn't take anyone in, and they gave him a huge suite, so everyone will fit in…'

'Angelina is coming here?' he said slowly.

'Yes. Well, not here! Not to your house, to the hotel, like I was saying…'

Silence.

'With Nonna being so unwell, she wants to see her before… before anything happens.'

More silence.

'Giuseppe?'

'Yes? No, no, don't worry about that. It's good. Please, do ask them to stay. There's plenty of room, I…'

'Of course not, don't be silly… But we'll come and see you for sure!'

'Yes. Yes. That's good. I'm… I'm glad.'

His reaction had left me bewildered. The last thing I wanted was to give that kind man something else to worry about. I'd thought the news would make him happy.

'Well, I suppose I'd better go, now…'

'Please, don't go. Why don't you wait for her here? We can welcome her together,' he said, and gave my hands a gentle squeeze.

*

Giuseppe and I sat on the front step of his house, waiting in comfortable silence. Neither of us felt the need to make small talk, each of us lost in our thoughts. My mind was still reeling from Pietra's letter…

I think of the tiny grave where we buried your baby, and pray for her every day.

Good God.

Who was in that grave? Neve, or Angelina?

Mamma – which baby was she, of the two? Which baby survived, and which one died?

I remembered the nightmare I had – Clelia walking away, her eyes black, and Nora's ghost following with her arms lifted…

'I think that's them,' Giuseppe said, and stood. I followed suit.

A yellow taxi was approaching, and the closer it got, the harder my heart beat. I lifted myself on my toes, to try and see who was inside – the silhouette of a small woman…

She was here!

I wish I could say I didn't cry, but I did, like a little girl. Mamma ran to embrace me while the taxi driver was taking her bags out of the trunk. It was an endless, wordless embrace – until we pulled away and looked into each other's eyes – there was so much to say! She cupped my face with her hands.

'Oh, *tesoro mio*…'

'Mamma!' She looked fresh and beautifully groomed in a long, rich red linen dress that offset her dark complexion. She opened her mouth to speak, but then shook her head, unable to find the words. 'Mamma, this is Giuseppe, remember him? He's Massimo's dad, you know, Matilde's fiancé… He's kindly letting me stay…'

My words trailed away. I'd seen Mamma's face.

'Giuseppe…' she murmured.

'Angelina,' he said, and I froze, and looked at them both.

Yes. She definitely remembered him.

*

Mamma and I stepped inside the hospital, arm in arm. She was very pale, and every step, it seemed to me, was an effort. She was about to meet her mother after over forty years, and neither of us had any idea of how it would go. I only prayed that Nonna would be strong enough to tell us the truth – and willing to do it.

'I'm sorry, Signora Nardini has gone home,' the receptionist said, after consulting her files.

'She has?' Mamma and I looked at each other.

'What's happening? Everything all right?' Ethan whispered.

'Yes. Nonna has gone home. To Carlo's house, I think…'

Mamma looked devastated. 'If she's with Carlo, I'll never see her again,' she said in English, so that Ethan would understand.

I couldn't allow this. I couldn't. I had to find a way.

'I'm sorry, would you know a nurse called Romina, by any chance? Would it be possible to speak to her?' I asked the receptionist.

'Of course I know her, yes. You're in luck, she's in now. Give me a moment,' she replied, and disappeared into the corridor I'd been down so many times.

'Don't worry, Mamma. I'll take you to Nonna, I promise,' I said, and held both her hands in mine. She shook her head and looked down – she seemed more desolate than determined. Well, no matter: if she was too frightened to fight, I would fight for her. I would be her strength.

Out of the belly of the hospital came Romina, her blue eyes smiling as always. 'Oh, Luce. Your nonna was discharged. Her son took her home,' she said.

'Romina, I know it's a strange question, but you probably guessed that everything is not well between my uncle and me. You wouldn't know, by any chance, if Carlo took her to his house?'

'Yes, I noticed. They didn't tell me, but I did overhear something. Signora Nardini asked her son to take her to Rosa Bianca, the Nardini home? She said she wanted to see it one last time, at least. I doubt that it'll be possible… they won't let such a frail lady up there… but Carlo seemed to agree. I'm not sure, though…'

Rosa Bianca! If she wasn't at Carlo's house, there was hope. '*Grazie, Romina, grazie!*'

'Obviously I didn't speak in a professional capacity… it stays between you and me?' She gave me an apprehensive look.

'Of course.'

'I hope you make up. I really do. It's terrible when these things happen in families…'

'I hope so too,' I replied, and, on impulse, I gave Romina a hug. 'Thank you for all you've done.'

'It's my job,' she replied simply.

'Mamma…' I began as we stepped outside under a white sky. Instead of the blazing sun I'd been accustomed to, the weather had turned, and it looked like a summer storm might come. 'Bosconero is…' How could I prepare her for what she was about to see? But I didn't need to say anything more.

'We're going to Rosa Bianca,' Mamma said. 'I want to go *home*.'

*

'I'm not sure this is a good idea,' Ethan kept saying under his breath.

We'd gone to the camp to find Massimo, and we were now driving up in a truck. This time, none of us was wearing a hard hat: our visit to the village was unofficial, illegal, and nobody needed to know.

'We have no choice,' I replied. 'Mamma wants to see her home, and there's a good chance that Nonna will be there.'

Ethan rubbed his forehead with his fingers and said nothing. We were silent for the rest of the journey, and silent some more as we arrived in Bosconero and took in the destruction once again – for the first time, in Mamma's case. She clasped both her hands on her mouth.

'It's been so long. So long. And look at it now… It's all gone…' she cried.

'We'd better go around the walls and through the back,' Massimo said gravely. 'Follow me.'

'I know the path you mean,' Mamma said and walked on. There she was. My fierce, strong mother.

We made our way around the ancient walls to the back of the village, hoping we would not be seen and sent back to Bastia. Ethan helped Mamma walk on uneven ground, until we reached a little dirt track in the woods surrounding the village. The path opened onto a grassy slope not dissimilar to Collina Cora – and on top of the slope was Rosa Bianca.

We stepped into the garden, through Nonna's lush plants, the hibiscus, the deadly passiflora, the angels' bells – only then did we see the crack running through the house from left to right, cutting it in half like a wound. It didn't run through paint and plaster only, then, but through the core of the building.

'They're here,' Mamma whispered; at first I had no idea how she knew, and then I, too, heard Carlo's voice carried by the wind.

Mamma strode on, all timidity lost, somehow, and circum-navigated the house to make her way inside. Massimo grabbed my arm before I could follow her: 'Please, don't be long,' he admonished me. I nodded briefly and walked on. 'I'll wait here,' he called after me.

Mamma walked in like she owned the place, like she lived there. Like she belonged. I was so proud of her, and yet I couldn't help the feeling of doom that was descending over me.

This will get much worse before it gets better, I sensed.

The house was in shade, Carlo having closed the shutters. The ever-present dust, a memento of the tremor, danced in the sunbeams that seeped through. There was a smell of damp and old in the air, a smell of heavy past; memories hung like cobwebs at every corner.

Nonna was sitting on an armchair in the living room, looking smaller and greyer than ever; Carlo towered beside her. When we appeared, so fast that they were taken by surprise, it was like they'd seen people who were long dead, and had come back to haunt them.

Mamma stood in front of Carlo and Nonna, with Ethan behind her. She had a commanding air at last, the confidence I thought she'd lost, and was wordlessly asking to take charge.

'Mother. Carlo,' she said calmly. It sounded formal, cold. I would have expected a tearful reunion between them, but she wasn't going to Nonna at all.

Nonna's face worked – why was she not crying Mamma's name, extending her hand like she had with me?

'Angelina!' Carlo called, and in his voice there was almost a hint of longing. Inside my mind and heart, a deep rumble began, just like an inner earthquake. There was something strange in the situation, something unexpected.

Nonna Clelia still wasn't opening her arms.

'You sent me away,' Mamma said simply. 'You said if I returned, you'd kill me.'

'Carlo! You said that to…' I began, but my words trailed away. Mamma wasn't talking to Carlo, but *to Nonna Clelia*.

'I had no choice,' Nonna said. 'And you know why.'

'To protect yourself!'

Nonna's voice was raspy, barely a whisper. 'To protect *Carlo*.'

'What are you talking about?' I blurted out. My eyes had been moving from one woman to the other. 'Can you please fill me in? With the truth, possibly?' I looked at Nonna.

Nonna's breathing was ragged, and her colouring even greyer. Every word came out with such effort, she seemed to use her whole body to enunciate them. It was as if every time she spoke, she had to choose between talking and breathing.

'This is the truth! For years, Carlo has held Arturo responsible for the death of his parents, even if Arturo loved him like a son!' Another ragged breath. 'It was the first day of the hunting season, and they went to the woods with their rifles. Angelina was supposed to stay home with me, but she went out to see a friend, without telling me. They carried back Arturo dead, his body full of bullets. I suspected Carlo, but I couldn't… I couldn't believe… Not our Carlo. Angelina told me she'd seen *something*. That I was never to know what it was. I insisted, and she confessed she'd seen Carlo shooting his father… By the morning, she was gone, and I could never find her again.'

'What?' Carlo was as white as a ghost. 'What—'

'No. It's another lie,' Mamma said, interrupting Carlo. 'I saw Papà dying, yes. And I saw you both with rifles…'

'I didn't shoot him, Angelina! I'm not a murderer!' Carlo almost implored. 'Yes, Arturo had given my parents away. They were shot like dogs up in the woods. I hated him with all my heart. Mother kept telling me how he had told his cronies the location of the camp that night. He knew that my parents would be murdered! And his sister-in-law! But he still did it. And every time I tried to bring it up, to ask him why, how he could do such a thing, he cut me short. He changed the subject. He couldn't face his guilt… But I never killed him or anyone. Mother, how could you say such a thing? Angelina, you couldn't possibly have believed this all these years…'

'I never believed it, no. Mother told me it had been you. She tried to tell me what I saw. She told me I had to protect you and disappear. But I knew you were innocent. I went away to protect you, Mother, because I knew if they asked me I would not be able to keep the secret! I've always known it was you, *because Papà told me*. When he was dying, he murmured into my ears with his last breath: *è stata Clelia.*' Clelia did it.

I shuddered.

It was with the comrades of our Brigata that I learned to shoot, and I was good at it, Nonna had told me. I felt queasy.

She'd killed my grandfather.

'Carlo, why do you hate Angelina, and me?' I had to ask. 'Why did you not want me here?'

'Angelina was going out with a boy our mother didn't like. She told me Angelina wanted her out of the way so she could be free to go out with him. That she would accuse our mother of shooting Arturo…'

'Because she did!' Angelina shouted.

'I know that now,' Carlo said, and took his face in his hands. 'My sister went away, all alone, and I lied for years… to protect you, Mother. Why? Why did you do all this? Why did you make sure I would hate him, why did you shoot him?' he said, tears flowing down his cheeks.

There was a pause, a heartbeat; I wanted to shout out what Nonna had told me, that it hadn't been Arturo, but Carlo, as an unknowing child, who had guided the Germans to them, and that she'd never told him so that he wouldn't have to live with that burden on his shoulders… but was it true? After what I'd found out about the swap between Neve and Angelina, I couldn't believe a thing she said. Did they know about Arturo's real identity?

'Carlo,' Angelina said. 'Mother kept telling you that my father was responsible for the murder of your parents, over and over again. Why? With such a secret in a family, wouldn't you try and bury it as deep as you could, instead of bringing it up as she'd done? Why? Maybe she was planning to make *you* shoot him, during a hunting trip? Wouldn't that have been perfect, Mother?'

Finally, Clelia spoke. 'Yes, it would have been. But Carlo wouldn't hurt a fly. It fell onto my shoulders. I did it because Arturo *knew*.'

'Knew what?' Carlo asked, bewildered.

'That it had been you, giving the camp away, unwittingly,' I explained. 'You were followed. You went looking for your parents, and… well, they didn't want you to know and feel responsible.'

'But I didn't go looking for my parents. I didn't go to the camp. I was only six years old!'

'But Nonna said… it was you,' I repeated.

Liar.

Suddenly, I felt the soft fur of the cat on my leg, still sitting there like a tiny statue…

'I didn't go to the camp,' Carlo said, and for the first time since we'd met, he spoke to me like a human being. His eyes were sincere, devoid of the anger and contempt he'd shown me since I'd arrived. 'Mother wasn't protecting me from knowing I had caused the murder of my parents. Because I didn't.'

He wasn't lying. I was sure. 'Maybe you're mistaken, you were only little…' I attempted to explain.

All eyes converged on Nonna.

'Why did you lie, Mother?' Carlo began. 'Why did you tell Luce I was responsible for my parents' death? It wasn't me. It was Arturo. That's what you always said to me. And he never denied it.'

Nonna spoke. Her voice was feeble, interrupted by shallow breaths. She seemed so ill now, so much worse than she'd been when I'd first met her, only a few days before…

'Fine. It wasn't you, Carlo. And it wasn't Arturo.' Carlo blinked, hunched under the weight of all these revelations. 'But Arturo *knew*.'

'What did he know, Mother?' Angelina asked, her voice icy.

'If I tell you, you'll hate me…' Nonna cried, and for a split second, I almost felt sorry for her. Almost.

I had to speak out. I took out Pietra's letter from my crossbody.

'I found this upstairs,' I said. 'It's a letter from a woman who was at the camp, that night,' I said, and began to read.

Clelia, or like you called yourself when we were at war, Bianca,

'That was Nonna's alias, in case you don't know.'

Finally I can use your fighting name without fear! This is a new life and a new world. Of course I don't blame you for not taking me with you, you couldn't know I was alive, I remember the dark and the snow… It's a miracle you and me survived. I'm so sorry you had to endure the death of poor Nora, just after you lost your daughter in childbirth…

I hope whoever gave us away burns in hell. Although we'll never know! Oh, my dearest friend Bianca, I'll never return to Bosconero, what for? My whole family is gone. I just hope you will be happy and healthy all the days of your life. I think of the tiny grave where we buried your baby, and pray for her every day...

Mamma faltered, and Ethan and I ran to support her.

'At least I won't bring my secrets to the grave with me,' Nonna said calmly. She knew there was no way out now; no way forward, but the truth. Her web of lies, to Carlo, to Angelina, to Matilde, to me – was coming undone, and the loose threads were strangling her. 'Nora and I gave birth in the woods. My sweet daughter was stillborn. And Nora's daughter suckled, all happy and rosy. That was the moment that broke me. Even more than not hearing my daughter cry when she was born, even more than seeing Neve in my sister's arms, her tiny head still encrusted with Nora's blood. No. What broke me was that moment – to see her suckle, and see my sister's quiet joy, the contentment painted all over her face as she held her second child. And mine, my fourth lost baby, had been taken away to be buried.

'I've always been a good girl. A good daughter, a good sister, a good wife. I would have made a good mother. And then, in a moment, I wasn't good any longer. All my life I had to see my sister happy, while I broke my back. She had a son already. And now my baby was dead, and hers was alive. I knew that I had to hold that baby. I had to suckle that baby with the milk I was full of, and that my own daughter couldn't drink. It was me who gave the camp away, in exchange for mine and Neve's life. And all these years, I lied. I always lied. To Arturo, to Carlo, to Angelina. Even to myself. I convinced myself that my betrayal never happened, that Angelina was my daughter. That Nora died because of Carlo's carelessness, and Neve died with her. But now, here it is. The truth. For all it's worth, so many years down the line. Nobody gave the camp away. Nobody attacked us that night. I did what I had to do to keep my baby with me. And nobody was left to tell the story – even if Pietra was left alive, it was too dark for her to see *who shot her*.'

I found my mother's hand and held it. We clung to each other and stood like trees against a stormy wind. The smell of old and damp, the gloom, the burden of all those memories weighed on me. Even in the heat, I felt cold. In the horrified silence that followed, Nonna clasped her fingers around her locket. I could hear my mother's heavy breathing beside me, and I slipped my arm around her waist.

My nightmare. Nora, dead, walking behind her sister, trying to get her baby back. And the scene she'd described – Mauro leaning against the wall, Pietra curled up under the tree.

It was her. Clelia. She had shot them all.

'I am Neve. Not Angelina, like I always thought. I am Neve,' my mother murmured.

'Yes. I'm so sorry, Angelina, Carlo. So sorry,' Nonna rasped. 'At least I did one thing for you, Carlo. I helped you keep Matilde. You didn't stand up for yourself when that whore wanted to leave you and take Matilde away! Did you not see how beautiful my angels' bells are? You complimented them, Luce, didn't you? Because the soil is good, right there where I planted them.'

There was silence for a moment – we were all too shocked to speak.

'It was the only way to keep my daughter. And it was the only way to keep my granddaughter.'

'You killed Martina. You killed Matilde's mother,' Carlo said.

'I helped you keep Matilde,' she repeated.

All of a sudden, Carlo, the tall, broad almost-monster I'd seen had become a haunted old man, betrayed by the person who should have loved him the most.

Nonna's feeble voice rose again. 'I didn't tell Arturo about Angelina not being our daughter – he guessed, because she was the picture of Nora. And when he mentioned it, my reaction gave me away. I lied to him, of course, but he wore me down until I had to tell him what I'd done. I implored Arturo to keep the secret, but he was a straight man, a righteous man. I knew it was only a matter of time. And one day he said to me exactly what you said: that he couldn't take it any more. That he had to come clean to our children. I knew that if the truth was revealed, they would have hated me forever. I couldn't lose you both. So, I did what I had to do. And how weird, that I should lose my daughter because of what happened. The daughter that was never mine in the first place. You weren't supposed to be there, when they went hunting. You were supposed to be home with me...'

But Nonna couldn't finish the sentence. It was then that the lamp began to sway, a small movement at first, and then creating an arc that grew bigger and bigger. I knew by now what it meant even before the noise began, and my system went into panic mode at once. Everything was whirling around me: Mamma's wide eyes as the lamp smashed on the ground, glass shards all over the room, the rumbling, that terrible rumbling that came from the ground under our feet. I felt someone grabbing my waist – Ethan – and something primal, instinctual inside me made my arms shoot forward and grab my mother. But the moment my fingers made contact with her, the ground convulsed again, and I missed her: I almost fell forwards, but not quite, because Ethan's strong hands were holding me, sinking into my flesh, dragging me away. Slivers of plaster from the ceiling fell on me, and then dust that blinded me. My arms flailed, trying to reach Mamma, but met only air. Stumbling, falling and getting up again, until the white sky was above me, and I was outside in Ethan's arms.

'Mamma!' I called her name as a soft drizzle began to fall on me, washing my hands and face. Ethan was stopping me from going back in – I saw Massimo try and run inside, but he fell on his knees.

Rosa Bianca shuddered hard, just like the tower did over Matilde, before it crumbled over her – a cloud of dust rose from it. I heard myself screaming, then I began coughing and heaving dust – in my mind, I was calling out my mother's name, but no sound was coming out any longer except ragged dust-breathing. My mother appeared on the doorstep, crowned with roses. Carlo was behind her, holding her up as they seemed to dance together with the shaking ground. He threw her forward, outside and into my arms; for the last time, my eyes met Carlo's, as the house crumbled on him.

CHAPTER TWENTY-THREE

We refused to be taken to hospital to be checked over, though they tried to insist; we were fine, and we wanted to be alone. We denied that anyone had taken us up there, maintaining that we were simply fulfilling an old lady's wish. There was no way we'd let Massimo get into trouble for something that was entirely our choice. We could have died, all of us.

Instead, we'd been set free.

We were in Giuseppe's house, huddled up in the spare room. Mamma had washed and changed, and she only had a few scrapes after the fall. Brave, the white cat who'd adopted us after surviving yet another crumbling building, was sleeping on the cool tiles, his coat now white again.

It was hard to believe that Rosa Bianca was gone, and that Carlo and Clelia had been buried under it. And Matilde's mother, who'd been there a long time, under the angels' bells.

It was hard to wrap our minds around the lies, the secrets. As I was translating for Ethan all that had happened, all that had been said, I almost couldn't believe it myself.

It would take a long, long time before all that I'd unravelled could sink in.

And still, the expression on my mother's face, even after the shock, was lighter than I'd seen in a long time.

In spite of the death and destruction, my mother was smiling. And not just that: she looked like a weight had been removed from her shoulders.

'He saved me, you know. In the end,' she said. 'My brother. I'm alive thanks to him. It was all so fast, but somehow it went really slow. It lasted a moment, but it was a long time. A long time to forgive.

'The ceiling was falling on us, Luce. The whole thing was falling on us. You want to know what Carlo did?' She fixed her eyes, shiny with tears, in mine. 'He grabbed me and dragged me towards the door. And then, like you saw, he pushed me out. Maybe he could have taken a step forward, and saved himself too. But I think he chose to stay behind. Everything that would have fallen on me, fell on him instead. Stones and bricks. He enfolded me so that nothing would touch me,' she said, and made a gesture with her hands, like a mother bending over her baby to protect her. 'And then, the second he pushed me out, he asked something of me.'

'What?'

'To forgive him. I couldn't answer, but in my heart I said yes, yes, I forgive you. I felt this incredible peace, Luce… A peace I haven't known since… Since I left.'

'Do you feel… strange, knowing that you were never Angelina, but Neve?'

'That Nora and Mauro were my real parents, yes. But I *am* Angelina. I have been since I was barely hours old. My identity, after all, doesn't change. I'm Angelina, and I'm your mother. Also, I know the truth about the man I knew as my father. The man I loved as my father. David Zevi.'

'At least between us, there are no secrets or lies any more,' I said.

'No. And there will never be again,' Mamma said.

At that moment, there was a knock at the door. It was Giuseppe.

'Would you come for a walk with me, Angelina? I think we need to talk,' he said to Mamma, and she took his hand, and then looked at me.

'No more secrets,' she said, and followed Giuseppe outside.

It was like being struck by lightning, because it was at that moment that I understood.

When they came back, they called us downstairs, and Giuseppe held me in his arms. He whispered four words in my ear.

And those four words changed everything.

*

Ethan and I stepped together under the warm flow of the shower, and he washed my body gently – he enveloped me in a towel and took me to bed. We lay side by side, too tired, too stunned for anything more than tenderness. For now.

I stroked the side of his face, looking in his deep, dark blue eyes. Oh, how I'd missed him.

'Ethan…'

'Yes, Lulu,' he said, and it was almost painful, the relief in hearing my old nickname, and the love in his voice. Why, why had it taken so long to destroy the wall between us?

'I never stopped loving you.'

'Just as well, because I never stopped loving you. Never.'

It was a long time, before we spoke again.

*

'You came to Italy to unravel your family's secrets, and you ended up finding your father as well,' he said.

'I had no idea…'

'Did you not notice the resemblance between you and Giuseppe, Luce? You look like two peas in a pod!' I shook my head lightly. Feeling his body close to mine was perfect happiness.

'I don't know how I didn't. He was always… I don't know, strange with me. He kept looking at me when he thought I wouldn't notice. One night he spoke to me about making a mistake, not knowing what he'd done… He meant he didn't know what he'd done to lose Mamma.'

'So that's what she was going to tell him, that day. When she took the shortcut through the woods. She was going to tell him she was pregnant.'

'Yes. Pregnant with me.'

'What a coincidence. That Matilde should fall in love with your father's stepson.'

'Coincidence or fate, who knows.'

'Fate, Lulu. I'm sure,' he said, and kissed me again. The last thing I wanted was answer my cell phone but with everything that had happened, I couldn't have ignored it – in case someone needed me.

'Massimo?' I spoke into the phone, and then my sobs and laughter joined his through the microphone.

'What happened? Lulu, what happened?'

I could barely speak through my tears of joy. I took Ethan's face in my hands. 'It's Matilde. Ethan, Matilde is awake.'

EPILOGUE

Ethan and I sat at Collina Cora, on the grass, under the Italian sun burning in a cloudless sky. Up on the hill in front of us was what was left of Bosconero.

'I'm going to stay, Ethan. For a little while,' I said tentatively.

'I know. I was sure you'd say that. I'm going to stay too.'

'You are?'

'Well, if you want me to!' He smiled.

'Oh, yes. I do. I really do.'

'Just as well I've accrued months of holidays, at this point! I've been a workaholic for too long.'

'Well, that's in the past. We are here now,' I whispered, and kissed him on the cheek.

'It only took a journey overseas, a slew of family secrets and an earthquake to draw us back together again,' Ethan whispered. 'Ethan and Lulu, again. Remember?' He slipped an arm around my shoulders, and I breathed his scent, the scent I knew so well. The scent of Ethan, the young man I met years ago; the father of my son, who was beside me when Eli came into the world. Ethan and Lulu, who shared twenty-five Christmases, three homes, a son, happy days and terrible days, and were now sitting in front of a place destroyed, to be rebuilt and made to thrive again.

Just like us.

This book is dedicated to the De Martino family, for letting us sleep in their garden the night of twenty-third of November 1980, when the Irpinia earthquake hit Naples.

LETTER FROM DANIELA

Dear everyone,

It's so good to find you here! Maybe you've followed me all the way from Glen Avich, through Seal Island and to Italy; maybe it's the first time you've picked up a book of mine. If you would like to be updated on what's coming next, then join my mailing list here:

www.bookouture.com/daniela-sacerdoti

I often wonder where you are in the world, what your circumstances might be right now, in Covid times, and how you've been during this spring's lockdown, when *The Lost Village* was written. Living in Northern Italy, I was in the eye of the storm when it all broke out – the rules imposed here were draconian for a while, to the point of not being allowed out of the house at all unless for emergencies. We were allowed, though, to take our dog for a daily walk – no more than two hundred metres away from our home, and only one person at a time. Needless to say that our puppy, Sasha, never had so many walks in her life! For months, all I saw was my home, my garden and the orchard across the road – I was lucky, to have so much nature around me, and in spite of the solitude and sense of alarm, I felt reconnected with the slow rhythms of life past more than ever before. It was surreal how the news called for constant panic, while all around me spring bloomed quietly, in the void left by people and traffic.

For a month I couldn't write, while like so many of us I tried to negotiate the onslaught of news, of harsher and harsher rules imposed on us – for good reason, but still traumatic – and navigate my children's online schooling. During this time I took solace in reading about other women's experiences around the world, because I very much felt we were united in this and while isolated, still not alone. It was only after a conversation with my editor that I got back on track with my writing: she pointed out to me that we could frame our work as service, giving our readers an escape from all we were going through.

After that, I found it much easier to concentrate on *The Lost Village* as my tiny contribution to make things better. Behind the heroes on the front line, the little people can only do their bit – but that bit does matter. Everything is easier if we stick together, especially in these divisive times – together as human beings, before anything else. So thank you, dear readers, for being part of my world and for reading my stories, thus giving me the very reason I write.

With all my love to each and every one of you,
Daniela Sacerdoti

        🖥 Danielasacerdoti.com

        📷 @danielasacerdotiauthor

AUTHOR'S NOTE

Although this novel is based on real events – in particular, the 2016 earthquake in central Italy – all stories and characters are the fruit of my imagination. I have also taken some artistic licence in the dynamics of the immediate aftermath of the earthquake and the unfolding of the events in relation to the emergency responses.

ACKNOWLEDGEMENTS

My thanks go to:

Jessie Botterill, my editor – I'm so grateful for the way you guide me, and yet you let me be free in my creativity. A true 'writer whisperer'!

Everyone at Bookouture, for giving their authors the chance to be truly faithful to their inspiration – a rare and wonderful gift, in the publishing landscape. Like a perfect music producer, to (often) unmalleable composers.

My community, both in the flesh and online, for the way we kept each other going during the long, long lockdown – for all the times a conversation, whether via email or across a field during the allotted daily walk, soothed our solitude and reminded us that human contact is also a human right.

My tribe, by blood or by choice – in particular, I'd like to thank Simona Sanfilippo (illustrator) and Cinzia Tarditi (accordionist) because they know and understand the curse and delight of being a freelance artist.

Thank you from the bottom of my heart to my husband, Ross, for putting up with having a writer for a wife – no mean feat!

More than ever, thank you to my boys, Sorley and Luca – you've been an example of resilience, hard work and optimism in these strange times. Your words and laughter, whether I'm listening to you play your music or chatting about *Skyrim* or laughing at our silly in-jokes, are my oxygen. I love you more than words can say – thank you for being the best sons a mother could have!

Printed in Great Britain
by Amazon

71761413R00159